CONTENTS

Introduction   VI

Important Note About this Book   VII

Dedication   VIII

Introduction   IX

1. Prologue   1

2. Chapter One   9

3. Chapter Two   13

4. Chapter Three   17

5. Chapter Four   22

6. Chapter Five   26

7. Chapter Six   30

8. Chapter Seven   36

9. Chapter Eight   39

10. Chapter Nine   44

11. Chapter Ten   50

12. Chapter Eleven   54

13. Chapter Twelve   58

14. Chapter Thirteen   61

15. Chapter Fourteen   66

16. Chapter Fifteen 71

17. Chapter Sixteen 75

18. Chapter Seventeen 79

19. Chapter Eighteen 83

20. Chapter Nineteen 88

21. Chapter Twenty 94

22. Chapter Twenty-One 99

23. Chapter Twenty-Two 104

24. Chapter Twenty-Three 109

25. Chapter Twenty-Four 114

26. Chapter Twenty-Five 119

27. Chapter Twenty-Six 124

28. Chapter Twenty-Seven 131

29. Chapter Twenty-Eight 135

30. Chapter Twenty-Nine 141

31. Chapter Thirty 149

32. Chapter Thirty-One 154

33. Chapter Thirty-Two 160

34. Chapter Thirty-Three 165

35. Chapter Thirty-Four 171

36. Chapter Thirty-Five 175

37. Chapter Thirty-Six 179

38. Chapter Thirty-Seven 183

39. Chapter Thirty-Eight 189

40. Chapter Thirty-Nine 192

41. Chapter Forty 196

42. Chapter Forty-One   199

43. Chapter Forty-Two   202

44. Chapter Forty-Three   215

45. Chapter Forty-Four   220

46. Chapter Forty-Five   224

47. Chapter Forty-Six   231

48. Chapter Forty-Seven   234

49. Chapter Forty-Eight   241

50. Chapter Forty-Nine   244

51. Chapter Fifty   246

52. Chapter Fifty-One   249

53. Chapter Fifty-Two   253

54. Chapter Fifty-Three   263

55. Epilogue   265

Also By   273

Acknowledgements   275

About The Author   276

Sign up for exclusive content and Heidi's newsletter here.

You can also find out more about Heidi and her upcoming books on social media:

Facebook Page

Facebook Group

Instagram

TikTok

This is a dark romance, which I'm guessing is why most of you are here.

It contains a number of triggers, including graphic violence and gore, graphic murder and torture, mentions of PTSD, depression and anxiety. It mentions sexual assault and other forms of abuse, as well as child abuse, child death and suicidal ideation. It also contains several graphic sex scenes including group activities.

This book does contain components of BDSM and polyamory. In no way is this intended to be an accurate, realistic representation of the many rules, guidelines and other aspects of these lifestyles. This is a book of fiction, not a guidebook for real life, and is purely intended to be read for enjoyment and entertainment.

ARC READERS

Thank you for joining me on this 6-book journey! To say I'm thrilled to share this final book in the series with you is an understatement, although I am sad to see these characters go (although in typical Heidi fashion, I wouldn't be surprised if we see them pop up again ;))! This book has been professionally edited, but—as always—if you notice a stray typo and send it my way, I will be forever grateful. Enjoy!

This is for everyone who needs a good beach vacation with something dark and smutty to read by the pool.

If you dream of morally grey men who are gentle with the women they love.

And if you, like the snakes and the worms, believe that we can flourish even within the darkness and turn it into something beautiful.

If you haven't read any of the other books in the Blood and Sand series, please read this section!

I **highly recommend** you go back and read the previous books in the series to get the most out of this one.

While some people have been able to jump into *Sea of Demons* (Book 5) without having read the previous books in the series, and still understand what was going on and enjoy the book, most would have preferred to go back and get to know the characters and the dynamics and history between them before diving into that one. This book, *Sea of Redemption*, is only going to be more confusing.

But, if you're stubborn like me, and determined to jump right in, by all means please do. Who am I to stop you, anyway?! You know what you like better than anyone.

Some info that might be helpful in making your decision:

The Blood and Sand series is built around three groups, one of which only made their appearance in book 5.

Sea of Snakes

This introduces Devon and the Snakes (Skyler, Zeke, Dom and Rake).

Sea of Sinners, Sea of Rage and Sea of Pain (also available as Sinners, Rage and Pain: The Brixton Trilogy)

This introduces Angel and the Brixtons (Aidan, Roman, Brick and Slade). There is one brief interaction between Angel and Devon, and minor mention of the other group, during these books. So, you could be perfectly happy and informed reading these three books before Sea of Snakes, if you prefer.

Sea of Demons

This continues the story of Devon and the Snakes, and Angel and the Brixtons, and the two groups are prominently featured together through this book. So it's very helpful to have the back story. This is also the book where Aria and her men (Dimitri, Florian, Josef) make a brief—and frankly unexpected—appearance. They become quite pivotal by the end of the book, and it will be helpful to understand their relationship with the other two groups before you jump into the final chapter. Again, that's your call.

CHAPTER ONE

BRICK

"**S**hut it, Fucker!"

The sickening stench of rotting flesh assaults my senses as I drag the rusted metal cart across the cold concrete floor. My latest prize cowers in the corner, his trembling limbs rattling the chains that bind his wrists and ankles.

Fucker has been screaming at me for the past ten minutes, spitting venom and curses in a pathetic attempt to rile me. That's what I've decided to name him. Fucker. As if a few empty threats and insults can undo the damage he's done.

The rage simmers in my gut, clawing up my throat in a roar.

I slam the cart to a stop, sending a violent clatter through the basement. Fucker flinches but that insolent sneer stays plastered on his face.

My hands curl into fists, knuckles cracking. "You think this is a fucking joke?" Each word is punctuated by a slam of my fist against the metal tray.

He jerks against the chains. "Go to hell!"

I grab a wicked knife from the tray, testing the edge with my thumb. A thin line of red wells up, the sting sharp and sweet.

"I've already been." My lips twist in a humorless grin as I stalk toward my prey.

He tries to scramble away on the cold floor but the chains won't give.

"Now, you get to see what hell really looks like."

The knife flashes under the dim light as I bring it down in a graceful arc. A strangled scream fills the air, echoing off the basement walls.

This is just the beginning, and I can already tell it's going to be fun.

A floorboard creaks behind me. I glance over my shoulder to find Devon descending the stairs, a wicked gleam in her eye.

"Can I join in?" she asks, practically purring.

My lips curl up. "By all means."

Devon strides over to the cart, surveying the array of tools with a calculating gaze. She selects a small blowtorch, the flames dancing in her eyes as she tests it. "I've been wanting to check this out for a while now."

Fucker's eyes widen in terror, flitting between us. But instead of accepting his fate, he renews his struggles against the chains, spouting off curses and empty threats. As if he has any say in what's about to happen. You'd think my little trick with the knife would have given him a clue. Some people just aren't very smart.

Devon saunters over, the blowtorch in hand. "Now, now. There's no need for that kind of language." She clicks her tongue, and then glances over at me. "We're going to have so much fun together. Aren't we, Brick?"

"Absolutely." I hand her a knife, watching in dark delight as she drags the tip down the bastard's cheek. His screams fill the air, high-pitched and desperate.

She laughs, the sound light and airy. "Music to my ears."

The blowtorch ignites with a roar, casting an orange glow over Devon's face. She wields it with expert precision, searing the bastard's skin inch by agonizing inch.

His shrieks pierce my skull but I relish every moment.

Devon is a vision of beauty and death, embodying cold perfection. Together, we'll make this bastard suffer in ways he's never imagined.

Because he deserves it, and because we want to.

Devon withdraws the blowtorch, tilting her head as she regards our victim. He's sobbing and trembling, reduced to a whimpering mess. Pathetic.

"Why have we chosen this guy, anyway?" Devon asks, curiosity etched into her tone. "He seems rather unremarkable."

"You would think, based on his appearance." I fold my arms, admiring her handiwork. The bastard's torso is a ruin of burns and blisters, the acrid stench of charred flesh hanging in the air. "He's been drugging women at the island's nightclubs, including ours, and assaulting them. Left the last few in hospital, and from the way he's escalating, it's not long before he'll begin to murder."

Devon's eyes narrow, flickering with cold rage. "Is that so?"

Fucker cowers under her gaze. "N-no, I swear it's not true! I didn't do anything, please, you have to believe me!"

Devon smirks. "Liars get punished. Isn't that right, Brick?"

"Always." My hands clench into fists as I stalk toward Fucker. He's still lying, even now, the worthless piece of shit. I grab his hair and yank his head back, baring his throat. "Perhaps you'll be more forthcoming after I skin you alive."

Fucker screams, writhing against his restraints.

Devon watches with a predatory gleam, blowtorch at the ready.

"Please! I'll tell you everything, just stop, please stop!" The bastard dissolves into hysterical sobs.

Devon sighs. "How disappointing. I was hoping for more of a challenge." She shrugs, flicking on the blowtorch again. "But if you insist on giving up so easily..."

Fucker's shrieks echo through the basement, like music to my ears. Tonight, he'll get exactly what he deserves.

And Devon and I will have our fun.

After a few more ministrations with the blowtorch's cruel flames, Fucker passes out, his ruined body slumped in its restraints.

Devon wipes her brow. "Well, that was entertaining."

I chuckle and squeeze her shoulder. "It was. You're a natural."

Devon grins, sharp and wicked, her eyes gleaming. "I learned from the best." She glances at Fucker and her lip curls with contempt. "He didn't last long."

"Pathetic," I scoff. A wry smirk tugs at my lips as I notice Devon's knuckles, stained crimson with blood. She's been training again, for moments just like this. "Lucky for us, we have all night."

Devon's eyes darken, meeting mine. "Oh really? What did you have in mind?"

A low chuckle rumbles in my chest. "Patience, Devon," I growl. "We've only just begun."

Fucker stirs with a groan. Devon's eyes light up as she turns toward him, blowtorch at the ready. She grins as she fires it up again.

Fucker screams, thrashing against his bindings in a futile attempt to escape.

I watch, entranced, as she works the flame over his already scorched flesh. His screams rise in pitch, ragged pleas for mercy tumbling from his lips.

Devon ignores them, her focus intent upon her task.

The scent of charred flesh fills the air, stronger now. I breathe it in deep, arousal stirring low in my gut at the heady combination of pain and fear.

Devon glances at me from under her lashes, her eyes dark with desire to inflict more pain. "Like what you see?"

Fucker's screams fade to whimpers, his pleas trailing off into incoherent babbling.

Devon clicks her tongue in annoyance, switching off the blowtorch, and shakes her head. "Pathetic."

"It seems our friend lacks stamina," I remark dryly.

Devon huffs out an irritated breath, and crosses her arms over her chest. "I was just starting to have some real fun." She glares at Fucker, her eyes narrowed. "He's no fun when he's unconscious."

Amusement flickers through me at Devon's disgruntled tone. "There's always next time."

Devon's lips curve into a slow, wicked smile. She leans up on her tiptoes, whispering in my ear, "Promise?"

A throaty chuckle sounds behind us. We break apart to find Angel descending the stairs, one brow arched in amusement.

"Don't let me interrupt," she says lightly. There's a teasing lilt to her tone and her lips twitch at the corners.

Devon smirks, leaning into my side. "You're not interrupting anything. Our friend passed out before the real fun could begin."

"Pity." Angel's gaze flicks to Fucker's unconscious form, a glint of humor in her eyes. "I was rather looking forward to the show."

Heat floods my veins at the thought of Angel watching Devon and I torture this man together. I gaze at Angel through hooded eyes. "There's always a next time."

A slow, Cheshire smile spreads across Angel's face. She saunters over to us, trailing her fingers down my chest. "Is that a promise?"

"A guarantee," I murmur, fisting a hand in Angel's hair. I crush my mouth to hers, kissing her with a raw hunger that leaves us both breathless.

When we break apart, Devon grins at us.

"Shall we finish off this bastard now?" she asks. "We've let him hang on for entirely too long at this point." Her tone is teasing. She's enjoying every moment of this as much as I am.

Heat floods my veins at the promise in her voice. I grip Fucker's hair, wrenching his head up. He blinks blearily up at me, his eyes glassy with pain.

"Time to talk," I growl. "Tell me everything about the bastards trying to infiltrate my clubs, or your suffering will seem like paradise compared to what comes next."

Fucker spills the details in a rush, desperate to avoid more pain. His intel is useful, giving me names and locations of the scum trying to encroach on our territory. The people supplying him with drugs, how he chooses his victims, the people who specifically encouraged him to target our venues.

Once I have the information I need, I snap his neck. His body goes limp, the light fading from his eyes.

I turn to find Devon and Angel watching me with lust darkening their gazes. Tonight will be filled with pleasure of the most sinful kind.

"As fun as this has been, I'm off to see Skyler," Devon says, eyes gleaming. "Care to join me for round two once you've finished here? I'm sure there's some deserving bastard somewhere not too far away."

She cracks me up. Ever since her taste of torture at Tane Brown's compound, she's obsessed, and always looking for more. A torture addict, just like me. Plain and simple.

I sense she's struggling a little with this new unhinged side of herself, but we all go through that at the beginning. I remember those days, although I was only a child. Dad, after all, taught me just about everything I know.

"Tempting," I say. "But I have plans for Angel that will likely keep us occupied for some time." I wiggle my eyebrows.

Devon smirks. "In that case, just make sure you don't start without me next time. This was a lot of fun."

I smirk. "You're a wicked girl, Devon."

"You love it," she says, and sashays up the stairs.

Once she's gone, I turn my full focus to Angel. Her lips are swollen from our kisses, her eyes dark with need.

"Shall we?" I ask, lifting a brow.

Angel smiles, slow and sinful, and saunters toward the stairs. "Catch me if you can."

I'm on her in a second, pinning her to the wall as I crush my mouth over hers.

She moans, tangling her hands in my hair to pull me closer.

My fingers hook under the bottom of her top, and drag it up her torso.

She arches into me with a throaty moan, her fingers unbuckling my belt.

Our breaths come fast and sharp, the air around us charged with need. I lift her shirt higher, baring her breasts to my gaze.

"Gorgeous," I murmur, palming one mound as I lower my head to take a nipple between my teeth.

Angel cries out, her nails biting into my shoulders.

I soothe the sting with my tongue before switching to her other breast, lavishing it with equal attention.

Her hands move to my jeans, shoving them down along with my boxer briefs.

My erection springs free, hard and aching.

Angel wraps her hand around my length, stroking firmly.

Pleasure rockets through me.

"Inside me," she gasps. "Now, Brick."

I lift her, pinning her to the wall as her legs wrap around my waist. Our mouths fuse as I position myself at her entrance and thrust home with one hard stroke.

Angel throws her head back and screams.

Devon

I walk out into the balmy night, still tingling with excitement from what took place in Brick's basement. My hands flex at my sides, itching to inflict more pain.

Brick understands me in a way no one else does. He sees the darkness that lurks inside, that craving for violence, and doesn't judge me for it. If anything, he nurtures it, helping me hone my skills.

I'm not as far gone as Brick, not yet, but I aspire to his level of viciousness and complete lack of remorse. He's a psychopath, no doubt about it, but it's not like the movies portray. Brick has depths, layers to his personality. He can be kind, in his own way. Witty and charming.

And he's the only one who truly understands this warped, ugly part of me—and teaches me how to do better. Like I'm his twisty little sister, and he's my unhinged mentor of torture tools.

Don't get me wrong—my guys love every part of me, too, but they don't get my newfound need to torture, to inflict pain, in quite the same way. They do it out of necessity, whereas Brick and I do it for pleasure.

My phone buzzes in my pocket. I pull it out to find a text from Brick.

Brick: Enjoy your time with the surfer boy. You did well today. I'm proud of you.

A smile curves my lips and warmth blooms in my chest. Brick's praise means everything to me.

I'm on my way to being just like him, embracing the darkness that lives inside.

Brick is helping me become the monster I was always meant to be.

CHAPTER TWO

ANGEL

Tension crackles in the air as we gather in the dimly lit warehouse, our groups eyeing each other warily. Shadows dance on the concrete walls, broken only by beams of moonlight filtering in through the high windows. The constant hum of traffic outside is a stark reminder of the world beyond these walls.

Devon takes charge, her voice echoing through the cavernous space. "We are proof that all of the groups vying to take down Tane Brown have been at odds for too long. We all have a common goal, and our conflicts with each other are a useless and damaging distraction. Tane is the real enemy here."

Flashbacks of past conflicts between our crews flood my mind, a reminder of the long-standing animosity that has divided us for so long. But now, faced with a common enemy, we have no choice but to set aside our differences with rival factions and unite against a greater threat. Hell, based on how things have gone between the Brixtons and Snakes, we might even find some new friends.

"I don't know about this, guys," Aidan voices his doubts, skepticism etched into every line of his gorgeous, rugged face as he runs his hand through his closely cropped, dark hair. "How do we know we can trust the others? They're liars and criminals by definition!"

Stepping forward, I address Aidan directly, my voice firm. "Because we want Tane gone just as much as they do, Aidan. The enemy of my enemy and all that shit."

"And, if they don't do what we want them to, we'll just torture them! Win-win!" Brick's voice booms through the warehouse, echoing off the dusty walls. His eyes sparkle at the thought of getting to harm yet another group that stands in our way. Brick's ability to find a silver lining in even the darkest of circumstances never ceases to amaze me, and it's one of the things I love about him most.

Devon's conviction is unwavering as she meets my gaze, nodding. "Loyal or not, let's assume they're in this with us. And, like Brick says," she adds, gesturing toward her torture buddy, "there will be consequences for those who don't meet their end of the bargain."

Dom quirks a brow in her direction. "I'm in complete agreement. But... real question. Even with the additional support, do we really think we can do this?" He pauses. "We came pretty close last time, but... ultimately we failed."

Devon's smile is sharp and fierce. "I know we can."

As Devon outlines our plan, excitement builds among us, a shared determination uniting us in purpose. The road ahead may be fraught with danger, but together, we are stronger than any obstacle that stands in our way.

The thought of our crew allied with others makes my pulse quicken. United, we could be unstoppable. But it won't be easy to convince the guys, and they're already expressing their doubts. It took enough trust and suspension of belief to get these two groups together—the Brixtons and the Snakes—and looking back, it's wild to think how far we've come.

They know in their heart of hearts it's the only way we'll get to Tane, but it's always been their goal to take him down on their own. Needing to partner with others isn't only risky, it's a blow to their egos. They're proud of who they are and where they've come from, and needing to rely on others isn't the way they ever wanted to play this. But that's something they need to get over, and soon.

Flashbacks of the fist-fights between some of the Brixtons and the Snakes, the barbed comments, they all come rushing back. And the Snakes are some of the good ones, guys we've come to know and trust despite our initial differences.

The people we may need to ally ourselves with now can't be counted on in the same way the Snakes can. Their loyalty hasn't been tried and tested in the same way. Yet, Aria and her men recently proved that not all strangers are dangerous, and they might come to your aid when you least expect it.

I survey the room, noting the uncertainty etched on everyone's faces. I don't love the idea of joining forces with our rivals either, and I know it won't be easy. But I don't see any other choices. Sink or swim.

"I get why you're hesitant," I say. "We've been fighting with some of these groups for years. But Devon's right. Tane's the real threat, and he needs to be taken out. I think Aria and her guys are proof that there are people who can be brought into the fold, who can really help us do this once and for all."

I lock eyes with Aidan, always the most resistant to anything involving risk, and someone the others all look to in times of uncertainty. As much as Skyler and Zeke are in charge of the Snakes' operations, Aidan has become the unofficial leader of our combined crews. "You've always had my back. I'm asking you to trust me on this."

Aidan holds my gaze for a long moment before nodding. "If Angel says it's the right move, I'll ride with her." He glances at Devon. "And you as well. Alliances are my personal kryptonite, and it's because of you two that we got as far as we did last time. I'd be an idiot not to listen."

My eyes shift to Skyler and Zeke, and their faces are serious as usual.

Aidan runs his fingers through his hair, his trademark tell that he's anxiously contemplating something important.

Zeke and Skyler glance at each other in silent conference, and they both nod.

Skyler is the first to speak up. "Yeah, you're right. I don't love it, but we need to take a leap of faith. It feels like we either do this or drown in the wake of Tane's terror. Neither seems like a great option, but this really is our only chance to finish this."

"I don't like it, but you're right," sighs Zeke. "I don't see any other options."

I turn to Devon, my breath unsteady as the weight of what we're about to do starts to settle. "Alright, sounds like we're all in. What's the plan?"

Devon grins, a predatory glint in her eye. "First, we reach out to Dimitri. His crew clearly has beef with Tane, too, and they've proven themselves worthy of an alliance. They saved our lives back there for goodness' sake, and put themselves in harm's way in the process. With their help, we'll just about have the manpower needed to launch an all-out assault on his stronghold."

Excited murmurs ripple through the room.

"Once we join up with Dimitri and the other guys, we hit Tane hard and fast before he knows what's coming," Devon continues. "We take away his money, his products, his territory. We destroy his entire operation…"

"We make him rot from the inside out? Go out with a bang?" Brick's eyes are gleaming now, his interest piqued by the possibilities.

A savage smile tugs at my lips. We've spent so long fighting Tane's goons, barely surviving by the skin of our teeth. The promise of finally crushing him fills me with dark satisfaction that I know Devon and the rest of the group shares.

"Let's do this," I say, fire in my eyes. "Let's end this bastard once and for all."

CHAPTER THREE

ANGEL

The warehouse explodes into action as both crews rally. United by a common purpose, former enemies stand shoulder to shoulder, ready to wage war against Tane Brown. It's amazing how past differences melt away in the face of a common goal.

I scan the room, buoyed by this new energy, adrenaline pumping through my veins. We just might pull this off.

My gaze lands on Roman across the warehouse. He's watching me intently, an unreadable expression on his rugged face. Our history is complicated, full of passion and pain, defined by an undeniable magnetism between us, ever since he walked into my hair salon and killed a man right in front of me.

He strides over, his movements graceful and predatory. "You sure you're ready for this, Angel?" His voice is low, meant only for me. "Taking on Tane again is gonna get messy. People are gonna die. Hell, we almost died last time we tried. I can't bear the thought of anything bad happening to you—"

I lift my chin. "I know exactly what I signed up for, Roman. Death and pain are nothing new to me—you know that. The question is, can you handle it?" I search his dark eyes. There's desire there, and concern. But also ruthlessness.

He steps closer, invading my space. "Don't worry about me, princess. I was born ready for this fight."

I swallow hard as his woodsy scent envelops me. "Good," I manage. "Just don't get in my way."

His mouth curves into a wicked grin. "Wouldn't dream of it."

Before I can react, he turns and stalks off to confer with the rest of the guys. I release a shaky breath, thrown by the way he still affects me after all this time. But it's not just him, because Aidan, Brick and Slade all have their own magnetic pull on me as well.

Shaking it off for now, I focus on the task at hand. The battle against Tane will be brutal and bloody. But with Roman and the other Brixtons at my side, I know I can face anything.

Aidan comes up beside me, his presence steadying. "You seem...tense. Which is understandable... I just want to make sure you're okay."

I scoff. "Tense...that's one way of putting it. But we do what we have to do." I shrug, not wanting to discuss my complicated feelings. "Right now, that means taking down Tane. Nothing else matters."

Aidan studies me for a long moment before nodding. "You're right. We have a job to do." His hand finds mine, giving it a gentle squeeze. "Just remember I'm here for you. Whatever happens with Tane."

I smile, grateful for his unfailing support. "I know. You always have been."

"And speaking of which, thank you for giving me a kick in the ass and reminding me of what really needs to be done," he adds, his expression serious as he gazes into my eyes. "You and Devon are right. It's the only way."

Butterflies dance in my stomach. This is a huge compliment coming from Aidan, who's usually cynical and skeptical about any plans, including his own.

Across the room, Skyler joins Roman and the others, his large figure moving with purpose.

Roman's eyes flick to mine for the briefest second, a silent acknowledgement passing between us.

We have a future to fight for, Together with my men beside me, I know we'll triumph over the darkness that threatens to consume us.

I survey the warehouse, taking in the determined faces of my family. The Brixtons and Snakes have formed a strong bond, united in our common goal to bring down Tane Brown and dismantle his empire of evil, brick by bloody brick. We may not have been successful in our most recent attempt, but we came pretty damn close.

Devon speaks up again. "Tane has evaded us for too long, hiding in the shadows while he destroys everything we hold dear. And gloating in plain sight. But his time is up. It won't be easy, but he will pay for the lives he's ruined and the havoc he's wrought. We'll make sure of it."

I exchange a glance with Slade and Brick, seeing my own fierce determination reflected in their eyes. Roman appears at my side, his presence a silent promise. Whatever happens, we'll face it together.

"Tane thinks he's won," Devon continues, "that we'll crumble under the weight of his tyranny just like the people of these islands have been forced to do for far too long. But he's wrong. Our spirit isn't so easily broken. We've endured too much, and come way too far to give up now." Her gaze sweeps the room, meeting each person's eyes in turn. "These are our islands. Our home. And we will defend this place with our last breath—sacrifice everything—to rid the world of Tane's evil."

No words are spoken, but the room is buzzing with an almost audible energy.

"Are we doing this?" Devon demands, her eyes blazing.

"Yes!" The shout is deafening, a battle cry that shakes the walls.

Devon smiles, sharp and fierce. "Then let's go to work."

I survey the determined faces around me, pride swelling in my chest. We've come so far, endured so much to reach this point.

All the pain, all the loss and sacrifice has led us here, to this moment of reckoning.

I think of the friends we've lost, their lives cut short by Tane's cruelty.

I remember the devastation left in the wake of his ambition, the trail of bodies and ruins he has left behind.

So much needless death and suffering, even by many innocent people, all for the sake of power and greed.

No more. The time has come to make him pay for his crimes, to bring him to justice once and for all.

I meet Devon's gaze across the room, seeing her own steely resolve reflected there. Together we've helped to lead our people through darkness, but now a new dawn is rising.

The future is ours to shape, a future without fear, without oppression. A future of freedom.

We turn to Aidan, Skyler and the others, our brothers in arms and so much more. The bonds between us have been forged in fire, an unbreakable loyalty that transcends words.

We're ready for this fight, and without even knowing it, we've been preparing our whole lives for a moment like this.

Roman appears at my side, his presence a steadfast comfort. I know that whatever comes, he'll be there with me. Just as I'll be there for him, and for everyone who has placed their trust in me.

I smile, slow and sharp.

Let Tane come.

I have an army at my back, and they are hungry for justice. The real battle is about to begin.

CHAPTER FOUR

ARIA

I'm breathless, my heart pounding. The thrill of the chase still sings in my veins.

Dimitri pins me against the wall, his hands roving over my body. He was the first of the three to catch me, as usual. "Such a bad girl, Aria. You need to be punished."

Heat coils low in my belly at his words. I arch into him, craving his touch. "Please, Dimitri..."

He growls, fisting a hand in my hair and yanking my head back. His lips scorch a trail down my neck as his other hand squeezes my breast.

"On your knees," he commands, his voice rough with lust.

I sink to my knees, trembling in anticipation. Dimitri unzips his pants, freeing his thick cock. I lick my lips, aching to taste him.

He rubs the head of his cock over my lips, smearing pre-cum. "Beg for it."

"Please, Dimitri," I moan. "I need your cock. Fuck my mouth."

With a snarl, he drives into my mouth. I relax my throat, taking him deep. Dimitri's hands tighten in my hair as he uses my mouth, his hips pistoning.

The taste of him floods my senses. I moan around his cock, my own arousal pooling between my legs. I slip a hand under my skirt, my fingers seeking my clit.

Dimitri glances down and growls in approval. "Look at you touching yourself. Good girl, Aria. Keep going. I want to see you come when I fill your mouth with cum."

His words send a jolt of heat through me. I rub circles over my clit as Dimitri's thrusts grow erratic. With a shout, he empties himself down my throat.

I swallow greedily, climaxing at the taste of his release.

Dimitri pulls out, tugging me to my feet.

Before I can catch my breath, Josef and Florian descend, their hands and mouths seeking to give me the pleasure Dimitri promised.

Dimitri steps back, chest heaving, and watches with a satisfied smirk as Josef maneuvers me into position.

I brace my hands on the dining table, arching my back. My skirt is shoved up around my waist, baring my ass and pussy to Josef's heated gaze.

"So wet and ready," Josef rasps, sliding two fingers into my dripping cunt.

I moan, rocking back onto his hand. "More, please."

He withdraws his fingers and replaces them with the thick head of his cock. "Is this what you want, Aria?"

"Yes!" I gasp as he sinks into me with one hard thrust.

Josef sets a brutal pace, pounding into me.

The table creaks under my hands, my breasts bouncing with each snap of his hips.

Dimitri moves closer, pinching and rolling one nipple between his fingers. "Come for us again, Aria. We want to watch you clench around Josef's cock."

The dual sensations send me tumbling over the edge with a wail. My inner walls clamp down on Josef, dragging his own climax from him.

Josef collapses over my back, his weight bearing me down onto the table. His cock slips free, followed by a trickle of cum.

A warm, wet tongue laps at my sensitive flesh, cleaning Josef's release. I lift my head to see Florian kneeling behind me, his eyes glowing.

Florian rises, wiping his mouth. "My turn."

Florian lifts me off the table and spins me around to face him, desire etched into his handsome features.

"On your back," he commands, helping me onto the table.

I obey eagerly, spreading my legs in invitation. Florian settles between my thighs, gripping my hips to pull me closer to his mouth.

His tongue swipes through my lips, flicking my clit. I gasp, fisting my hands in his hair.

"You taste so sweet, Aria," Florian murmurs against my flesh. "I could feast on you all night."

He seals his lips around my clit and sucks, shooting sparks of pleasure through my body. I writhe under his skillful mouth, chasing another climax.

Florian slides two fingers into my cunt, crooking them to stroke my g-spot in time with his laving tongue.

"Oh god, Florian!" I cry out, feeling my inner walls start to flutter. "Don't stop!"

He increases the pressure, driving me higher and higher until I shatter with a scream.

Florian laps at my pussy, prolonging the waves of ecstasy. "You're so gorgeous when you come, Aria."

He stands, freeing his thick cock from his slacks. I lick my lips at the sight, desire stirring low in my belly again.

Florian braces his hands on either side of my head, leaning down to capture my mouth in a searing kiss. I can taste myself on his lips, musky and tangy.

He nudges my entrance, sliding in slowly. We moan in unison as he fills me inch by inch.

"So tight and wet," Florian breathes against my lips. "You feel like heaven."

He draws back and thrusts deep, pulling a cry from my throat. Our bodies move as one, climbing higher with each snap of his hips.

I drag my nails down his back, clutching at him. "Harder, Florian. I'm so close."

Florian pistons into me, the table rattling under us. "Come for me, Aria. I want to feel you come all over my cock, too."

His words tip me over the edge. I shatter around him, my inner walls clamping down.

Florian follows with a roar, his warmth flooding my core.

We collapse together, our sweat-slicked flesh pressed close as we struggle to catch our breath.

Florian lifts his head, brushing a tender kiss over my lips. "You are exquisite, Aria. You are absolutely perfect."

He eases out of me slowly, his release trickling down my thighs.

I whimper at the loss, already craving his touch again.

He scoops me into his arms, carrying me down the hallway and into bed.

The other men crowd around us, their large hands stroking and petting.

Dimitri presses a cool glass of water to my lips. "Drink, baby. You need to stay hydrated."

I sip gratefully, too blissed out to argue.

Josef drapes a soft blanket over me, tucking it around my body.

"Get some rest, beautiful," he murmurs, dropping a kiss on my forehead. "We'll take care of you."

Surrounded by their warmth and affection, I drift into a peaceful sleep. My men shield me from the world, a barrier of muscle and sinew guarding what belongs to them.

I've never felt so cherished, so utterly possessed. Whatever comes next, we'll face it together. Bound as one by lust and love, there's no force that can stand against us.

The Next Day

I wake to the sensation of calloused fingers carding through my hair. Blinking open my eyes, I find Dimitri gazing down at me, a soft smile curving his lips.

"Good morning, princess. How do you feel?"

I stretch languidly, my muscles pleasantly sore. "Wonderful. Though I could use a shower."

He chuckles. "We were hoping you might say that."

Florian and Josef appear, each balancing a tray laden with food. My stomach rumbles at the sight of pancakes, fruit, and coffee.

"Breakfast is served," Florian announces with a grin.

"And we have plans for the rest of the day as well," Josef adds, eyes glinting with promise.

A delicious shiver runs down my spine. "Do tell."

Dimitri strokes a finger down my cheek. "Patience, little one. All in good time."

His touch ignites a slow burn in my blood, awakening my desire once more. I've only just sated my hunger for these men, yet their latest sweet actions have me craving them again already.

Our future is uncertain, fraught with danger and the unknown.

But as long as we are together, I have no fear of what's to come.

CHAPTER FIVE

ARIA

A *couple of days later*

The neon lights streak across my vision as we stroll down the busy street, the buzz of the city pulsing around us. My men trail behind me, their footsteps echoing on the pavement, but my focus stays locked ahead, assessing each building we pass for its potential.

Before was time for pleasure. Now it's time for business.

Excitement wars with doubt in my chest. This new venture sparks with possibility, but the shadows of our pasts and the uncertainty of our future linger at the edges, waiting. I square my shoulders against their weight.

I pause at a corner storefront, picturing the warm lighting and intimate booths it could become. "What do you think?" I ask.

Dimitri steps up beside me, his brow furrowed. "It has potential, but we'd have stiff competition in this area."

Josef nods. "I agree. We should consider location carefully."

I sigh, but determination steels my spine. One way or another, we'll find the right place. My men and I have faced far worse than choosing a location. Together, we can build something beautiful from the ashes of our past lives.

I turn and gesture them onward into the neon night. Shadows loom ahead, but with my men at my side, I'm ready to face them.

I lead my men further down the street, possibilities swirling through my mind. The scent of frying oil and spices wafts from a nearby restaurant, making my stomach rumble.

"I envision a vibe that's trendy but enduring," I say. "An intimate atmosphere, but not stuffy. Instagram-worthy but not some lame flash-in-the-pan gimmick where everyone takes a picture of the one signature dish. We'll have an eclectic menu—local produce and proteins, interesting ingredients. A fusion of all the best this area has to offer, really. And a top-notch cocktail list including a whole selection of booze-free options."

I glance back at my men. Excitement gleams in Florian's eyes, but doubt creases Josef's brow. Dimitri looks pensive.

I know they're wondering, like me, if we can really do this. If we can keep the more violent aspects of our operations going and build something good together from the ground up. A legitimate business, an honest living, in addition to everything else. They have their business interests, and now it's time for me to live my dream. It won't be easy, but when has anything worthwhile ever been easy for people like us?

"Just imagine what we could create," Florian says, a smile in his voice. "A little oasis among the chaos. Somewhere people can come to celebrate the best moments of their lives, or just escape the fray for a moment and build some enjoyable memories."

Josef shakes his head. "We can't rush into this. It's too big of a risk without doing our research. Do you know how many new businesses fail within the first year? And it's a huge investment. We need to get this right."

He's right, of course. We need to be smart, despite our eagerness. The shadows of the past still lurk, waiting to swallow our hopes, as do the myriad snake oil merchants who'll only be too happy to snap up our money on a shitty deal before we know what's happening.

But with care and patience, we can outmaneuver them. Together, step by step, we will make this dream real.

I squeeze Josef's shoulder and nod to Dimitri and Florian. "Come on. Let's keep looking."

The city hums with potential around us. Our future is out there somewhere, waiting to be claimed. All we need is the courage to reach for it.

I take a deep breath, inhaling the crisp night air as we round the corner onto a quieter street. My phone buzzes in my pocket. I pull it out, glancing at the screen. A message from Devon.

My eyes widen in surprise.

Devon: We need to have a sit-down. You and your guys. The Snakes and the Brixtons. It's time to discuss next steps, and this can't wait.

This could be dangerous. The Snakes and Brixtons were at each other's throats for a long time, but their bond has recently grown strong. They seem unbreakable.

We showed Tane that our loyalty is not with him, and now we expect that he'll come at us harder than ever.

And by doing so, we showed the Snakes and Brixtons that we can be trusted.

We are, after all, determined to achieve the same goal—taking down Tane Brown. This carries risk, of course, being the new ones... the group that is the least known and therefore the most easily discarded. The most likely to be used to take the fall, or as collateral damage.

But there's opportunity here, too. Together, we'd be a force to be reckoned with. Able to hit back and protect our own.

"Devon wants to talk," I say, looking up at my men. "She's called a meeting with us, with the Snakes and Brixtons."

Florian's eyebrows shoot up.

Josef frowns, wary.

"Is that smart?" Dimitri asks. "Getting in the middle of their feud with Tane?"

"It's risky," I agree. "But we really showed our colors over on the other island. We're already smack bang in the middle of things as far as Tane's concerned. And if we want to take Tane down, we need numbers. Isn't that why we helped them over there in the first place?"

Josef shakes his head. "I don't like it. We've only just broken free of one viper's nest. Why crawl into two more?"

"Because these are our islands, too," I counter. "Our home. We have a right to fight for it." I meet each of their eyes. "And they might be dangerous, but we're not the ones they have their eyes on. We all want the same thing. I can't force you into this. But I won't hide from Tane anymore. With or without allies."

Florian grips my shoulder, resolute. "We're with you."

Dimitri and Josef exchange a look. Josef sighs.

"You know we'll follow wherever you lead. But promise me we'll be cautious?"

I squeeze his hand, moved by their loyalty. "Always."

This won't be easy.

But together, we can take back control.

One ally, or in this case, two. One day at a time.

CHAPTER SIX

DEVON

I sit in my room, the morning sound of bird calls loud through the screen on my window. The heavy air presses down on me as I replay the dark events that brought me here, grappling with this twisted new thrill coursing through my veins.

Because while the birds are light and happy and free, I feel the opposite. And it has both nothing and everything to do with the guys.

I pace back and forth, my mind racing as fast as my pulse. I've always been the calm in the storm—okay, that's a complete lie. I'm sassy, and occasionally a bit of a brat. Yet when it comes to our group, I've consistently been the voice of reason in our morally gray crusade against Tane Brown. The need to ally. To think things through calmly and deliberately without rushing in, no matter how tempting.

But now something primal stirs within me, something that hungers for the fight, for the blood.

I can't ignore it anymore.

"What's happening to me?" I mutter through gritted teeth. This isn't who I am, who I'm supposed to be. I'm losing myself in the violence, and I'm terrified by how much I crave it.

I hear the fall of footsteps down the hall and spin around. There's a gentle tap on my door, and Skyler enters, his face etched with concern.

"Talk to me, Devon. Let me in," he says gently.

My hands tremble. "I don't know if I can stop this darkness inside me," I confess, my voice ragged. "Hurting them, it's starting to feel too good. I can't stop thinking about the way Denzo's eyes looked when we..." My voice trails off, my mind warring with itself, simultaneously horrified and delighted by the memory.

Skyler steps closer, his eyes boring into mine. "You don't have to face this alone. We're all struggling in our own way. But we have each other."

His words steady me, but my blood still sings for the fight. I don't know if I can resist its siren call for long. But, looking into Skyler's eyes, I find a flicker of hope. Maybe together we can lead each other out of the shadows, back into the light. He's been through so much himself. Maybe we can grow through this together like we have so much else.

But I can't get the image of Tane's man out of my head—the satisfying crunch of bone and cartilage under my knuckles as I pummeled his face. The thrill of delight I get each time I think about the way Brick painstakingly disemboweled the man, stringing his intestines up on a rack like authentic ramen noodles.

Or the intense FOMO I have of not being present when the guys put Angel's stalker through a twisted game where he had to eat his cousin's dick and his own tongue, finally being decapitated by Angel herself. The artistry... just... incredible.

It's got to the point where these types of thoughts make my pussy clench. Yep, I really do need help.

"I'm losing myself," I rasp. "When I'm in the thick of it, I don't see enemies anymore. Just targets. And I'm consumed by thoughts of this stuff all the time. Who will be next... how far we can push the boundaries."

Skyler's jaw tightens, his eyes clouding with concern. "Maybe we need a break from all this. Get away for a while, clear our heads." I know his words are meant to provide comfort, to give me an out if I need it. He's just as eager to end this as I am.

I let out a harsh laugh. "A vacation? Isn't that what we just had, kind of? You really think Tane will simply let us walk away? This is the time we need to galvanize and strike, not think about 'getting away from it all'."

Skyler's gaze meets mine and he studies me for a moment, and then nods. "So we'll make him," Skyler says, determination in his voice.

Loud footsteps echo in the hallway. I whirl around to see Dom striding into the room towards us, his face unreadable.

"Am I interrupting something?" he asks coolly.

Skyler shakes his head. "We were just talking options."

"The only option is finishing what we started," Dom says. His eyes bore into mine, and I feel a spark of that primal hunger flare up in my gut.

He's right. The only way out is through. I curl my hands into fists, ready to drown my doubts in violence once more. I can worry about any lasting effects after the fact. For now, I need to embrace my bloodlust and do what needs to be done.

I nod slowly, the fire in my veins overtaking any lingering doubts. If this is who I need to become to protect my family, then so be it.

"You're right," I say to Dom. "It's time to end this, once and for all."

Dom's mouth twitches into a sly smile. He can sense the darkness taking root inside me, feeding on my rage and desperation. He recognizes the same darkness in me that exists deep within himself. Maybe he should come along next time Brick and I are exploring our dark sides.

"That's the Devon I know," he says. "Ruthless when it counts."

Skyler frowns, clearly uneasy with how readily I've embraced Brick's violent counsel, and the way Dom is egging me on. But he doesn't argue further, just gives my shoulder a gentle squeeze.

"Just promise me you'll be careful," he says softly.

I meet his worried gaze steadily. "I promise."

But we both know it's a hollow assurance. There are no half-measures in this world we inhabit. And I've already crossed lines from which there is no coming back.

All that's left is to charge forward, consequences be damned. Tane and his men will feel my fury soon enough. I'll paint the walls red if I have to, and to be honest, I very much want to.

My hands curl into claws, ready to tear into warm flesh and break bones. I take a deep breath, steadying myself before I speak again.

"You're right, Dom. We'll face whatever comes together. But I'm still struggling with these violent urges inside me. It's like there's this primal part of me that hungers for the thrill of the fight, for the taste of blood."

I pause, hating to admit these dark desires out loud.

"I don't want to become a monster, but I can't deny that hurting Tane's men made me feel powerful. Unstoppable, even."

Dom regards me with concern, but no judgment.

"That rush of power can be addictive," he says. "But we have to remember who we are—and what we're fighting for. We're Snakes, not animals. But, that said, I think we've realized that the ends do justify the means if we really are going to take Tane down. And it's not terrible if you get some enjoyment out of it." He shrugs. "I know that's the way I've come to deal with the more violent aspects of this lifestyle."

I nod, but uncertainty gnaws at me.

"We've learned that defending ourselves isn't enough anymore. The only way to win this war is to fully embrace the darkness. We just need to hope that we're able to return to our usual principles when we're on the other side of all this."

Skyler nods his head firmly. "We'll find a way, Devon. When this is all behind us."

His unwavering faith gives me hope. I meet his gaze with renewed resolve.

"You're right," I nod. "We've all learned that we can't always stick to our code... it's just not practical these days. Everything is getting more ruthless, more fierce, more deadly. But no matter what Tane throws at us...our approach might just need to change in the meantime. I won't completely lose myself to the shadows... I'll just lean into them a little more than I usually do."

The darkness still calls, but if we stick tightly enough together, we can hold on to the light.

CHAPTER SEVEN

SKYLER

The ocean stretches before me, endless and eternal. The salty breeze tangles my hair as the sun beats down, causing the water to sparkle in a wild dance. Waves crash against the shore in a hypnotic rhythm, and I close my eyes, letting the sound soothe my troubled mind.

I've come so far to get here. Running a surf school was never part of the plan, but somehow I turned my passion into a thriving business. Pride wells up inside me as I look back on everything I've accomplished. And all of it, surrounded by constant danger.

I take a deep breath, letting the salty air fill my lungs. The beach is buzzing with activity—surfers of all ages and abilities dot the shoreline, waiting to catch the perfect wave. This place is like a second home to many of us, a tight-knit community bound together by our shared love of the ocean.

Out on the waves, I spot a familiar colorful board—Rake, goofing around as always even as he expertly rides the swell. He's been here since the beginning, since way before my little surf school was even just a fledgling operation. Now he helps me run the place, his humor and easygoing nature making even the newest students feel at ease.

Watching Rake, I can't help but smile. He's part of the family I've built here. My father may have put this place on the map, but I've made it my own, surrounding myself with people who encourage me to embrace my passions.

Devon's right—the future is mine for the taking. I just have to let go of the past and all its expectations. This life I'm building, it's not my father's. It's mine.

I think back to the advice I just gave her. I'd be a hypocrite not to apply it to myself. We have each other to lean on in challenging times, and I don't have to face my demons alone. This is just something I need to work through, until I get to the place where my father's legacy finally stops haunting my every moment.

With newfound resolve, I grab my board. "Come on," I say to myself. "Let's catch some waves."

The ocean swells before me, and I paddle out to meet it head on. The salt spray mists my face as I sit atop my board, rising and falling with the rhythm of the waves.

Rake paddles up beside me, flashing his trademark goofy grin. "Great day for a little surf, isn't it?" he says.

I nod, squinting against the bright sunlight glittering off the water.

The swells around us begin to grow, and Rake's eyes light up. "Incoming!" he shouts.

We both start paddling furiously, positioning ourselves to catch the growing wave. It swells larger and larger until suddenly we're both up, popping to our feet in perfect unison. The wave cradles us as we fly across its face, carving back and forth in exhilarating bursts of speed.

I glance over and see Rake with his arms spread wide, hollering and whooping as we share this moment of pure joy. My earlier doubts seem to wash away with the tide. This right here is everything—the thrill of the waves, the salt spray on my skin, the camaraderie of riding alongside a friend.

As we kick out in the whitewash, Rake gives me a high five. "Yeah, Skyler!" he exclaims. "That's what I'm talking about!" His enthusiasm is contagious, and I can't help but laugh.

The ocean sets me free in these moments. Out here, I'm not living in anyone's shadow. I'm just me—Skyler—chasing the thrill of the surf.

I nod and give Rake a fist bump, but as we paddle back out, I feel the darkness creeping in again. No matter how hard I try to lose myself in the surf, my father's legacy weighs on me like a leaden anchor.

It doesn't seem to matter how much I accomplish, because his voice always rings in my head telling me the many ways I'm not good enough in his eyes. Too soft, too weak, why can't I be more like my brother, and so on. It's like the better I do with anything, the louder the voice gets. And right now, it's almost deafening. Willing me to fail.

They say when your parents die, it can bring relief for some. But 'they', whoever they are—they're lying. You might not hear the voice of your actual parent anymore, but the version of them that lives rent-free in your head—which is almost certainly worse than the real thing—can take up a full-time residency and put on a nightly show if you don't watch out.

Rake senses the shift in my mood. "You good, bro?" he asks, brows furrowed with concern.

I hesitate. Rake's one of my best friends, a chosen brother, but will he understand? I take a deep breath and decide to open up. Besides, there's something magical about words spoken when you're sitting on your surfboard out in the ocean. Bonds are formed, deals done, out here. There's no judgement, only a shared love of surfing and a reminder that we're all tiny little ants in the overall scheme of things.

"It's just...my dad," I say quietly. "No matter what I do, I can't escape being his son. I'm so sick of living in his shadow." I sigh. "And you know this is something I've struggled with my entire life... I thought it would get better with all... this," I gesture at the expansive ocean glimmering in the sun before us, "but the better I do, the more it feels like he's judging me from wherever he is now."

Rake nods, his expression thoughtful. "Yeah man, that's gotta be tough," he says. "But you gotta know—you're killing it with the surf school. You built this whole thing yourself. Your dad didn't do that, you did."

I smile halfheartedly. Rake means well, but he doesn't fully get it.

Out of the corner of my eye, I spot Devon walking down the beach toward us. Her red and pink hair whips in the wind, glinting in the sunlight. Walking daddy issues. If anyone will understand, it's her.

"Thanks Rake," I say. "But there's only one person who really knows what it's like." I gesture toward Devon as she approaches.

Rake follows my gaze and nods in understanding. "Ha, yeah. Her father was one for the books. I'll catch you later, bro," he says, clasping my shoulder supportively before paddling away.

"Hey." Devon's voice breaks me from my reverie as I reach the shoreline.

I turn to see her approaching, her feet sinking into the sand. Her ponytail whips in the wind, strands escaping to frame her face. It seems like so long ago that I first set eyes on her, this gorgeous surfing student turned captive turned life partner. I never imagined things would work out this way, but I'm so glad they have.

"Hey yourself," I say.

She comes to stand beside me, gazing out at the darkening water. "You okay?"

I sigh, shoulders slumping. "Just thinking about everything, you know? There's a lot to take in at the moment. Tane, the business, just... there's so much going on." Devon's the only one who has ever truly understood the demons I wrestle with, maybe because of the oppression of her own father. I pray she can help me now, before I drown in my dad's towering legacy.

I lift the board from the water and hoist it under one arm.

Devon slips her hand into my free one, squeezing gently, her touch instantly soothing. She gives me a knowing smile, her eyes radiating warmth and understanding. "You've got this, Sky. You've accomplished so much. You know this. And you should be proud of what you've done here."

I nod, my throat tight. "I just can't seem to escape his shadow," I confess. "No matter what I do, how far I come...I'm still my dad's son."

"I know it's hard," she says, squeezing my hand again and bringing instant comfort. "But you can't keep comparing yourself to him, Sky. You're amazing in your own right. I really thought you'd worked through most of this." She pauses, and while her gaze meets mine she reaches up and tenderly traces her finger along my jawline. "But I know, more than most, that just when you think you've worked through something it can rise back up and bite you... hard. And not in a good way."

I sigh heavily, glancing out at the darkening ocean. The dying sunlight glints off the waves—waves that seem ready to swallow me whole.

Devon's expression turns to concern, her brow furrowed and her lips pressed in a thin line. God, she's gorgeous even when she frowns. "You need to remember we're here for you, and he can't get to you anymore. You can't let him win. You need to move forward."

"I'm trying, Dev," I say quietly. "But sometimes it feels hopeless, like I'm fighting against a rip current I can never overcome."

Devon moves closer, forcing me to meet her intense gaze. "You listen to me, Skyler. You are not your father. You get to choose who you become. Who you already are. You've stepped into your leadership role alongside Zeke, just like we all knew you were capable of."

She's right—the future stretches before me, vast and limitless like the sea. I don't have to let the past pull me under. I stare searchingly into her eyes, desperately wanting to believe her.

"Serious question for you, Skyler, and I'm not afraid of the answer. But do you ever hold me up to some standard of how my father was? What if you did, and I didn't measure up to what he or others expected me to be... especially if they expected me to be just like him?"

Her words sink in. "Of course, I would never..."

She pushes further. "I know you wouldn't. Why though?"

I shrug, my brow furrowed. It seems so obvious when she puts it this way. "Well, you're not him. And he's hardly the type of person that I'd ever expect you to *want* to live up to."

"Even though sometimes he *was* there for me? That I have some good memories of him, and other people even go so far as to emulate him in business? Doesn't that find me lacking, that I don't follow along in his shadow?"

I think of her father and all the baggage that he came with. Tales of formidable power, and at one stage, untold wealth. A life full of business deals and accolades. But then, under the covers, a mountain of shady business practices and questionable decisions in his personal life. Someone who would ultimately give up their daughter to pay off a debt, and then flee to avoid the consequences. Someone we ultimately had to kill just to set her free, and because he deserved it. There's no way I'd ever expect her to follow in his footsteps, and I'd think she was mad if she tried.

She gives me a knowing glance.

Slowly, I feel a sense of calm wash over me. My past doesn't have to dictate my future. I'm more than my father's legacy. I know this. I just need to remember it and have it stick.

I pull Devon into a grateful embrace. My shadows of self-doubt still lurk, but they're dissipating a little.

We stay here, locked together, as the sun finally sinks below the waves.

Tomorrow brings new challenges, but tonight, I am simply Skyler. A man with an incredible woman by his side, and so much potential to live his own dreams, not someone else's. And for now, that is enough.

"Come on, Sky." Devon tugs my hand. "Let's go grab some dinner. We'll figure the rest out later."

Together, we turn and walk down the beach. The dying light gleams on the water, leading us forward.

With her hand firmly encased in mine, I can't help but feel like there's nothing we aren't capable of facing together.

CHAPTER EIGHT

AIDAN

Our headquarters are a stark contrast to the chaotic energy of the city streets. Within these walls, surrounded by maps and data charts, it feels almost monastic. A sanctuary for strategic thinking, safe from prying eyes.

I sit at my desk, illuminated only by the glow of my laptop screen, and try to focus on the task at hand. My eyes scan the latest intel in preparation for the critical meeting ahead. The rhythmic tapping of my fingers against the keyboard is the only sound piercing the heavy silence.

Risk assessment. Contingency plans. I wade through my analysis, evaluating every potential outcome. The weight of responsibility feels heavy on my shoulders. One misstep could unravel everything we've built.

As I analyze the details for the meeting with Dimitri and the rest of his team, my mind keeps drifting to Angel. Her fearless spirit fuels me even when we're apart. I can almost see her determined gaze, feel the heat of her touch. She invades my thoughts, my senses—she's with me even when she's not.

I try to refocus, to think logically about the risks and potential outcomes. But logic falls away and there is only Angel—her passion, her fire, the way she sees right through me. I ache for her in a way I've never ached for anyone. My fingers still over the keys as I give in and let myself imagine her here with me now...

The harsh trill of my phone startles me from my daydream. I curse under my breath, angry at the interruption. With effort I push Angel from my mind, steely determination settling over me. I have work to do. I can't afford distractions, no matter how tempting. And she is extremely tempting...

I take a deep breath and turn my focus back to the task at hand, my fingers flying over the keys once more. The endless what-ifs and statistical models. The meeting must go smoothly, no matter the cost. And I cannot let emotion cloud my judgment now. Too much depends on it, on me keeping a level head. Angel will just have to wait.

My fingers clatter on the keys, inputting notes with machine-like precision. I immerse myself in cold logic and probability, pushing away any thought of Angel's smile, her laugh, the fire in her eyes... the way she...

For now, I must be a machine. Everything else must wait until the mission is complete.

I take a deep breath and rub my eyes, trying to refocus. But my mind keeps drifting back to Angel. Her passion, her fire—it's what gives me purpose beyond the endless calculations and contingency plans.

The click of the door opening jars me from my thoughts.

Zeke strides in, his face an unreadable mask. There's always been an uneasy alliance between us. Different styles, different visions for moving the Brixtons and Snakes forward. We might have bonded in our last attempt to take down Tane, but I'd hardly call us identical twins when it comes to our strategic approach. But despite our differences, I still respect the shit out of this man.

"Zeke," I say evenly, meeting his gaze. "We need to present a united front for this meeting. No mixed signals or power plays."

He holds my stare, then gives a curt nod. "Agreed. We have the same goal here, even if we differ on how to achieve it."

I resist the urge to argue. Zeke loves playing devil's advocate, questioning my every strategy. But we can't afford dissent right now.

"I know we clash at times," I reply. "But when it matters most, we come together."

Zeke's expression softens slightly. "You're right. We're a team, Aidan. I've got your back—you know that." He extends his fist and I bump it with my own.

A moment of silent understanding passes between us. We're united now against a common enemy. The mission takes precedence over everything else.

With Angel's spirit to guide me and Zeke and Skyler's support at my side as co-leaders, I feel ready for whatever this meeting with Dimitri brings. The Snakes and Brixtons will show our strength.

I nod at Zeke, a silent acknowledgment of our truce. There's too much at stake to let personal differences get in the way.

My gaze drifts across the room, landing on a picture of Angel that hangs on the wall. It's candid, with her hunched over a laptop, her brow furrowed in concentration. A lock of vibrant purple hair falls across her face and in the image she's brushing it back absently, focused on her task.

Seeing her steadfast dedication renews my own resolve. Angel came to us broken, searching for meaning after a life of pain. Over time, she's blossomed into a capable leader. If it wasn't for her and Devon insisting that we park our differences and unite around our common goal, we'd never have come close to taking Tane down. Her inner light guides us forward, even in the darkest times. She can see potential where we see only chaos, and vibrant color where we see only darkness.

I force myself to look away, refocusing on the plans before me. There will be time for sentiment later—for now, we have a job to do.

Zeke and I work steadily, finalizing strategies and contingency plans. The mood between us has shifted. We operate in easy tandem these days, synchronized in our ability to map out strategy and identify potential threats even if our means of doing so don't always align.

After hours of preparation, I lean back in my chair. "I think we're as ready for this meeting as we can be," I say.

Zeke nods. "We've got all our bases covered. Now it's time to put our plans into action."

A sense of shared purpose settles over us. Zeke extends his clenched fist once more and I bump it with my own. No matter what lies ahead, the Snakes and the Brixtons will face it together.

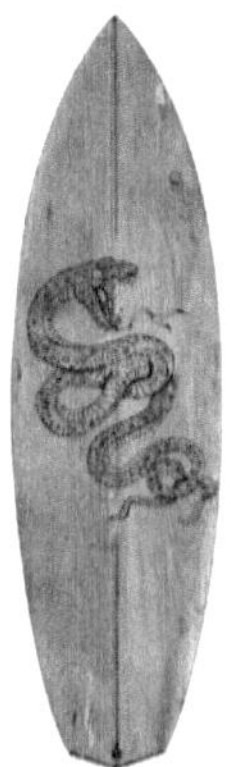

DOM

The scent of sizzling spices hits me like a punch to the gut as I step into the dimly lit meeting room. My eyes dart to the platter of fiery samosas in the corner, their red-orange filling practically glowing beneath the low lights.

A knot forms in my stomach. I've never been able to handle anything spicier than black pepper. The thought of it has me sweating. I'm ravenous, but I've learned my lesson and I guess I'm going to have to go without.

"Don't worry, Devon has got you covered, and sent in a special request." Aria's husky voice breaks through my rising anxiety. She emerges from a side room holding a tray marked 'Dom's Special Order' in her elegant script. "Can't have you sweating bullets in the middle of negotiations," she says with a wink.

A snort comes from the head of the table where Slade sits, arms crossed, with a scowl on his chiseled face. "Should've started a damn cooking school instead of getting mixed up in all this," he grumbles. "Dom's the kind of customer who goes into a Michelin star restaurant and asks for grilled chicken and rice, hold the pepper."

Aria laughs, the sound warm and musical. "We'd make a hell of a team. I'll handle front of house, you can be in the back working away over a hot stove."

She sets the tray down in front of me with a flourish. Plain rice, roasted chicken, a small bowl of yogurt. My comfort food. A swell of gratitude rises in my chest, momentarily easing the roiling anxiety within. I have an evil mob boss to take down, and I can't be worrying about Scoville units right now.

No matter what happens, at least I'll have bland food in my belly.

Slade eyes the dish and smirks. "Exactly..."

I take my seat at the heavy oak table, the wood smooth and cool beneath my fingers. Across from me, Aria and her men sit with an air of easy confidence, though I can detect a hint of tension in their postures.

My eyes drift over the maps and charts covering the walls, each one marked with details of Tane Brown's far-reaching criminal empire. A web of red strings connects his legitimate businesses to the illegal operations lurking in their shadows.

I have to admit, what Tane has managed to create is impressive. The façade of legitimate businesses—primarily restaurants and a few other tourist-oriented interests—spans the island chain. It would be difficult for anyone visiting the islands to avoid interacting with at least one of them if not more.

It's a stark reminder of what we're up against. The immense challenge of toppling a man who has the islands firmly in his grasp.

But as I meet Aria's steely gaze, I also feel a swell of hope. She and her crew took a massive risk to get us out of Tane's trap on the other island. I feel like I—we—owe them all a debt I may never be able to repay.

Whatever happens next, we're in this together. A motley band united by a common goal—bringing down the tyrant who has terrorized these islands for too long.

With allies like these by our side, I know we have a real shot at victory—side by side until the bitter end.

Aidan rises from his seat, his shoulders squared with determination. Zeke and Skyler flank him, presenting a united front. Our co-leaders—Zeke and Skyler from the Snakes, Aidan representing the Brixtons. Three strong men who have repeatedly proven their ability to take a long-term view and make decisions in our best interests. I trust the three of them implicitly.

"Thank you," Aidan begins, his voice unwavering despite the storm of emotions I'm sure is raging within. "You didn't have to help us escape. But you chose to put your lives on the line anyway. We won't forget that." He meets Dimitri's gaze, gratitude shining in his eyes. "We owe you more than we can ever hope to repay. But we'll stand with you until Tane is brought to justice."

Despite Aidan's show of strength, and my agreement with his words, I can't shake the icy fingers of fear creeping up my spine. The thought of facing Tane again makes my blood run cold. He's cunning, ruthless, willing to do anything to protect his empire and punish those who defy him. There have been too many close calls already, and he's only growing stronger.

But when I turn back to Dimitri, I see the same steely resolve reflected in his eyes. He knows the risks better than anyone, and he must be just as terrified as we are. Yet here he sits, ready to take the fight to Tane once more. Aria, and the other guys in their group, too.

Bolstered by their courage, I push aside the doubts clawing at my mind. We come from different worlds, different factions. But in this moment, we share one purpose.

"We may not have hoped to need allies," I say, holding Aria's piercing gaze. "But we share a common enemy. And if we stand together, Tane doesn't stand a chance."

Around the table, heads nod in agreement. In this room, faction lines melt away. We're a team now, united by a single goal.

And with these people at my side, I truly believe we can tear Tane Brown's empire down, once and for all.

Dimitri speaks now, determination etched into the hard lines of his face.

"We've been fighting Tane on our own for too damn long," he growls, fists clenched. "It's time we joined forces and showed that bastard he can't keep dividing us." He slams a fist on the table, rattling the glasses and plates. "Together, we'll bring him to his fucking knees."

Josef, Florian and Aria murmur their assent. I feel a swell of hope in my chest. With Dimitri's ruthless persistence and his team's intricate knowledge of the islands, we might just have a real shot at toppling Tane's regime.

But as we delve into the details of our plan, the gravity of what we're attempting starts to sink in. Storming each of Tane's compounds, hacking into his networks, turning his most trusted men against him—it won't be easy. There are a million ways we could fail.

My stomach twists into anxious knots as I think of everything that could go wrong.

If we slip up even once, Tane won't hesitate to make us suffer. Vivid images of torture flash through my mind, chilling me to the bone. He's infuriated that we managed to get as close as we did last time, no doubt plotting his own revenge.

I force myself to take a deep breath, steadying my nerves. I just hope we get to him first.

Because one way or another, his reign of terror needs to end. Here and now, we make our stand. We have to. There is no other choice.

I take a deep breath and try to focus on Aria as she outlines possible entry points into Tane's main compound.

Her voice is cool and collected as she analyzes structural weak spots and security rotations.

Looking at her, you'd never guess the trauma she's endured at Tane's hands. She and her crew have been fighting him far longer than we have. If anyone understands the risks we're taking, it's them.

But that doesn't stop them. Aria is fearless, driven by an unshakeable sense of purpose. She won't stop until Tane is dead and her family avenged.

Her determination rekindles my own flickering courage. I don't trust many people, but something tells me I can trust these guys. We can do this. We will do this.

The conversation flows late into the night as we hammer out the details. Adrenaline thrums through my veins, banishing my earlier doubts. I can almost taste victory on my tongue, rich and sweet.

When we finally call it a night, I catch Aria's eye across the table. Her gaze conveys a silent promise. We're in this together now, bound by vengeance and purpose.

With allies like these, Tane doesn't stand a chance.

His days are numbered.

CHAPTER TEN

ANGEL

I step out of the meeting room, the weight of our new alliance pressing down on me like a ton of bricks.

Devon follows close behind, her usually cheerful face now etched with concern as we make our way down the dimly lit corridor.

My heels click sharply against the concrete floors, echoing in the empty hall. I can't shake the knot in my stomach—have I made a deal with the devil himself by joining forces with Aria and her men? They seem like they're on our side, but...

Devon places a gentle hand on my shoulder and gives it a squeeze, as if sensing my inner turmoil.

Her unwavering support anchors me, keeping me from being swept away in the riptide of doubt threatening to pull me under. She's been my rock through all of this, never wavering, even when I was ready to crumble.

As we reach the heavy wooden door leading to our shared office space, I'm filled with gratitude for my steadfast friend. Her faith in me gives me the strength I need to see this alliance through, come what may. Together, we can accomplish anything.

I push open the door, the familiar smell of paper and ink washing over me. Our office is a reflection of our partnership. It's an organized chaos that we've cultivated together over time. A space where we can let our creativity run wild, bouncing ideas off each other as we bring our visions to life.

Typically, my side of the room is covered with catalogs showcasing all the latest innovations in hair coloring and cutting techniques. But lately, things have been different. Instead of info on hair products, the entire room is filled to the brim with sketches, swatches, and designs pinned haphazardly across the walls. Bolts of colorful fabrics are stacked precariously in the corners while our large wooden desks sit cluttered with supplies.

Devon sinks into the overstuffed chair behind her desk, leaning back and closing her eyes for a moment. Her brow is furrowed in thought as she too processes the weight of our new alliance.

"That was intense," she finally says, breaking the heavy silence hanging between us. Her voice is tinged with uncertainty. "But I'm glad we're on the same side."

I nod, perching on the edge of my desk across from her. "Me too. It's better to have Aria and her men with us than against us."

Devon opens her eyes, determination shining through. "We've got this," she says firmly. "We can do this."

I feel myself relax as her confidence washes over me.

A surge of excitement stirs within me as thoughts of the meeting flee my mind. The possibilities of partnering with Devon on a new business venture seem endless, and frankly, much safer to think about. There are so many opportunities we could explore by combining our resources and skills.

"What if we created an athleisure line together?" I suggested a few months back, my voice rising with enthusiasm. "We could blend your amazing design talents with my marketing experience. I know we could build something incredible."

I still remember Devon tilting her head, considering. "That's an amazing idea. But would you have the time for that on top of the salon?" It was a fair question back then.

"Definitely," I nodded at the time. "I just brought on a new manager last week to oversee the day-to-day operations. That frees me up to focus on expanding into new ventures."

I could see the excitement building in Devon's eyes as my words sunk in. A smile spread across her face, still etched in my mind now for its warmth and genuine joy at the idea. "I love it," she was quick to reply. "We could really make something special—clothing that's stylish yet functional. Empowering women to feel strong and confident, both in and out of the gym."

And now, look at us. Our office is filled with all the things we need to kick this off properly. Our passion project, friends and co-entrepreneurs. This feels good.

Devon and I dive into fleshing out ideas for the athleisure line, our creative juices flowing. She sketches some more designs while I jot down thoughts on branding and marketing strategy.

Her sketches begin to take shape—sleek leggings with mesh paneling, sports bras with crisscross straps, tops with inspiring mantras. I find myself getting swept up in the creative flow, grabbing my own notebook to jot down ideas for branding and marketing.

Devon's eyes light up at one of my suggestions, a smile spreading across her face. "I love it," she says, her enthusiasm infectious. "That's going to give our customers the confidence to try something new, to safely push themselves harder."

She returns to her sketchpad, pencil flying across the page as she begins bringing our ideas to life. Her passion is palpable, completely absorbed in translating our vision into tangible designs.

I watch in admiration as leggings, sports bras, and tops take shape before my eyes. Bold prints, fun colors, sleek lines—each piece radiates the confidence and strength we want to inspire.

"The fabrics need to be high performance," Devon muses, brow furrowed in concentration. "Something that can handle intense workouts."

Her eyes shine with enthusiasm as we dive back into planning. "I'm thinking we could do a whole activewear line," she says, sketching out ideas with swift, sure strokes of her pencil. "Not just leggings and sports bras, but jackets, tennis skirts, the works."

I nod, leaning in to examine her drawings. "Love it. We could do some edgier, sexier pieces too. Push boundaries. Create outfits that look just as at home at a cardio session as they do in the bedroom."

She grins. "Hell yes."

My mind races with ideas and inspiration. This athleisure line symbolizes everything Devon and I have built together—independence, self-reliance, feminine strength. And the ability to put ourselves first and take what we want, not be dictated by what society tells us is 'our lot'.

We're so engrossed in brainstorming that we don't even hear the office door swing open.

"Well, well, what do we have here?"

Aidan's teasing voice cuts through our concentration. We glance up to see him and the other guys crowded in the doorway, mischievous grins on their faces. They tend to stay away from our little section of the compound, leaving us to our 'girl time', but occasionally they visit just to check up on us.

"This looks cozy," says Slade, an eyebrow cocked.

Brick steps further into the office, peering down at the sketches and notes spread across our desk.

"What's all this about... are you building some kind of babe empire?" He picks up one of Devon's drawings, examining it with a smirk. The guys know we've been working on something, but we've largely kept them in the dark while we've started figuring things out ourselves.

Devon rolls her eyes at Brick's comment but continues sketching, undeterred. I feel a swell of admiration for her ability to stay focused on our goals.

After a moment, she reaches out and snatches the sketch from his hand. "It's none of your business," she says crisply, though there's a hint of amusement behind her eyes.

I feel a swell of pride for my strong, stubborn friend. The guys may joke and tease, but Devon and I share an unbreakable bond. We have a vision and we won't let anyone shake our determination to make it a reality.

"We're creating an athleisure line to empower women," I explain. "Combining fashion, function and inspiration."

Aidan and the guys gather around to look at Devon's sketches. There are murmurs of approval and appreciation for her talent.

"These designs are hot," Roman says with a wink.

Devon smirks. "That's kind of the point."

I can't help but smile, excited by their positive reactions. This feels like a pivotal moment, our collective vision taking shape.

My mind races with ideas as we continue brainstorming. Marketing campaigns, photo shoots, pop-up shops. Each new concept adds to the momentum building inside me.

With Devon's artistry and my business savvy, I know we can build this into something amazing. Something that impacts lives, inspires confidence, sparks change. The possibilities feel endless.

There's a synergy in the room that wasn't there before. By including the guys and getting their buy-in, they now feel invested in seeing this succeed.

"We'll leave you ladies to it then," says Slade, holding his hands up in mock surrender. "But we expect VIP access to this...babe empire."

"Oh my god, please stop calling it that," Devon rolls her eyes in exasperation. "Or we'll start referring to your operations as the 'big boys club'."

As we wrap up and the guys file out, laughing, Devon and I share a determined look. The future is ours for the taking, one step at a time.

I run my fingertips over the desk's smooth surface. "You know, I was thinking we could convert one of the spare rooms upstairs into a proper design studio for you. Natural light, space to pin up inspirations..."

Devon looks up, eyes wide. "Seriously? That would be amazing. I love sharing this space with you but it is starting to get a little cramped."

"Of course," I say softly. "We're partners. Your dreams are my dreams now."

She reaches across the desk, squeezing my hand gently. Our eyes meet in a moment of silent understanding.

The men may tease and doubt and think of this as our funny little cottage business, but we have each other. And together, we are unstoppable. Our empire, built by women, for women.

The click of my boots echoes down the empty corridor as I step out of the meeting room. Devon trails behind me, her brows knitted together, lost in thought.

The weight of allying with Aria still sits heavy in my gut, and while being in the office offered a brief reprieve, it's hard to stop thinking about the huge, dangerous challenge before us.

Still, with Devon and the guys by my side, it's the best shot we have.

CHAPTER ELEVEN

DOM

The scent of blood permeates the dank basement air as I descend the creaking steps.

Brick's hulking frame is silhouetted against the dim light, his muscular arms flexing as he works. The wet smack of flesh impacting flesh echoes off the cold concrete walls.

My pulse quickens at the visceral display before me. This nameless fool dared to cross the Brixtons and now pays the price. I yearn to join in the savage dance, to feel the slick warmth of blood on my knuckles. But this is Brick's stage tonight.

Brick pauses, his chest heaving, to admire his tools lined up neatly on the scarred wooden table. He selects a short, serrated blade, the overhead light glinting off its eager edge.

A low groan escapes the bloodied mess of a man bound to the chair.

Brick grins, all white teeth and roiling menace. He goes to work with renewed fervor, and the basement rings with agonized screams.

I ache to participate, to unleash the feral rage that simmers within. But I merely observe for now, bearing witness to Brick's gruesome artistry. This fool's torment has only just begun.

Brick pauses, breathing heavily as he admires his handiwork.

The man in the chair is now barely recognizable, his face a pulpy mass of torn flesh and broken teeth.

"Want to join in on the fun?" Brick asks, turning to me with a savage grin. His hands are slick with blood, droplets speckling his white tank top. "I needed to do something to relieve the tension after that meeting. This just feels right."

My heart pounds with anticipation. I've watched Brick ply his trade countless times, but rarely does he offer to share his toys. This is a gift I won't refuse.

I approach the sobbing, shuddering wreck of a man. His pleading eyes meet mine, wide with pain and terror. I bare my teeth in a smile. Slowly, deliberately, I pick up a pair of pliers from the instrument table. The cool metal calms my raging bloodlust.

With Brick observing approvingly behind me, I set to work.

The man's muffled wails rise in pitch as I apply the pliers with surgical precision.

Brick chuckles, a deep rumble from his broad chest.

We share this sacred communion, bonding through blood and agony.

This fool will regret the day he crossed us.

I nod in satisfaction as the man's screams turn to whimpers. His spirit is nearly broken.

Brick claps me on the back, his hand leaving bloody prints on my shirt. "Not bad for your first time," he says.

I'm no stranger to violence, but my approach usually involves knuckles and the sound of bones being crushed. Torture like this... well, it's just a different way of getting your point across.

Before I can respond, a voice calls out from the top of the stairs.

"Are we interrupting?" Angel descends into the basement, Devon following close behind. Angel's nose wrinkles at the thick, coppery scent of blood hanging heavy in the air. Her eyes flick dismissively over the sobbing man.

Devon remains impassive, gazing at the gruesome scene with detached interest. I expected her to be more excited, but I know she has a lot on her mind. We all do.

Brick grins, clearly pleased by their arrival. "Not at all, ladies. We were just getting started. Checking out your athleisure range reminded me of how much I enjoy creating things myself..." He grabs a serrated hunting knife from the table, testing its edge with his thumb.

I step back, letting Brick take over. With practiced ease, he carves into the man's flesh, his victim's cries rising in intensity once more.

Angel circles slowly, observing Brick's work. A small, cruel smile plays on her lips.

Devon stands motionless, no hint of disgust or horror on her beautiful face.

These women understand. The Brixtons and the Snakes look after their own. And those who cross us pay the price.

Devon steps forward, her steps echoing off the concrete floor. Without a word, she picks up a pair of pliers from the table. Our captive's eyes go wide with terror as she approaches.

In one smooth motion, Devon grips his pinky finger and twists. The snap of bone echoes through the basement, followed by a raw, primal scream.

"Oh, hush now," Devon says softly. "We've only just started on you."

She drops the mangled finger and grabs the next one. I watch in fascination as she efficiently breaks each finger, her face never changing from its neutral, angelic expression.

I've never seen her quite like this... so composed, so utterly dark. And I've never been more in love.

Finally, she sets the pliers down and turns to us, brushing a strand of pink-highlighted hair from her eyes.

"Are you guys hungry?" she asks casually. "I'm starving."

Brick barks out a laugh. "I like you, Dev," he says. "You've got guts."

Devon smiles blithely, not bothered in the least by the sobbing, bleeding man before her. Without another glance at our victim, she pivots on her heel and heads for the stairs.

"Come on. I want pancakes," she calls over her shoulder.

Angel shakes her head in amusement and follows.

Brick claps me on the back again.

"Let's go get some grub," he says.

I take one last look at the broken man chained to the wall, then turn my back and head upstairs with the others.

Devon is right.

Torture works up quite an appetite.

CHAPTER TWELVE

DIMITRI

The Next Evening

The rumble of the waves crashing against the shore fills my ears as I take a sip of my ice-cold beer.

Zeke leans back in his chair, gazing out at the moonlit ocean.

Skyler and Aidan also sip on their beers, enjoying the calm moment before the storm we all know is on its way.

After yesterday's meeting, we agreed to meet up today in an attempt to get to know each other. The co-leaders of our fragile little alliance—the Snakes, the Brixtons, and my team... I guess you could call Aria, Josef, Florian and I the Unknowns. Because we all have secrets. Double lives, if you will. Although I'm guessing my business is about to become front and center of the conversation.

"So, what's your line of work, Dimitri?" Zeke asks, turning his attention to me. I knew this question was coming. It was only a matter of time.

I can't help but smile, because I don't know if they're prepared for my answer.

"I mean, other than the obvious? You must have a front for another business, at least. Laundromat? Convenience store?" Aidan asks, his nose slightly upturned.

I hesitate for a moment, swirling the beer around in my glass. Do I trust these men enough to reveal the truth? Or do I stick to my usual vague response?

Ah, what the hell. We're plotting to take down the most dangerous man on the island chain. I think it's time for some honesty between allies.

"I run an exclusive club downtown. We cater to a...particular clientele with specific desires. A club where we make people's darkest dreams come true."

Zeke's eyebrows shoot up, but he doesn't interrupt.

Skyler almost chokes on his drink. "Wha—we have one of those here?"

Zeke's eyes fly to meet mine. "You mean..." The rest of his words escape him.

Aidan looks at me with a blank stare, his brow furrowed.

"Yes, several actually. A collection of sex clubs. Our flagship is here, and we have outposts on every island. I'm looking at expanding to the mainland soon."

"Oh, so it's thriving then?" Zeke leans in, intrigued.

I smile and shrug. "Sex is an evergreen business. It doesn't matter if there's a recession, war, famine, general societal anxiety... people are doing it, people want to do it. They can't get enough. And in uncertain times when they're cutting back, well... they want more from clubs like mine."

Skyler whistles. "Really..."

"It started out many years ago as an underground spot for people looking to live out their deepest, darkest fantasies. No judgement, no shame. Just a safe place to indulge. Over time, word spread among certain circles. Now... well let's just say business is booming."

I take another swig of beer, letting that sink in.

Skyler leans forward, curiosity glinting in his eyes. "So what do you do there, exactly? Other than the obvious."

I chuckle. "Our services are broad. We've got private rooms for every taste. Costumes, props, you name it. We also have themed events, live entertainment. It's a full sensory experience."

Aidan shakes his head in disbelief. "And that actually pays the bills? There's enough people into that stuff here to keep multiple clubs running?"

"You'd be surprised," I reply with a smirk. "Let's just say, an island paradise like this, it brings out people's wild side. And we're there to facilitate it. And there's a mixture, too... people who live here and have made it part of their lifestyle, and visitors who like to let their hair down while they're on vacation."

The guys all look at each other, a mix of shock and intrigue on their faces. This conversation has taken an interesting turn, but I don't mind indulging their curiosity.

In our line of work, we take our thrills where we can find them.

I take a long pull from my beer, savoring their rapt attention. There's an art to spinning a good yarn, and I've had plenty of practice over the years.

"Like I said, we offer a judgment-free environment. Client privacy is paramount. We screen all our staff thoroughly and they're discreet as can be." I pause for effect, letting the anticipation build. I take a sip of my drink, the ice clinking in the glass. "Have you been to a club like this before?"

Aidan shakes his head. "Well, no..."

"We pride ourselves on discretion. It's why clients rely on us, why we've built such a loyal following."

Skyler nods in understanding. "That makes sense. So what kind of fantasies do you help fulfill?"

"We've got private playrooms for every kink—medical, dungeon, schoolgirl, you name it. Clientele can get trussed up in full leather and latex outfits. We've got equipment for suspension bondage, hot wax play. Anything to get the adrenaline pumping."

Zeke's eyes gleam with interest. "I could see how that would be entertaining for the right crowd."

"Absolutely. We cater to all sorts of fetishes and roleplaying fantasies. As long as everything is safe, sane and consensual, anything goes within our walls."

"What are some of the wildest things that happen there?" Skyler asks, his eyes gleaming with interest.

I smirk. I'm used to this level of intense interest in what I do. "We've got private dance rooms with poles, cages, even trapezes if you want an aerial performance. Our dungeon area is fully equipped for bondage, discipline, you name it. We host costume parties, have specialty nights like Schoolgirl Wednesdays and Leather Fridays."

I have their full focus now. Aidan leans in, eyes wide. I smile indulgently as the men barrage me with questions, their curiosity piqued about my illicit empire.

"Leather Fridays, huh?" Skyler nods thoughtfully. "I could see how that would be entertaining for the right crowd."

I take another swig of beer, licking the foam from my lips. "Like I said, sex sells. And we provide the ultimate adult playground. Our clients trust us to make their fantasies come to life, no matter how dark or taboo. We offer them an escape from the mundane."

"What does Aria think about all this?" Aidan quirks a brow. "Doesn't she get jealous? You must see... all sorts of things in your line of work."

I nod. "It took a lot of conversations to get to the point she was comfortable with it. Now, I can barely tear her away. She's very involved in the operations of the business, and has helped our client list grow exponentially through her sheer creativity with discreet marketing. It turns out there's a whole network of influencers specifically focused on this type of club, and I had no idea until I met her."

Skyler whistles. "I can only imagine what Devon would think if we tried to open a sex club."

Zeke laughs. "Right? I know she'd have a lot to say."

Aidan smirks. "Angel, too."

"You'd be surprised," I say. "It's one of those things where you get an idea of it in your head and it can come across as quite unsavory. Dirty. Gross. But in reality, it's clean and professional. We're providing a service, and everything is done on the participants' own terms. General feedback is that it's life-changing and cathartic in a way that keeps people safe, if anything. Once Aria wrapped her head around that, she became a super fan."

The guys nod as my words sink in.

Zeke raises his glass in a toast. "Well gentlemen, I think we could all use a little escape from the mundane right about now. What do you say we pay this infamous club of yours a visit sometime soon?"

I give him a devilish grin. "It would be my pleasure. I'll make sure you get the VIP treatment."

CHAPTER THIRTEEN

SLADE

I scowl as I enter the kitchen, my usual grumpy demeanor in full force. The smell hits me first—pungent garlic, earthy mushrooms, rich tomato sauce. And as I glance over the array of fresh ingredients laid out on the counter—ripe tomatoes, fragrant herbs, plump vegetables—a thrill races through me. My fingers twitch with anticipation. It's a familiar scent, one that brings a reluctant smile to my face despite my usual morning grumpiness. Okay, who am I kidding—my regular grumpiness.

This is my domain. My sanctuary. In here, I'm not just some sullen thug. I'm an artist. A master chef. My knives flash, slicing and dicing with expert precision. Spices rain down, filling the air with intoxicating aromas. Oils sizzle in pans, the promise of succulent dishes to come.

I shuffle further into the kitchen, my shoulders hunched in my soft t-shirt. But as I survey the ingredients spread across the counter, a glimmer of excitement flickers in my chest.

Angel glances up from chopping vegetables, her eyes crinkling with amusement. "Hey there, sunshine. Ready to work your magic?"

I grunt in response, even as warmth blooms through me. Angel knows how much I love cooking, that it's my language when words fail me.

Before her, this kitchen was my domain that few dared to enter. And while I enjoyed the solitude, sometimes I missed having a partner to enjoy the ingredients and the whole process as much as me. When Angel showed an interest, and an appetite for the fun we could have in here, it changed things for me.

We move in sync, an orchestrated dance. I drizzle olive oil in a pan, and it sizzles as Angel adds the garlic. The scent is heavenly. My hands work on autopilot, dicing, seasoning, stirring. Muscle memory takes over.

"Looking good over there," I call out gruffly, a hint of affection peeking through.

Angel laughs, her voice sparkling like champagne. "Why thank you, chef. I learned from the best."

We cook side by side for a while in silent companionship.

"This reminds me of that hole-in-the-wall place we found on the other side of the island," Angel says. "With the little Italian chef yelling at us the whole time."

I chuckle at the memory. "You thought he was gonna kick us out."

"I didn't know asking for hot sauce with pasta was such a sin!" Angel laughs. The sound wraps around me like a warm blanket.

"Speaking of which, don't burn anything this time," I warn gruffly, giving her a pointed look and gesturing at the pasta on the stove. Angel just sticks her tongue out at me in response. I have to fight to keep a straight face.

We trade stories as we cook, laughter filling the space between us.

"Who do you think is having more fun right now? Us, or Aidan on his little 'leadership outing?'" I smirk, and Angel sticks out her tongue and grins, pointing at her, me and the mess we're making in the kitchen.

In Angel's company, I find it possible to drop my prickly armor. My thoughts drift to many good memories together, her steady presence through my storms.

The sauce simmers, rich and fragrant. Angel dips her finger in for a taste, closing her eyes in bliss. Pride swells in my chest. Normally meals are my gift to her, my way of showing what I'm really shit at telling. That she's my family, and I am hopelessly in love with her. But now it's her time to spoil me.

As we plate the pasta, Angel squeezes my arm, a wordless thank you. I duck my head to hide my smile.

My Angel. Her smile as bright as the summer sun. Her laughter as melodic as wind chimes. She sees through my thorns to find the man within. The only one who truly understands me.

We work in syncopation, an effortless duet. The sizzle of oil in the pan, the thunk of the knife on wood. Our movements weave together like music.

As we cook, we continue to chat and joke, the conversation flowing as smoothly as our teamwork. No one makes me smile like Angel does. With her, I can be myself, thorns and all.

The kitchen comes alive with our combined passion. The rich aromas of simmering sauces mingle with the sound of our laughter.

When we finally sit to eat, I'm filled with contentment. The meal we created together nourishes so much more than just my stomach. Here with Angel, I've found the missing piece I've long searched for. My friend. My heart. My home.

"Angel, pass me the salt," I grumble, glancing over at her with a hint of affection in my tone. Though I come across as perpetually grumpy to most, Angel knows it's just a front. She's seen the real me, and she likes me for who I am.

"Here you go, chef grouchy pants," Angel says with a smirk, passing me the salt shaker. Her eyes dance with mischief, always ready with a witty response.

I shake my head, biting back a grin. Only Angel can get away with teasing me so mercilessly. With her, my prickly exterior softens. My grumpy soul has found its home.

"I think this is our best one yet," she declares after a few bites.

I nod, a smile creeping onto my face. "Not bad for an amateur chef like you."

Angel swats me with the dish towel again, but her eyes shine. We both know this meal is special.

In the kitchen, I found more than great food. I found the missing piece of myself.

CHAPTER FOURTEEN

ARIA

A few days later

The sun's rays glint off the restaurant's glass storefront as I stand outside, hands on hips, pride swelling in my chest. This will be my haven, my palace of culinary creativity. The traffic's roar and pedestrians' chatter fade away as I envision white linens, gleaming cutlery, the sizzle of meat on the grill.

I push open the door, my pulse racing. The empty space echoes my footsteps as possibilities swirl through my mind. I trail my fingers along the bare walls, imagining cozy booths, an elegant bar. This blank canvas is mine to transform. The responsibility weighs heavy, but so does the thrill.

I'm grateful that we were able to find this space. Dimitri's business comes with a network of contacts in high places, as most discreet and exclusive sexy ventures do, and one of his most frequent clients just happened to have an empty commercial space right in the area we were looking. It's everything I'd hoped for and more, with an indoor-outdoor flow that brings the exquisite beauty of the outside in.

I stop in the middle and turn slowly, picturing the magic to come. "We'll put the kitchen there," I say, pointing. "An open concept, so diners can see the action."

My partners nod, their faces alight. "I can see it now, my queen," Dimitri rumbles. "This place will be incredible."

"With the right decor, it'll be stunning," Josef adds, squeezing my shoulder.

I lean into him, craving his strength. We have so much to do, so far to go. But together we'll create something extraordinary. I know it in the depths of my soul.

"It won't be easy," Florian says quietly, "but we'll make this work." His eyes meet mine, lit with purpose. "And I'm so excited to watch your dream come to life!"

I reach for his hand, hope and fear mingling within me. The future gleams, tantalizing, just out of reach. We have to grab it with both hands, refusing to let go.

This empire will be ours.

I take a deep breath, steadying myself. The future is unknown, especially with everything going on with Tane, but I need to stay focused on the present. There's so much work to be done before we can open these doors.

"We should start unpacking the equipment," I say decisively. "Josef, can you handle the ovens? Florian, the walk-in fridge needs assembling."

They nod, heading off to their tasks. I turn to Dimitri. "Let's unpack the dishes and smallwares. We'll need them organized for prep."

Soon the space hums with activity.

Josef curses under his breath, wrestling with an oven door.

Florian frowns at the fridge instruction manual, tools spread around him.

Dimitri and I sort through boxes, lining up gleaming stacks of plates and pots.

The work is tedious but satisfying. With each box unpacked, each piece of equipment assembled, we inch closer. This empty shell will soon hold life—the sizzle of sautéing garlic, the chatter of happy diners.

As afternoon fades into evening, weariness seeps into my bones. But I force it back. There will be plenty of time to rest when the work is done... and when Take is taken care of.

I straighten, rolling my shoulders. "How about some dinner? We could all use a break."

The men's eyes light up. Josef grabs takeout menus from his bag. "Pizza or Chinese? Some guys were handing these out on the street earlier and both look good."

Within about thirty minutes, our food arrives. An array of Chinese takeout, packed into little cardboard containers. The aroma is intoxicating, and I heap my plate high enough that the guys give me stunned looks.

We settle on the floor amidst the organized chaos, fueling up for the tasks ahead. The road is long, but we will walk it together.

I glance around at my partners as we eat, pride swelling in my chest. We've already accomplished so much today—this empty space is slowly transforming into the restaurant of my dreams.

Dimitri catches my eye and smiles softly. "How are you holding up?" he asks. "I know this is a lot to take on."

I take a deep breath. "It's overwhelming," I admit. "But also thrilling. This restaurant represents everything I've worked for."

I think of the long hours, the sacrifices, the single-minded pursuit of this goal. All the blood, sweat and tears will be worth it in the end.

"Just remember, you're not alone," Josef says, squeezing my shoulder. "We're here with you, every step of the way."

"Through thick and thin," Florian agrees. "We'll make this happen, together."

Their steadfast support fills me with renewed energy. The future gleams, bright and full of potential. With my partners beside me, I can weather any storm.

"Let's get back to it," I say, standing up decisively after taking one last bite of delicious noodles. "We've got a restaurant to build."

The men rise, determination in their eyes. As we get back to work, I know that we will triumph over any obstacle. With shared purpose and strength, we are unstoppable.

The night stretches on, but we don't stop. Piece by piece, our vision takes shape. And when the sun rises, it will illuminate the beginnings of our dream.

The hours fly by as we work to transform the empty space into a warm and welcoming restaurant. My earlier anxiety melts away as I focus on the tasks at hand—unpacking dishes, arranging tables, hanging light fixtures. The steady progress fills me with growing excitement.

As the day draws to a close, I step back to admire our work so far. The once-barren room now holds the beginnings of the cozy, elegant space I've envisioned.

"There's a lot more to do, but it's really starting to come together," I say with a satisfied smile.

"It looks great already," Dimitri agrees. "Just imagine how it'll look on opening night, filled with happy customers."

His optimism is contagious, spurring me on. But underneath the buoyant mood, I feel time pressing down. There is still so much to do, and only a finite number of days left before opening. That's without even considering the elephant in the room—Tane Brown, and our fragile alliance with the Brixtons and the Snakes.

I take a deep breath, steadying my nerves. "Let's keep up the momentum," I say decisively. "I want to get the kitchen set up tomorrow. At least enough to be able to train people and try out some of the dishes I've been conceptualizing."

The men nod, rolling up their sleeves. Their solid reliability calms me. As long as we work in sync, we can accomplish anything.

Step by step, we will make this dream a reality. The path stretches before us, both thrilling and daunting. I'm just so grateful to have these loyal, supportive men by my side.

As the last of the lights are switched off, I take one final look around before locking up for the night. A sense of deep satisfaction washes over me as I survey the space. Though still a work in progress, the beginnings of something special are emerging.

With the door secured behind me, I step out into the cool night air, the day's urgency fading away. In its place, a quiet confidence settles in my chest.

This journey won't be easy. There will be long hours, tough decisions, and unforeseen obstacles ahead. But when doubt creeps in, I need only remember this feeling right now—the thrill of watching a vision come to life. I've always wanted this, and to see it coming into fruition is a life's dream.

And all three of my men share this dream as wholly as I do—not because they care about restaurants, but that they're diligently focused on enabling me to do what brings me joy. Together, we'll celebrate each milestone, and pour our souls into creating something extraordinary. I help them with their dreams, and they do the same for me. Because—and I've only learned this since being with the three of them—that's how true partnerships are meant to work.

The restaurant awaits, my dream brimming with promise. And though the road is long, I know with absolute certainty that we'll reach our destination. For now, I allow myself to bask in the satisfaction of a day's work well done.

Tomorrow brings new challenges, but also new opportunities.

As I walk to our car, I smile softly to myself, my mind already racing with ideas. One thing is clear—with passion and perseverance, we'll turn this empty space into something truly remarkable.

Step by step, we will get there. Together.

CHAPTER FIFTEEN

FLORIAN

*L*ater

Aria's body fits against mine perfectly, our sweat-slicked skin sliding together with every breath. Her hair fans across my chest as she gazes up at me, her eyes glazed and lips swollen from kissing.

"You inspire me," I rasp, cupping her face in my hands. My fingers tangle in her hair as I stare into her eyes. "The way you move, the sounds you make...fuck, baby, the way you come for me. You're my muse."

My words are true, and she knows it. The way this whole restaurant venture is making her light up... it goes beyond a smile. I can see it in her eyes. If it's possible, I'd say her soul is glowing.

Her lips curl into a sultry smile, her hips rocking against mine.

The friction makes me groan, my cock already hard and aching again.

"Is that so?" Her voice is husky, filled with lust and delight. "Show me. Show me how I inspire you."

Fuck, she's going to be the death of me. I crush my mouth to hers, kissing her with a savage hunger that makes her whimper. My hands roam her body, squeezing her tits, gripping her ass, my fingers sliding through her wetness.

"The softness of your skin," I growl against her neck, nipping at the delicate skin. "The way you arch into me, so eager and willing. The way you scream my name when you come."

I suck a mark into her collarbone while thrusting two fingers inside her. She cries out, her inner walls clenching around my fingers.

"Florian," she gasps, shuddering against me. Her nails rake down my back and I hiss in pleasure, the sting heightening my arousal. I'm on fire for her, every nerve ending alight with need. Only she can inspire this raging inferno inside me, this all-consuming passion that threatens to burn me alive.

"That's it, baby." I thrust deeper, curling my fingers just so.

She screams, her body convulsing as she comes for me again. I watch her fall apart with hooded eyes, groaning at the sight. "Just like that. My perfect muse."

I withdraw my fingers slowly, watching her twitch and whimper.

She's panting, her eyes glazed over with pleasure.

I bring my fingers to my lips, tasting her essence with a satisfied groan. "You're delicious," I growl.

Kissing along her jaw and down her neck, I suck a mark into the swell of her breast. "But I still have plans for you and your gorgeous body."

I grip her hips and flip her onto her stomach. She gasps, startled, and I smack her ass playfully. "Stay."

She stills obediently, though I can see her trembling in anticipation.

My cock throbs, leaking precum against my thigh. I run my hands over the curve of her ass, squeezing the soft flesh, and she moans, craving more.

"So responsive," I murmur. "So eager to please."

I part her legs further, exposing her to my gaze. Her pussy is glistening, pink and swollen from her orgasms. I lick my lips, craving another taste.

"Please," she whimpers, wriggling her hips enticingly.

I grin and deliver another sharp smack to her ass.

"Patience, Aria." I grip her hips to still her movements. "Or I'll have to punish you."

She shudders at the threat, going pliant beneath me.

I caress the red mark on her ass, leaning down to press a soft kiss to her heated skin.

"Good girl." I position myself behind her, the head of my cock nudging at her entrance. "Now, let's see how many times I can make you come."

I thrust inside her in one smooth stroke, groaning at the feel of her tight heat enveloping me. She cries out, her fists clenching in the sheets. I give her no time to adjust, setting a brutal pace as I pound into her.

"Yes, just like that," I growl, fingers digging into her hips. "Take it, all of it. You're mine."

She's sobbing in pleasure, incoherent pleas spilling from kiss-swollen lips. I feel her inner walls start to flutter, and I drive into her deeper, chasing our releases.

"Come for me, Aria," I demand harshly. "Now."

She shatters with a wail, her orgasm triggering my own.

I spill inside her with a shout, my hips stuttering as I fill her.

We collapse onto the bed, a tangle of sweaty limbs as we struggle to catch our breath.

She nuzzles into my chest, a content smile on her face.

I wrap my arms around her, pressing a tender kiss to her forehead. "My perfect muse," I whisper again, sated and in love.

I pull out of her slowly, watching in fascination as my cum trickles from her swollen lips.

She whimpers at the loss, clenching to try and keep me inside.

I chuckle, giving her rear a light smack. "What a greedy girl you are today. But I'm not done with you yet."

I maneuver her onto her back, spreading her legs wide. Her pussy is flushed and dripping, lips puffy from our activities.

I kneel between her thighs, grasping the base of my cock and guiding it to her entrance once more. "Look at me," I order sharply.

Her eyes fly open, meeting my heated gaze.

"Watch me fuck you."

I push into her with a groan, watching her face contort in pleasure. Her mouth falls open on a gasp as I bottom out, my hips flush against hers. I give a slow, hard thrust that has her arching off the bed with a cry.

"Yes, just like that," I pant, setting a brutal pace.

I lean forward to capture one nipple between my teeth, biting down just shy of breaking skin.

Her inner walls start fluttering again and I straighten, grabbing her hips to pull her onto me. "Come for me. Now."

She shatters on command with a wail, back bowing off the bed. I follow soon after, spilling deep inside her warmth. We collapse back onto the bed, chests heaving from exertion.

I gather her close, pressing soft kisses over her face and neck. She hums contently, nuzzling into my chest.

"I love you, Florian," she whispers softly. "My own personal rockstar."

My heart swells at the words, a brilliant smile crossing my face. I tilt her chin up, kissing her sweetly. "And I love you, my darling. Always."

We lie tangled together, our limbs heavy with satiation. Aria's head rests on my chest, her fingers tracing idle patterns through the hair dusting my abdomen.

My own hands run up and down her back in a soothing caress, relishing in the feel of her soft skin under my palms.

She's curled into me like she was made to fit there, a perfect complement to my body. Our breaths have slowed to a steady rhythm, our hearts beating in time.

There's a bone-deep contentment settling through me, a peace I've only found with her in my arms.

She tilts her head up, her eyes meeting mine. They're glowing with warmth and affection, brighter than any star. A soft smile graces her lips and I can't help but return it tenfold.

"I never want to leave this bed," she mumbles, tucking her face into the crook of my neck with a happy sigh.

"Then don't," I whisper, tightening my hold on her. "Stay here with me forever."

She laughs, the sound vibrating against my skin. "As tempting as that is, we do have lives to get back to eventually. And Dimitri and Josef might have something to say about it, too."

I groan dramatically, pulling a giggle from her. "Must you always be the voice of reason?"

"One of us has to be," she teases gently. "You can play the role of the oblivious artistic genius, and I'll help you to remember the things you need to."

"I suppose you're right," I concede with a put upon sigh. "But just know, you're always welcome in my bed. In fact, I insist on it."

She smiles, brushing a sweet kiss over my jaw. "Lucky for you, Florian, it's one of my favorite places."

My heart swells at her words and I cradle her closer, beyond grateful for the woman in my arms.

Together, sated and content, there's nowhere else I'd rather be.

CHAPTER SIXTEEN

SKYLER

The ocean breeze caresses my skin as I stand at the water's edge, the rhythmic crashing of the waves calling to me. This is my sanctuary, where I find solace from the violent storms that rage within the city streets.

As I stare out at the swirling blue, I'm reminded of my purpose. As co-leader of the Snakes, it's my duty to ride these waves in search of secrets that will keep us steps ahead of our enemies.

With each crest I conquer, I gather whispers and clues to maintain our power. It's a dangerous dance that I've mastered over bloodied years. Only now, more recently, have I had the chance to operate the surfing school on my own terms. The profitability has changed, as has being my own boss, but the rest is the same.

"Hey man, ready for my lesson?"

I turn to see my latest student sauntering towards me, his chest puffed out in a transparent display of bravado. His voice booms over the ocean's roar.

He's one of those guys where everything about him is flashy. The type who always likes to pull out a hundred dollar bill or a black Amex while making sure everyone else in the room sees. Whose clothes are always brand name but you know he didn't just pick them out by himself. Like now, for instance... his

Tommy Hilfiger boardshorts with floral print scream tourist who was accosted by a pushy salesperson.

He's the grown equivalent of a twelve-year-old motoring past you on a segway with a smirk, or maybe one of those electric skateboards. He's the guy who wears the superbowl replica ring without having ever played football.

You know, you just want to kick them on sight.

The kid that shows up to sports practice in the top-of-the-line equipment when everyone else is wearing hand-me-downs and loaner gear, and he makes sure they know it. But this man has to be in his 50s, so he's a walking compensation for a very small penis. I have no doubt he drives a convertible and is onto trophy wife number three or thereabouts.

They say you shouldn't judge a book by a cover, but in this case, you one hundred percent can.

Still, he's a client, and I have a lesson to teach. I'll be professional as possible, and keep my judgements and eye rolls on the inside. And who knows, while I teach him a few basics I might just learn a thing or two myself.

"I gotta say, when I heard the best instructor in town could teach me to surf, I jumped at the chance." He steps closer. "Maybe afterwards you and I could grab some drinks, get to know each other. Introduce you to some of my friends who are in town. They're all business owners, you know...they'd love to meet a real-life surfer. Someone who sacrificed the ability to make real money for their love of the ocean. They'll find you fascinating..."

I force a tight smile, biting back a scathing retort. As much as he repulses me, I need to keep up this act, stay focused on digging for any useful details behind his arrogant façade.

We paddle out past the break and I feel him watching me, his eyes tracing my body, not as if he's checking me out, but as if by taking one of my surfing lessons he'll also get a pack of killer abs like mine. I fight the urge to plunge his leering face into the churning water. I work hard for these muscles.

"You know, a guy like you is real quality," he booms. "You should be spending time with people who raise you up, not these street thugs I've seen around here." He shouts above the wind, drawing looks from some of the said 'street thugs' surfing nearby. "I've got connections, access to deals that'll shake up this whole damn place."

I catch the swell of an approaching wave, using the momentum to steer closer while feigning impressed interest. "Oh really, what kind of deals?"

As he brags about shadowy criminal alliances, I pick out shards of information from his bragging, clues that may prove invaluable. By the lesson's end, I've gathered whispers that could shift the tide of power in our favor, or at least start to. He is here to do business, after all, and given the island chain's small size, it's almost inevitable any big deal involves Tane.

With each wave, I gather scraps of knowledge—names, places, plans. Pieces of a puzzle I can now assemble. The picture comes into focus—the shadowy deal, its architects, its intentions laid bare.

By enduring this man's inane waffling for fifty minutes or so, I've uncovered a vein of precious ore—one we can now exploit to shift the balance of power in this city. Our team will strike with precision, guided by the map I've sketched from this chance surfing encounter.

The man blathers on, oblivious to the damage he's wrought. And I nod along, already tasting the victory to come. Every nod seems to fill him with the urge to tell me more. When I make my eyes grow large in pretend awe of this 'amazing guy', that's when he seems to share the most.

The ocean's bounty once again fills my sails, just like it always does, carrying me to the shores of a new future. One where the Snakes rise ascendant, enemies scattered like sand.

As we paddle back toward shore, I feel the thrill of a hunt well-executed. The arrogant man provided more insight than he realized, his loose lips sinking his masters' ships. I steered our talk with subtle skill, mining nuggets of intel from his bloated ego.

This day marks a turning point, the waves of fate crashing down around us. I can't wait to bring this hard-won knowledge back to the others, to set our plans in motion. The man's arrogance will be his downfall—and our salvation.

I leave him on the beach with a false promise to meet again for drinks with him and his impressive buddies. I'm sure he wants to show me off as some kind of tanned, muscly trophy—his top-of-the-line surf instructor honing him to become the next Kelly Slater or whatever surfer he grew up admiring. Actually, he probably never even grew up watching surfing—he's the type that probably flicked through a glossy magazine in his first class cabin on the way here and decided a surfing lesson would make for a good story to impress people. Whatever floats your boat, man.

As I look back at the ocean's endless dance, I'm renewed with purpose. Despite me having to grin and bear these types of infuriating lessons, they do pay pretty well, not just financially but in terms of the information I'm able to gather. The secrets the ocean yields today could be the key to victory, if I'm willing to ride the waves.

Back at Snakes headquarters, I'm greeted by the usual chaos—Rake cracking jokes to lighten the mood, Dom threatening to beat people with his trademark scowl, and Devon muttering snarky comments as she helps Zeke with something on his laptop.

I quickly shower and change, then return to the living room. "Hey, it's time to go. We need to be there on time, there's a lot to discuss."

As we make our way to the Brixton's compound, I briefly give them the lowdown on what I was able to learn during today's lesson. Rake gives a low whistle as he takes it all in.

I can't wait to tell Aidan and the rest of the Brixtons.

Because this information is life-changing.

CHAPTER SEVENTEEN

SKYLER

When we reach the Brixton compound, the exterior is dark and still with only a small perimeter of security lighting, giving no clue to the action taking place inside. To a random person finding their way into this neighborhood, it looks boring and industrial as hell.

Inside is a different story. The five of us are beeped in, and we enter single file, coming to a stop in the center of the room. In the corner, Brick is sharpening some of his blades, while Slade prepares dinner, the sizzling aromas of garlic and chili permeating the air.

I make my way to Aidan's office, where maps and surveillance photos cover the walls.

He turns as I enter, his piercing gaze searching my face. "You got something?"

I nod. "My arrogant client from today's surfing lesson was more than happy to brag about a new deal going down. He couldn't help but namedrop and tell me way too much about his plans. It may be the break we need."

I relay the details—shadowy alliances, major players converging, the operation that could 'shake the foundations of this damn city.' Aidan listens intently, his brow furrowed.

"This is big. We need to act fast, get all our informants on this. I'll call Dimitri and see what he's able to dig up with his team."

"Right? I thought so too, which is why I wanted to fill you in straight away. Even if we can't use this deal front and center of our plans, he's still going to be very distracted for the next few weeks while these guys are in town. I'm sure his calendar is filled with mandatory events. He won't have a ton of down time to be worrying about us, or plotting revenge."

Aidan grabs a burner phone, then turns to me. "Good work Skyler. The ocean's given us a rare gift today. Now we ride this wave as far as it takes us."

His words resonate as I gaze out the window at the darkening ocean. The tide is turning, and with it, our fortunes in this endless war for the soul of these islands. But as always, I'm ready to ride.

I nod, letting Aidan make the call while I retreat into my own thoughts. This new intel has lit a spark in me, awakening that familiar thrill I get when a promising lead presents itself.

As I stare out at the roiling ocean, I think back to the surf lesson earlier. Beneath the man's arrogant exterior, I detected subtle cracks—flashes of worry, odd pauses, eyes darting about. It was only with time and patience that I drew out the nuggets of valuable information, like a prospector sifting through sand to find specks of gold.

I asked my questions in a way designed to make him feel like I was in awe of his 'big Mr. businessman who I could never hope to be like' persona. That I was way too much of a simpleton surfer bum to ever understand a big business deal involving more than Monopoly money. And he drank it up like a thirsty kid with a Slurpee on a hot summer day.

The man was a font of knowledge, bloated with secrets begging to spill out. And I was there to catch them, to gather the bits and pieces into a larger mosaic. Surfing is simply the pretense that allows me access to these powerful men and their incredibly loose lips.

I smile inwardly, knowing that the ocean has blessed me yet again. With each wave I ride, I'm that much closer to understanding the shadowy forces that grip these islands.

And with that knowledge comes the power to fight back, to loosen the stranglehold and clear a path into the light. The Snakes and the Brixtons ride with me, trusting in my skills to steer us through the churning unknown. And now, Dimitri and his team, so strong in their knowledge of these islands, filling in the gaps and making us a well-rounded powerhouse.

Soon we'll be crashing down on our enemies, the full force of our gathered intelligence driving us forward. But for now, I bide my time and wait for the next set of waves. The ocean always provides.

With Aidan's phone call completed, we both stride into the main living room where everyone else is making themselves comfortable, men on a mission. The others gather around, alert to the urgency in our steps.

"It's time," I announce. "The intel is solid. I know the players, the location, the nature of this mysterious deal."

Aidan nods. "I made a quick phone call and was able to verify some of the key parts of this. It's all legit."

Slade crosses his arms, his face intense. "Tell us everything."

I launch into the details, laying out all I learned between waves. Aidan and the team listens raptly, hanging on each new revelation. I can see the gears turning behind their eyes as a strategy takes shape.

"This is just what we've been waiting for," Roman says, a slow smile spreading across his face. "We can use this."

The mood in the room shifts, anticipation charging the air. We've worked so long for an advantage and now, finally, we have one. A crack in our enemies' armor we can exploit.

In low voices we make our plans, united by purpose. We all have scores to settle and this intelligence will let us exact the vengeance we crave. The streets will run red before this is finished.

Night falls, the strategy set. I stand at the window, gazing at the glimmering lights of the industrial neighborhood. Somewhere out there, our targets laugh and scheme, ignorant of the forces now aligned against them. But not for long.

Soon, the mighty will fall and the Snakes, Brixtons, and now Dimitri and his team, will claim what is ours by right. The waves have delivered us to this moment and we will ride the growing swell to victory.

CHAPTER EIGHTEEN

AIDAN

The flickering bulbs cast shadows on the concrete walls, amplifying the unease that hangs thick in the air. We're gathered in our warehouse, another usual meeting spot away from the compound, but this time Dimitri and his crew are here too. I scan their faces, looking for any sign of deception.

Can we really trust these guys who just showed up out of nowhere? I find myself going back and forth, the constant push and pull of 'we need to and we have no other choice' warring with 'what if this is the worst decision we've ever made?'

"I don't like this," Brick growls, folding his muscular arms across his chest. "How do we know they aren't spies for Tane?" He's trying to be quiet, but his voice is so deep and resonant the whole room can't help but overhear him.

Dimitri steps forward, unflinching under Brick's glare. "We're here for the same reason you are—to take Tane down." His voice is steady, but I sense the anger simmering beneath the surface. "He's taken as much from us as he has from you."

I study Dimitri, searching for any hint of dishonesty, but find none. Beside me, Angel places a comforting hand on my arm. "They're risking as much as we are by being here," she says softly. "We have to give them a chance."

I know she's right. If we're divided, Tane wins. I take a deep breath and make my decision. "You'll get your shot to prove yourselves. But betray us, and you won't live long enough to regret it."

Dimitri inclines his head in acknowledgement. His crew fans out, mingling cautiously with my own. There's still tension in the air, but with a common purpose, we just might have a chance. I feel a flicker of hope at this . Together, we can take Tane down.

Brick's eyes narrow as he sizes up Dimitri, looking for any sign of deception. When Dimitri meets his gaze unflinchingly, Brick steps even closer, using his hulking frame to intimidate.

"Pretty words," he sneers. "But they don't mean shit." He pokes a meaty finger into Dimitri's chest. "You think you can just waltz in here with your outsider crew and we'll just trust you?"

Around us, the atmosphere turns volatile, the rest of my crew murmuring at the disrespect shown to our tentative allies. The newcomers bristle, their hands drifting toward concealed weapons.

Before it can escalate further, I step between them. "Back off, Brick," I warn. "Some of us wouldn't be here if these guys hadn't helped us over on the other island. That has to count for something." He hesitates, then takes a reluctant step back.

Turning to Dimitri, I say more calmly, "You'll have to earn our trust. But threatening and posturing gets us nowhere." I sweep my gaze around the tense gathering, my eyes coming to rest on Brick. "We have enough enemies out there. Fighting amongst ourselves only helps Tane."

Brick scowls, but doesn't argue. The others relax fractionally. There's still an undercurrent of suspicion, but the potential for violence has passed. For now.

"Let's focus on the mission," I continue firmly. "We need to be smart and work together if we're going to succeed." I make eye contact with Dimitri and Brick in turn, willing them to set aside their differences. At last, Brick gives a curt nod. The alliance is uneasy, but holds. For now.

I take a deep breath as the tension in the room slowly dissipates. We've stepped back from the brink, but distrust still simmers under the surface. It's scary, trusting a group of people you barely know, and essentially giving them the power to use your information against you, to fuck up everything you've worked so very hard to build.

I can't blame Brick for his over-the-top response, because the same feelings are simmering just under the surface of my calm exterior.

Dimitri meets my eyes, a glint of gratitude in his gaze. I gave him a chance to make his case, despite Brick's hostility. Now it's on him to convince us that his intentions are true.

"I know you have limited reason to trust us," he begins, his voice low and earnest. "But Tane took everything from me too. I don't know if you're aware of how deep our issues with him go, but for starters, he murdered my wife and son." Pain flickers across his face.

"Oh my god," blurts Angel, her hand flying to her face. "Dimitri, I had no idea..."

"How would you be expected to know?" He shrugs, his mouth set in a firm line. "And I'm sure you're wondering, but I don't care about revenge... I'm past that and found something that's worth more." He pauses and glances at Aria, and something passes between them, no words needed. "Now, I care about justice. Same as all of you."

His words seem genuine, and I feel some of my doubts melting away.

Dimitri continues. "Hopefully the assistance we provided on the other island is enough to show you we're in this for the long haul, whatever it takes. We've put ourselves directly in the line of fire with Tane again. And to be honest, I'm scared. I couldn't bear for him to take away someone I loved again..." He glances at Aria, and I detect a slight tremor in his lips.

Around the room, I see heads nodding, faces softening. We've all lost massively to Tane's cruelty. Dimitri's raw admission strikes a chord. It sounds like out of all of us, Tane has caused the most destruction for him.

"We want the same thing," Angel says softly. Though wary, she's willing to give him a chance. The others murmur agreement.

"One wrong move and you're out," Skyler warns. But the threat lacks heat.

Slowly, subtly, attitudes are shifting. We're seeing each other as allies bound by trauma, not rivals. There's hope yet for this unlikely alliance.

"Let's focus on the plan," I say. "Together, we can defeat Tane and make sure he doesn't inflict this type of atrocity on anyone else ever again. Once we're done, the people of these islands will finally be free from his ongoing oppression."

Resolute, we turn our minds to strategy. The road is long, but for the first time, it doesn't seem so lonely. Side by side, we just might make it.

As the meeting breaks up, I catch Angel's eye across the room. She gives me a small, hopeful smile.

"We need each other," she says, echoing my thoughts. "Let's make this work."

I know how hard those words come for her. How deep her distrust runs. But she's willing to try, for the greater good.

Beside me, Brick claps a heavy hand on Dimitri's shoulder. "Don't make me regret this," he rumbles. Though his tone is gruff, I sense the offer of friendship behind it.

Dimitri meets his gaze steadily. "You won't," he vows.

Together, we file out into the night. The air practically vibrates with cautious optimism. This unlikely union still feels fragile, but the seeds are sown.

Tomorrow we prepare for war. Tonight, we prepare our hearts for trust.

CHAPTER NINETEEN

ANGEL

The loft is flooded with sunlight, the warm glow dancing across the stylish outfits adorning the mannequins. My heart races as I take it all in—this is it. Everything Devon and I have worked for, sleepless nights and endless revisions, leading to this moment.

"Today's the day we show them," I say, adrenaline and anxiety swirling within me. "Our vision, our hard work. It's all coming together."

Devon squeezes my hand in a silent gesture of reassurance. We're backstage, making final tweaks, smoothing out invisible and actual wrinkles. I fiddle with the hems of the shorts and adjust the straps of the sports bras, keeping my hands busy to subdue the nervous energy.

"You ready for this?" Devon asks, her eyes bright with anticipation. "They're going to love it."

I nod, swallowing hard. "I hope so. We've put everything into this."

My stomach flutters as I imagine their reactions. Will they understand what we've tried to create? The long hours, the creative struggles, distilled into this collection. More than clothes—a vision of who we are. Strong, united, invincible.

I want them to see it, to feel it like we do. To run their fingers over the fabrics and find meaning in each cut, each seam. We're revealing a part of ourselves in an entirely new way. And it terrifies me as much as it exhilarates me.

"This is it," Devon says, with a deep breath. Side by side, we step forward, ready to unveil our new baby.

The buzz of conversation fills the loft as members of the Snakes and Brixtons arrive, as well as Dimitri and his team. I peek through the curtains, taking in their curious expressions. Skyler's gaze sweeps over the space, the runway, the decorations.

"This place looks amazing," he says. "You two did all this?"

I step out from behind the curtain, nerves making my lips quirk into a timid smile. "Yeah, lots of late nights. But it's worth it."

Brick grins, his eyes crinkling at the corners. "Look at us, taking a break from torture for fashion." He strikes a pose with his big hulking frame and I can't help but laugh, easing some of my tension. Thank goodness for Brick's humor in moments like these.

I laugh under my breath, the sound strained. My palms tingle and I rub them against my jeans. This is it. The moment we reveal ourselves.

Devon steps onto the small stage, commanding the attention of the room. I stand beside her, my pulse hammering in my ears.

A hush falls over the group as all eyes turn our way.

"Thank you all for coming," Devon begins. "Angel and I have been working on something special..."

Her voice fades into the background as I study their faces—skepticism mingling with intrigue. This is our chance to show them who we are. Beyond the violence, the darkness, there is so much more. Creativity, passion, vision. I've been able to channel a lot of that into my salon, but this... this is entirely new territory.

My heart thrums with anticipation. We poured our souls into this collection. Now comes the moment of truth—will they understand? Will they see us in a new light? Will they come out of tonight believing in us?

I cling to Devon's words like a lifeline. This is just the beginning, I tell myself. Today we take the first step toward real connection and a positive entrepreneurial venture. Toward understanding the light that exists beneath the shadows.

Devon's voice rises with conviction as she concludes her opening remarks. "We wanted to create something that represents all of us—our strength, our resilience, our unity."

I take a deep, steadying breath as the first model steps onto the makeshift runway. She's wearing a racerback sports bra with mesh and lace and faux leather, and matching bicycle shorts. The color palette is dark grays and black with pops of bright neon pink and yellow.

"Each piece is designed with you in mind," Devon pronounces. "Strong, ready for anything. When wearing any of our pieces, they should help you to feel like you could take on a fierce workout, a boardroom meeting, running errands, or finally tackling that project you've been putting off."

The model stalks down the runway, confidence in her stride. As she turns, the tailored lines of the outfit accentuate her curvy form. She looks strong, capable, comfortable in her own skin. Appreciative murmurs ripple through the audience.

Our creations come to life, imbuing those who wear them with a subtle power. More models follow, showcasing pieces blending elegance and durability. Faux leather merges with more lace. More dark hues mix with vibrant pops of color. The clothing pieces move with our models as they walk and pose, light and fluid.

I scan the audience, reading their reactions.

Skyler's eyes widen in interest.

Brick nods in grudging approval. "This racerback top...it's pretty badass."

My heart swelling, I address the group. "We wanted to create something that makes you feel invincible. Something that represents who we are. Women, empowered and strong, unapologetically unafraid to be who we are at our very core."

I meet Devon's eyes, shining with triumph. No matter their reception, we've unveiled our vision. Our true selves. And we have plenty more ideas where these ones came from.

The models exit the runway to applause and chatter. The audience moves in to examine the collection up close, their hands gliding over fabrics, fingers testing the fabrics. I drift through the space, a butterfly fluttering from flower to flower as I explain my inspirations.

"The lining is tear-resistant but breathable," I tell Skyler as he tests the sleeve of a workout top. "Moisture-wicking and cooling while you wear it."

Zeke runs an appraising hand over a pair of yoga pants. "This material, it's durable yet lightweight. How'd you source it?"

"Lots of research," I reply with a smile. "We wanted gear that could withstand anything."

As I connect with them over each piece, their body language opens up. Guards drop, shoulders relax. We find common ground in the clothes' simple functionality.

The hard shells they wear to survive this harsh world transform into something more. Armor infused with creativity, with meaning. With me—and with Devon.

Seeing that subtle shift, their curiosity transforming into connection...it makes all the sleepless nights worthwhile. Because I know that while our future customers' approval will be extremely important for our success, I couldn't do something like this without the unwavering support of my guys.

Devon appears at my side, her expression mirroring the accomplishment swelling in my chest.

"We're stronger together," she affirms. "This proves it."

Our creation has unified us more than ever. Given us new purpose. We stand on the edge of something greater, together.

The crowd begins to thin as the night winds down. I take a step back, leaning against a concrete pillar to observe the scene.

Seeing our combined team like this, united and intrigued, fills me with a different sense of achievement. Through creativity and trust, we've brought them just a bit closer. Built a bridge between worlds that rarely intersect.

Devon appears beside me, two glasses of champagne in hand. She passes one to me, her eyes scanning the room.

"We did it," she says, her voice warm. "They really liked it."

I take a celebratory sip, the bubbles light and effervescent on my tongue. "Yeah, we did. And there's so much more to come."

I meet Devon's gaze, seeing my own optimism reflected back. No matter what comes next, we have each other.

And we have the trust we've built tonight, one stitch at a time.

I nod to Devon as we both take a final look around the loft, now empty except for the two of us. Mannequins stand sentry along the walls, adorned in pieces from our collection.

It's hard to believe that just minutes ago, this space was filled with the dangerous energy of the Snakes and Brixtons. Now only hints remain—a few discarded champagne flutes, rumpled throw pillows, the lingering smell of cologne and perfume.

I run my hand along a rack of athleisurewear as we make our way downstairs. Each one personalized, molded to its owner. Symbols of the unity we're building, step by step.

Outside, the night air is crisp and electric. Our group stands on the sidewalk, lit by the red glow of the loft's sign.

Devon and I pause in the doorway, soaking it in. This moment, this energy, is everything we envisioned.

"We're more than just a team," I say softly. "We're a family now."

Whether that leads us into fashion or further down the criminal path, it doesn't matter. We have each other, woven together by trust and vision.

I lace my arm through Devon's as we walk out to join the others. The night stretches before us, filled with potential.

Together, we are unstoppable.

CHAPTER TWENTY

ROMAN

The Next Day

The blaring TV jolts me awake. I peel my eyes open and wince at the harsh morning light flooding the safehouse. The news anchor's voice drones on about some new discovery, but I'm too groggy to care. I drag myself off the couch, joints cracking, and shuffle to the kitchen.

I'm pouring my third cup of coffee when Aidan's shout makes me spill it all over the counter.

"Turn that up. We need to hear this."

There's an edge in his voice that gets my attention. I hurry back to the living room, the caffeine already kicking in.

Devon is staring intensely at the TV, her face taut.

"...authorities have discovered mass graves on the neighboring island, confirming rumors..."

I freeze as the words sink in. They found them, just as I knew they would. My gut twists.

It's too late to stop this now. Fuck. The images on screen make that clear—cops swarming like ants over the island, excavating body after body. Bile rises in my throat.

Aidan whips around to face me, eyes blazing. "Was this you?"

I force myself to hold his gaze. "Yeah. I leaked it."

"Why the hell didn't you tell us? Surely this is something that we should have decided as a group. This is huge."

I take a breath, steadying myself. "It had to be this way. Tane's untouchable in the shadows. Exposing him is our only shot. I leaked it before we got wind of this new deal. But now, with that going down at the same time, he's going to be cornered so hard he won't know what to do except lash out recklessly."

Aidan curses under his breath. I know he understands, even if he hates my methods. The others are staring at me now too, uncertainty and anger swirling in their eyes.

But it's done. My play is in motion. Checkmate, Tane. Your kingdom's crumbling. Now we end this, my way.

I nod slowly, thoughts racing as I try to gauge everyone's reactions. Most seem pissed that I kept this to myself. Can't blame them. But I feel like they don't know Tane like I do.

Slade steps towards me, his eyes narrowed. "You're playing with fire here, Roman. This is gonna get people killed."

"People are already dying," I snap. "Or did you miss the mass graves on TV?"

He flinches. Yeah, cheap shot, but I need them to understand the stakes here.

"Enough." Angel's voice cuts through the tension. "We can stand here bickering or we can actually do something."

Brick grunts in agreement. Slade just watches me, his face as unreadable as ever.

"Angel's right," I say. "Look, I know you're mad. But this puts us one step ahead of Tane. We need to press that advantage now, before he recovers. He's going to be scrambling around trying to hide any sense of involvement while his business pals are here. All he's going to be focused on is salvaging this deal and avoiding any collateral damage to his business because of this discovery."

Aidan scans the room, then nods. "Roman's right. Surveillance and intel gathering are top priority. Anything that gives us further insight into how Tane operates." He levels his gaze at me. "And we'll need the media too. Can you handle that?"

I meet his eyes steadily. "Yeah. I've got contacts we can use."

"Good. Let's get to work then." Aidan heads for the stairs, barking out orders.

The others disperse, the buzz of activity replacing the tense silence. This is it. The point of no return. I take a deep breath and get moving.

No more waiting. The board is set, and I've made the first move. Now we play for blood.

I nod to Brick as he brushes past me, his expression unreadable. But I know he's got my back. Under that gruff exterior lies a heart of gold, even if he'd never admit it out loud.

My phone buzzes and I glance down to see a text from an unknown number. Looks like my media contacts are already reaching out. I forward the info to Zeke, our resident hacker. He'll vet them before we proceed.

In the other room, I can hear Angel and Aidan debating our next moves. Her creative spirit balances his ruthless pragmatism nicely. I'm glad he has her to keep him in check.

This whole mess started when Angel saw me kill someone right in front of her. Little did we know at the time she was on the run from a stalker who had tormented her for decades. She started out as a captive, but we soon brought her into the fold. Gave her a new family. A new life.

I failed to protect my own family, and I'll be damned if I fail Angel too. She's the little ray of light that keeps us from falling into the abyss. My north star guiding me back from the dark.

And I know one thing for certain—I will burn this whole city to the ground before I let anyone hurt her again. Tane's days are numbered. He just doesn't know it yet.

Angel's voice rises above the others as she makes an impassioned point, returning to the main room with Aidan. "I know Tane better than any of you. The man is paranoid on a good day. This kind of scrutiny will push him right over the edge."

She's not wrong. Tane operates best when he thinks no one is watching. But drag his misdeeds into the light, and that cool facade will crumble. He's used to other criminal groups vying for his power over the islands, but involving the media is something new and unknown, two of Tane's fears.

Aidan crosses his arms, mulling it over. He and Angel couldn't be more different, but they balance each other out in unexpected ways. She's managed to pierce through that ruthless exterior and find the man beneath. I think she reminds him of the person he wishes he still was.

"Alright," Aidan finally concedes. "We'll hold off on any direct strikes for now. But we need to keep him on his toes. Leak some new information to the press. Just enough to keep him guessing. But..." he pauses and glares at me, "...even if you think you have the best idea in the world, you *must* run it by the rest of the group first. Any more reckless one-man ideas, and it could result in a lot worse than us being mildly mad at you for a moment while we process the shock of it all."

Angel nods, a gleam in her eye. "I can work my contacts at the salon. Loose lips sink ships, as they say. Skyler may have the ocean and surfing lessons, but you'd be shocked at what all the wives and girlfriends of Tane's associates know, and what they'll spill over a deep conditioning treatment or a balayage. They're literally a captive audience for hours, and there's a reason I provide complimentary champagne while they wait."

Even now, she hasn't lost her playful spirit. It's what drew me to her in the first place. While the rest of us dwell in the darkness, she radiates light.

My phone buzzes again with an encrypted message from Zeke. He's identified my media contact as legitimate. Time to put the next phase in motion.

I catch Angel's eye and give her a subtle nod. We're in this together until the end. And when it comes time for the killing blow, Tane will never see it coming.

I crack my knuckles, my mind racing with possibilities. Tane's empire is vast, but even giants have weak spots if you know where to aim. The trick is finding the right pressure points.

"Okay, so I'll reach out to my media contacts again," I say. "We'll keep dropping hints about the mass graves, stir up speculation. I can also float some doctored financial records, make it seem like Tane's lost money on shady investments and imply a link."

Aidan grins. "Now you're thinking. Make him look reckless in business and sloppy with cleanup. At the very least, it's likely to sabotage this big deal he's apparently so busy working on."

Brick giggles from his perch on the arm of the sofa. "Ooh, I love watching empires fall. It's like Jenga!" He mimes pushing over a tower of blocks.

Angel playfully swats his leg. "Don't get too excited yet. Tane won't go down easy."

"Okay okay. But that gives me an idea for naked Jenga... stay tuned, Angel." Brick winks at Angel lasciviously and wiggles his brow, and we all laugh.

Angel's caution is valid, but I know with these latest developments, we have the opportunity to place Tane firmly on the ropes.

The game is on. Every empire has its breaking point, and we're about to find Tane's. All those bodies buried on the island are just the beginning. By the time we're through, his entire operation will be dug up and left in the light.

I clap my hands together. "Alright, let's get to work. We all know the drill."

The team springs into action, gathering equipment and dividing up tasks. Angel grabs a duffel bag full of hair styling supplies. Even in the midst of a mafia war, she insists on maintaining her cover as a hairdresser.

"I'll head to the salon, keep my ear to the ground for gossip. We really do hear everything in my line of work," she says with a wink.

Aidan pulls up a map on his laptop, studying our surveillance grid. "I'll coordinate the field teams from here. Brick, you take the docks. Roman, the casino. Stay invisible. Slade, you stay here with me."

We nod, already moving toward the weapons lockers to gear up. I turn to Aidan.

"You ready to stir up some digital chaos?"

He grins. "Born ready. I'll work with Zeke to infiltrate Tane's servers, and we'll leave some nasty surprises in his financials."

Brick briefly perches on Aidan's desk, peering at the screen. "Ooh, can you make it look like he spent ten grand at an alpaca farm? Embezzle money for llama feed? Oh man, we can imply he owns animals and treats them poorly...

and I'll get my vegan groups onto him. There's nothing louder than an angry vegan, let me tell you!"

I chuckle. Even in tense times, Brick's mischief lightens the mood. We have our assignments. Now it's time to dismantle Tane's empire, brick by brick, no pun intended.

He won't know what hit him until it's too late.

CHAPTER TWENTY-ONE

DEVON

A few days later

The jungle comes alive around me as I push my body to its limits. Leaves and branches whip past in a blur of green, my lungs burning with each ragged breath. Today, everything changes. I have to be ready.

I'm not sure what the future will bring, or if our mission to eliminate Tane will require any physical skill on my behalf. But when I feel physically prepared, I feel mentally stronger, and that's what I need right now.

Just as well I have several guys more than happy to teach me everything I need to know.

My feet pound down the winding trail, each footfall precise and focused. A fallen log appears in my path and I vault over it effortlessly, never breaking stride. I'm faster, stronger than I've ever been. I hurtle through the steamy air, using rocks and vines as stepping stones to test my agility. A misstep could mean disaster, but I simply won't let that happen today.

I round a bend and the facility emerges through the trees. My heart thunders in my chest. Almost there.

With a final burst of speed, I sprint into the clearing surrounding the combat ring.

Dom stands with his arms crossed, his mountainous frame casting a long shadow in the morning light. Our eyes meet and he gives me a single nod. He knows what today means to me. What I have to prove.

I circle the ring, visualizing my opponent, every muscle coiled and ready. I take a breath, centering myself. A bead of sweat trails down my back. I clench my fists and step into the ring.

I'm ready.

Across from me, Dom waits, shirtless and limber, lightly bouncing on the balls of his feet. His toned muscles flex as he rotates his shoulders, his eyes locked on mine. There's an intensity in his gaze that sends a shiver down my spine.

"Ready to go again?" he asks, his voice low and gravelly.

I drop into my fighting stance, my fists raised. "Always."

Dom moves in a blur, aiming a punch at my ribs that I deflect just in time.

I counter with a roundhouse kick which he evades.

We exchange blows, neither of us giving any ground.

He switches tactics, sweeping my legs out from under me.

I roll and spring back up, my adrenaline surging.

I unleash a flurry of strikes meant to overwhelm his defenses.

He blocks each one, cat-like reflexes on full display.

Our eyes remain locked as we circle each other, sweat dripping.

"Your form is improving," Dom says. "Keep your guard up."

I absorb his advice with a quick nod. No mistakes, not today. I visualize my true opponent, the one who won't stop until he's destroyed everything I care about. Rage wells up inside me, fueling my attacks.

I catch Dom's arm and use his momentum to flip him onto his back.

He grunts as he hits the mat then sweeps my feet again.

We both roll to our feet, chests heaving.

"I need to be perfect," I say through gritted teeth. "Tane won't give any of us a second chance."

Dom's eyes flash with understanding. He beckons me forward and we clash again, each strike ringing out into the heavy air.

Rake watches silently from the edge of the ring as I steel myself for the fight ahead.

After our intense sparring session, Dom pulls me aside to offer some personalized guidance.

"It's not just about strength, Dev," he says, his tone gentle but firm. "You need to anticipate his moves, stay one step in front."

I nod, absorbing his advice. Dom has always been able to see my weaknesses and help me improve.

"I'll remember that," I reply. "Thanks, Dom."

He squeezes my shoulder, his dark eyes radiating care and belief in me. With him by my side, I feel like I can do anything.

I leave the ring with renewed motivation, the cheers of my found family echoing behind me.

Now it's time to focus on a different kind of training.

I enter a section of the facility designed to mimic an interrogation room, complete with a single chair, stark table, and various tools meant to intimidate. Zeke waits inside, ready to run through scenarios with me.

"This part isn't about physical strength at all," I say, mostly to myself. "It's about breaking them down, finding their weaknesses."

Zeke nods. "Getting inside their heads. You ready?"

I straighten my shoulders, blocking out any hesitation. "Let's do this."

I take a seat across from Zeke, studying him intently. In interrogation, every detail matters—the twitch of an eye, a nervous tap of the fingers. I need to notice it all.

"Let's start simple," Zeke says. "I'm the hostage, you're the interrogator. Get me to talk."

We launch into the roleplaying, with Zeke pretending to be a captured enemy.

Under his guidance, I hone my ability to manipulate, threaten, and exploit psychological vulnerabilities.

I lean forward, keeping my voice low and commanding. "You'll tell me everything I want to know. Lie, and you'll regret it."

Zeke scoffs, staying defiant.

I slam my fist on the table, making him jump. "I know more than you realize," I hiss. "Cooperate now, and we'll go easy on you."

I can see Zeke processing my words, looking for any hint of deception. I keep my expression stern, unyielding.

"Nice try," he says. "But you've got nothing on me."

I stand abruptly, grabbing a nearby tool and brandishing it in his face.

His eyes widen. I've found a weakness—he fears pain.

"Last chance," I snarl. "Tell me what I want to know!"

Zeke swallows, breaking into a nervous sweat. "Okay, okay! I'll talk, just don't hurt me..."

I lean back, victorious. The interrogation training is paying off—I'm learning to exploit every vulnerability.

We continue practicing different scenarios, my skills growing sharper. By the end, I'm manipulating Zeke effortlessly, worming any information from him. I'll be ready for Tane. For our final confrontation.

The sun sets over the jungle canopy as I make my way to the campfire, muscles aching from another intense day of training. I need these quiet moments to process it all—the endless drills, the constant pressure to improve. But, as with most things, it's the pressure I place on myself that creates the most tension.

Dom is already there, flames dancing in his dark eyes. He pats the log beside him. "Come. Sit."

I ease down, staring into the fire.

"You've come so far, Devon," Dom says gently. "We all see it."

I shake my head. "It's not enough. I need to be better. For all of us."

Dom grips my shoulder. "You're not fighting this battle alone."

"I know," I reply. "But part of me feels like this all started because of me, so I feel compelled to finish it."

Leaves crunch as Angel approaches, her vibrant hair glowing in the firelight. She sits across from us, meeting my eyes.

"You're not alone in this," she says firmly. "We're all with you."

I give a small smile. "I know. But when it comes down to it, I need to be the one who ends it." Who ends Tane, once and for all.

We discuss the upcoming confrontation, the stakes involved. They listen as I voice my doubts and fears. Their support buoys me, and keeps me focused.

By the time we part for bed, I feel centered. Ready. Tomorrow will bring a new level of intensity. We need to be prepared when Tane comes.

The fire has died down to glowing embers as I make my way back to the training facility alone. Moonlight filters through the canopy, casting the jungle in an ethereal glow.

Inside the ring, I stand motionless, soaking in the heavy silence. This place has become a second home, every session pushing me harder, sharpening my skills for the task ahead.

I know Dom watches from the shadows, an ever-present source of strength.

"Tomorrow, we push harder," I say aloud. "We need to be ready."

"And you will be." His voice echoes through the empty space. "I believe in you, Devon."

I close my eyes, visualizing the fight, each movement swift and precise. When I open them, my gaze is steel. Resolute.

"I'm ready for you, Tane." My voice resonates with conviction. "This starts and ends with me."

Whatever comes, I won't falter. The others have faith in me, support me. And I have faith in myself. For their sakes, I can't fail.

Tane's cruelty ends here. I vow it with every fiber of my being.

The moon illuminates my silhouette as I stand tall, focused and unwavering. Ready for the battle ahead.

CHAPTER TWENTY-TWO

DEVON

*T*he Next Day

The sun's glare off the ocean is blinding, forcing me to squint as I stare out at the waves. The sand is hot beneath my bare feet and I dig my toes in, seeking comfort that won't come.

"Do you think we're doing too much?" I blurt out.

Angel turns, eyebrows raised behind her sunglasses. "What do you mean?"

"The clothing line, the surfing school..." I trail off with a frustrated sigh, raking a hand through my hair. "They're all big ventures on their own without considering the rest of our operations."

I start pacing, unable to contain the nervous energy thrumming through me. "Aria's opening a fucking restaurant, for god's sake. Is this really the time, when we're trying to overthrow the Bowser of the islands?"

Angel's lips quirk into a wry smile. "So we're meant to stop living until this is all over?" She steps in front of me, halting my frantic movements. "What if this doesn't end, Devon? What if this isn't the final act and there's more to come?"

"I know, but I just spent a couple of days in the jungle trying to turn into some kind of action hero. I have the basics down, but this type of thing takes years to fully master. It feels like we're taking Nerf guns to a nuclear war. Imagine if we really stepped back and focused until we knew without a doubt we were ready to take him down."

Her hands come up to frame my face, forcing me to meet her steady gaze. "Do you want to just wait and wait for the perfect time?" She shakes her head, tendrils of hair blowing in the breeze. "There is not, and never will be, a perfect time. He's only going to keep getting stronger, bringing more and more onto his side who will be loyal without question."

I close my eyes with a shaky exhale, leaning into her touch. Her words wash over me, equal parts reprimand and reassurance.

"I don't know about you," she continues, "well, I do actually. You're the same as me." Her thumbs brush over my cheekbones. "You don't want to spend your life living in regret and wondering 'what if'."

I nod slowly, the fight going out of me. She's right. Of course she's right.

"Okay," I breathe out, opening my eyes to meet her steady gaze again. In that endless blue I find the calm I've been seeking. "Okay, we do this."

Her answering smile eases the clench in my chest. As long as we're together, we can weather any storm.

As I realize the inevitable path ahead, my mind drifts and I consider the exhausting alternative she outlined so pragmatically—living each day on high alert, endlessly strategizing and trying to stay one step ahead of him. Never fully relaxing or letting my guard down, always anticipating his attempts to push us off the islands or eliminate us completely.

It's a mentally draining way to live and I'm tired of it. Tired of the scheming, the violence, the fear of what he might do next. As thrilling as outmaneuvering him has been at times, I'm ready for it to be over.

"I'm too tired for that, honestly... the thought of him getting stronger." I sigh, jaded at the thought of another round with Tane. "I think we all are ready for this to be over."

I sink down onto the couch, leaning my head back and closing my eyes. "Not that it hasn't been fun, plotting and scheming—and especially going along with Brick's wildly creative and—well, psycho...plans." A wry smile tugs at my lips. "But there's a lot of risk involved, and it can be... scary."

I open my eyes, gazing up at the ceiling fan as it lazily circulates the humid air. "The thought of a more normal life, something with a level of predictability, has its appeal."

Skyler, overhearing some of the conversation as he enters the room, perches on the arm of the couch next to me, mussing my hair affectionately. "We'll still have our operations running in the background, you know. While we pursue these other things."

"It's just... a lot," I sigh, overwhelmed by my rapidly growing mental to-do list.

He nudges my shoulder playfully. "I know my surf school hasn't taken me away from our regular business. In fact, it's enhanced it.

I roll my eyes, swatting his hand away. "But you use that to access intel from your clients. It's really complementary to the other things we do." I wave a hand vaguely. "I hardly think we're going to change the world through sports bras and yoga pants."

Skyler grins, undeterred. "Hey, you never know."

Angel's musical laugh rings out. "What do you mean? Spandex saves the day?"

Skyler snorts, shaking his head. "No, but you're going to have access to a whole new pool of people. And do you know what people have, Dev? Secrets and information."

He leans in conspiratorially. "Whether you gather it at a surfing lesson or a yoga retreat, information is information."

I raise a skeptical eyebrow, prompting him to continue earnestly.

"And, I don't mean to be sexist, but you get a group of women together at a fitness class, and from what I've seen on television—on those reality shows you watch—that's the prime time to share the juiciest news." He nudges me again. "People really seem to let their guard down in those environments."

I can't help but chuckle. "Come on, Sky...I've walked in and seen you checking out Real Housewives episodes by yourself, when nobody else was in the room. Is that where you learned how women operate in 'those environments'?"

A blush spreads up his neck and across his cheeks. "I was just...keeping up on pop culture so I could wow my clients." He rubs the back of his neck self-consciously. "Anyways, that's neither here nor there."

Rake walks up to us, overhearing Skyler's excuses. "Just own it, man. I watch it to perfect my table-flipping techniques. Hasn't come in handy yet, but I'm just waiting for the right time…"

We all smirk. Trust Rake to bring the levity and make Skyler feel better in the moment.

I wave a hand, taking pity on Skyler. "Message received, Sky. I shouldn't worry about this taking me away from our end goal. There's more to life than Tane Brown, and hopefully soon he won't even be part of the equation, and just a distant memory."

Skyler smiles, relief evident on his face. "Exactly."

I take a deep breath as Skyler's words truly start to sink in. He's right—there's more to life than constantly watching over my shoulder for Tane's next move.

Skyler's perspective helps give me hope. He and Angel make a compelling case that now is the time to go on the offensive. That we can still run our regular operations in the background even as we pursue new ventures we're passionate about.

The more I think about it, the more a plan comes into focus. My athleisure line with Angel will provide the perfect cover as we put additional pressure on Tane. And everyone else's new businesses will allow us to gather intel from entirely new networks of people.

I feel a spark of excitement begin to grow within me, replacing the uncertainty I'd felt before. We're going to take Tane down once and for all. And then we'll be free to build the lives we want, spreading our wings beyond the shadows of the past. The future is ours for the taking.

I look between Skyler and Angel, gratitude welling up inside me. "You're absolutely right. Both of you. I was losing perspective but I'm back on track now." I squeeze Angel's hand before pulling Skyler in for a quick hug. "Let's do this. It's time."

I feel myself shine with renewed purpose as I turn to leave the hideout, Skyler and Angel's words still ringing in my ears. This is far from over. But with my found family beside me, I know Tane stands less of a chance than ever before.

As I step outside into the humid night air, I take a deep breath, feeling it fill my lungs. The neighborhood sounds surround me with distant music, raucous laughter, a police siren wailing. This island is well and truly my home now, these streets course through my veins. And I'll be damned if I let anyone take that away from me.

My boots thump decisively on the pavement as I make my way through the maze of back roads, back toward the heart of the city. I can already envision the next steps—shoring up our existing operations, laying the groundwork for the new businesses, and hitting Tane where it hurts most. My mind whirs, strategizing even as I walk.

There's a lot to do, and nothing is for certain. But I'm back in the fight now, energized and determined.

I won't stop until Tane is nothing but a distant memory.

The future belongs to me and my family.

And I'll reshape it with my own two hands.

CHAPTER TWENTY-THREE

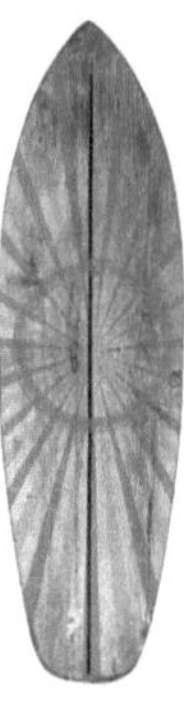

RAKE

*T*he Next Day

The jungle comes alive with the morning mist. Dewdrops cling to waxy leaves as birdsong fills the air. It's a new day, a chance to leave the past where it belongs.

My feet pound the muddy trail, my breath coming hard. Devon and the boys got me out of the gutter, but some stains don't wash off easy. The things I've done, the people I've hurt...like a lonely relative at Thanksgiving dinner, those ghosts aren't leaving anytime soon.

A branch whips my face, and I taste blood, salty and metallic. The pain grounds me, keeps me present. I run faster, my lungs burning, using the jungle as my personal punching bag.

By the time I reach the clearing, my shirt is soaked through. I double over, hands braced on my knees as I suck in air. Anger simmers in my gut, rage at the unfairness of it all. With a roar, I slam my fist into the nearest tree trunk, bark splitting my knuckles.

"Damn it!" I growl through clenched teeth. No matter how hard I try, the past won't let me be. Some days the weight of it feels like it'll crush me into dust.

But I'm not alone in this fight. Devon and the others have got my back. Maybe it's time I let them in, let them help shoulder the load.

I wipe the blood from my hand and head back down the trail. The ghosts are still with me, but having brothers like these makes them easier to bear. And Devon, my Devo... my sweet queen—she has the uncanny ability to make everything okay.

I take a deep breath and continue my run through the dense jungle trails, trying to clear my mind. But the memories come flooding back, unbidden. I'm transported back to the dark alleys and seedy underbelly of my past.

I see the flash of knives, hear the screams and taunts as we fought over turf. The metallic scent of blood heavy in the air. My brother's face appears, always by my side. Until that night when everything changed. An innocent little boy, suspended in time, his ghostly presence accompanying me through my darkest experiences as an adult.

The images are so vivid, it's like I'm there again. I can feel the slick cobblestones under my shoes, the frigid night air cutting through my jacket. My pulse quickens as the scene plays out once more.

My brother's cry pierces the din, a choked gurgle. I whirl to see him grasping his throat, blood spilling between his fingers. The light in his eyes extinguishes as he collapses.

"No!" The agonized scream tears from my throat. I run to him, clutching his limp body in disbelief. Around us the fight rages on, but I am deaf to it. In that moment my world narrows to my brother's still form. It doesn't matter that he drowned, that this entire memory is nothing but an illusion. In my mind, he dies a different way nearly every single day.

The false memory fades as I stop in a secluded clearing, my chest heaving. I lash out, pounding the tree trunk in anguish and frustration.

"Why won't you leave me be?" I cry out hoarsely. The ghosts of my past relentlessly haunt me, no matter how hard I try to outrun them.

I sink to my knees, the bark rough under my palms as I lean against the tree. Hot tears blur my vision. I thought I'd left that life behind, but the memories cling to me like shadows.

A snapping twig alerts me I'm no longer alone. I stiffen, hastily wiping my eyes before glancing up.

Devon stands a few feet away, concern etched on her face. Her presence is calming amidst the maelstrom inside me.

"Rake..." she begins softly.

I cut her off brusquely. "I'm fine. Just needed to blow off some steam."

She doesn't look convinced. "It's okay not to be fine. I know the past doesn't just disappear."

Her voice holds no judgment, only empathy. My defensiveness fades. If anyone understands, it's her.

"Come on." She nods towards a fallen log. I follow and sit beside her, the rich jungle providing a cocoon of white noise.

"Talk to me," she urges gently.

Haltingly I open up, sharing more than I have with anyone. The words pour out, so many memories I've tried to lock away. She listens without interruption, anchor-steady at my side. Just the way she was when I first told her about my brother, which seems like a lifetime ago.

"The things I've done, Devon..." My voice breaks. "How do I make peace with it all?"

"By realizing you're more than your past. It shaped you but doesn't define you." She squeezes my hand. "We've all got demons, Rake. They just take different forms. Even the people who seem to have it all together have them, sometimes the biggest ones. The trick is learning to live with them."

I absorb her words, feeling the weight on my shoulders lighten.

I nod slowly, letting Devon's wisdom sink in. She's right—my past is a part of me, but I don't need to give it the power to control my future.

"I never thought I could belong anywhere after..." My voice trails off. "But being here, with the Snakes, with you...it's different."

Devon smiles. "Because we're family now. We've all got damage, but together we're strong."

Her certainty makes me believe it too. I stand, suddenly eager to move forward. "Come on, let's head back."

We make our way through the lush jungle as the training facility comes into view. The physical exertion of the hike purges the dark thoughts that clung to me earlier.

Inside, I head straight for the combat ring, adrenaline pumping through my veins.

Devon joins me with a knowing grin.

We spar intensely, blocking and striking in a fluid dance. Her movements are graceful yet lethal.

"Good!" she pants, dodging a kick. "Channel it all here."

I pivot, unleashing a flurry of controlled strikes. Each blow releases more of the past's hold on me.

Devon counters expertly, her eyes blazing with approval.

We continue until collapse, dripping sweat.

"The past can fuel your future if you let it," she says, clasping my shoulder. "But make sure you harness it in a good way. Energy is energy, good or bad, it all ends up in the same place."

I nod, feeling lighter than I have in years. Shedding the past one piece at a time.

Dom's gravelly voice interrupts us. "Hey, save some for the rest of us!"

I turn to see the other Snakes entering the training area.

Skyler tosses me a towel with a wink. "Looking good out there, Rake. We've got an epic session planned today."

Dom cracks his knuckles, his imposing frame looming large. "Time to really put you through your paces," he rumbles.

Adrenaline surges through me again. Training with Devon was intense, but with the whole crew it's on another level. We divide into pairs to run drills, the room soon filled with grunts, thuds and shouts.

I'm paired with Dom, our movements fluid and in sync after months together. He grins as I counter his strikes.

"You've come a long way, man," he says.

I can't help but beam, buoyed by the camaraderie. The Snakes aren't just my brothers in arms, they're my brothers in life.

Hours later, exhausted but fulfilled, we lounge by the fire pit as the sun sinks below the horizon. Swapping stories and jokes, I marvel at the lightness in my chest. I haven't felt this content in forever.

For the first time in too long, I feel at peace. The shadows are still there, but fading. Surrounded by the people I now call family, I know I'm not alone.

The flames crackle, sending sparks dancing into the night sky. Laughter and banter fill the air as we pass around beers and snacks.

As the others chat, I gaze into the fire, mesmerized by the flickering glow. The events of the day play through my mind-the run, the heart-to-heart with Devon, the intense training session.

It's been a rollercoaster, but I feel stronger because of it. Leaning on the Snakes, opening up...it wasn't easy, but nothing worthwhile ever is.

The fire pops, pulling me from my reverie. Glancing around, warmth swells in my chest. These people accept me, scars and all. For the first time in forever, I feel like I truly belong.

A log shifts, sending up a fountain of embers. The sparks drift upwards, disappearing into the night. Watching them, a sense of lightness comes over me. The past will always be a part of me, but I don't have to let it define me.

As the last ember fades, I stand. My chosen brothers' voices fade behind me as I walk to the edge of the campsite. The moon hangs huge and heavy, casting silver light over the sleeping jungle.

Looking out at the moonlit vista, determination wells up within me. The past is done, but my future lies ahead. And I'll face it standing strong, backed by the people I now call family.

Tomorrow will bring new challenges, but together we'll meet them head on. Each day is another chance to heal, to grow. To become the man I want to be.

The shadows remain, but my path is lit.

And I know I don't walk it alone.

CHAPTER TWENTY-FOUR

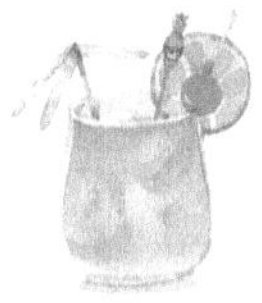

ARIA

*A*cross Town

I sit at the kitchen island, my hands wrapped around a warm mug as I stare into its dark depths, contrasted with the golden morning light that gently bathes the loft. The coffee does little to ease the tightness in my chest.

Across the room, Dimitri and Josef are locked in hushed conversation. Their brows are furrowed, and their jaws tense. I wonder if they're rehashing the fight—my shouted words echoing in their minds as they do in mine.

Everything was going fine yesterday, but at some point the stress of opening the restaurant combined with my fears of going up against Tane again, and I just snapped. The guys bore the brunt of it, and I'm not proud of some of the things I said.

In the moment, I questioned our relationship completely. Questioned their loyalty. I can only hope they can see my lashing out for what it was—someone under too much pressure taking it out on the people closest to them.

Florian bustles around the kitchen, apron around his waist, spatula in hand. The sizzle of eggs and bacon pops and crackles. He glances over his shoulder, offering me a small smile.

"Morning, Florian. Smells amazing," I say, trying to inject brightness into my voice.

"Morning, love. How did you sleep?" I just shake my head slightly, eyes downcast. Sleep has been impossible, my thoughts consumed by the rawness of our argument.

Florian seems to understand, nodding gently as he turns back to the stove.

The distance between us all feels like a chasm. I sip my coffee, the bitter liquid searing my tongue. Unspoken words hang in the air, yet I don't know how to voice them. All I can do is wait for the guys to join me, our breakfast a cold comfort.

I close my eyes as the scene shifts, transporting me back to the previous night. The living room fills my mind, the air thick with tension.

"You can't keep pushing us away, Aria!" Dimitri's voice booms, his usual composure fractured. "We need to know what you want from us."

My chest heaves, hands balled into fists. "I don't know what I want!" I yell, anger and confusion swirling within me. "I'm trying to figure it out, but I have a restaurant to open. I don't have time for walking on eggshells, or worrying about hurting anyone's feelings."

Dimitri steps towards me, his tall frame imposing. "This relationship requires compromise. You have to meet us halfway."

I stand my ground, glaring up at him. "And you need to give me space. I didn't ask for any of this!"

The memory fades as I open my eyes. My heart is pounding, residual adrenaline flooding my veins.

In the present, Florian calls that breakfast is ready. I smooth my hair, take a deep breath, and join the guys at the table.

The atmosphere is strained, the clinking of cutlery on plates too loud in the uncomfortable silence. I push my food around, avoiding eye contact.

After a few tense minutes, Josef clears his throat. "Aria, we need to discuss last night." His usually playful eyes are solemn, his mouth turned down.

I nod, poking at a piece of bacon. "I know. It's just...complicated." I finally meet their gazes. "But we do need to talk."

After breakfast, Dimitri suggests we go out to the balcony, away from the confines of the apartment. I follow him outside, the brisk morning air raising goosebumps on my bare arms.

Below us, the city is awake and bustling, a stark contrast to the heavy quiet between us. Dimitri turns to me, his expression serious.

"We can't keep having these fights, Aria," he says, a hard edge to his voice. "We need to understand where you stand with us."

I wrap my arms around myself, suddenly feeling small. "I'm trying, Dimitri," I say softly. "It's hard to balance my feelings between the three of you along with everything else that's going on. Everything is changing so fast."

He steps closer, tilting my chin up to meet his intense gaze. "Then talk to us. We can't read your mind."

I take a shaky breath, emotions swelling within me. "I care deeply for each of you, but sometimes it feels overwhelming. One minute I want space, the next I'm craving your touch." I pause, biting my lip. "I've never done this before. It's new and scary and...exciting."

"We don't mean to pressure you. We just need to know how to support you." His hand finds mine, squeezing gently.

I cling to him like a lifeline, my heart racing as I try to put my inner chaos into words. All I know is we have to find a way forward together.

Florian and Josef make their way outside to join us. I take a moment to collect myself, looking between the three men who have come to mean so much to me. The sun climbs higher in the sky, the open air helping to clear my cluttered thoughts.

"Maybe we should sit," I suggest, motioning to the balcony floor.

We arrange ourselves in a circle, the tropical cityscape stretching out behind us with rows of hotels that just about tease the clouds. I take a deep breath before beginning.

"I need space sometimes to process everything. This relationship is moving so fast, and my feelings are constantly shifting." I meet each of their gazes in turn. "But I also need patience and understanding. I want this to work, but it won't be perfect overnight."

Josef nods, his expression open. "We can give you space when you need it. Just communicate with us."

"And we'll go at your pace," Florian adds gently. "No pressure."

I feel a weight lifting from my shoulders. "Thank you. I know I'm not always the best at expressing myself. But I'll try to be more vocal about what I need."

Dimitri reaches for my hand. "We're in this together, Aria. Whatever you need, we'll support you."

His touch is grounding. I give him a small smile. "I appreciate that. I feel like we're finally getting somewhere."

The four of us continue talking as the morning sun climbs higher in the sky. There's a new sense of possibility, of hope for the future. For the first time in days, I feel we're moving forward together.

The day passes in a blur of normalcy—cooking meals together, watching movies, just enjoying each other's company. There's an undercurrent of intimacy to even our most mundane interactions.

While I'm thoroughly enjoying the restaurant setup, having a day to just be is working wonders for my mind.

Florian's arm brushes mine as we chop vegetables side-by-side. Josef squeezes my shoulder affectionately as he passes me the popcorn. Dimitri's fingers comb through my hair gently while we lounge on the couch.

After the rawness of our confrontation, this easy togetherness feels soothing. The little touches and glances soothe the lingering hurt, filling the spaces between us with warmth.

As evening falls, I find myself lying in bed, reflecting on the day. Moonlight filters through the curtains, casting a soft glow across the room. I feel a lightness in my chest that wasn't there this morning.

Despite the lingering doubts and fears, I'm filled with a sense of possibility. With patience and understanding between us, we can weather the storms yet to come.

My eyes drift closed as I sink into the pillows. The future is still uncertain, but I don't feel so alone anymore. With their support, I can find my way forward.

Today was a step in the right direction. And though the path won't always be smooth, with them by my side, I feel stronger, a spark of determination igniting within. I'm ready to face the challenges ahead.

With the understanding we've built today, I know I don't have to navigate it all alone. Florian's sly humor and steadfast support. Josef's intense wisdom and creative spirit. Dimitri's nurturing care underneath his dominant, gruff exterior.

Together, we make each other stronger. And though it's complicated and messy at times, I wouldn't trade it for anything. What we have is real, raw, and true.

I turn away from the window, a small smile touching my lips. The future is filled with possibility, and I'm no longer afraid to explore it. Tomorrow awaits, bright with promise.

And with my partners by my side, I'm ready to greet it.

CHAPTER TWENTY-FIVE

AIDAN

The air is thick with the scent of coffee and determination as I survey the hive of activity around me. The secure compound hums with purpose, our headquarters the beating heart of the machine we're building to take Tane down.

Maps, blueprints and live video feeds line the walls. Each person here is a cog with a role to play. And we only get one shot to get this right.

I stand at the head of the table, all eyes on me. The key players are gathered—my men, the Snakes, and Dimitri and his Unknowns. The room crackles with tense focus. This is it.

"Alright everyone, listen up. We've got one shot at this. Let's make it count." My gaze sweeps over them, this band of brothers and sisters in arms. I know their strengths, their weaknesses. Now it's time to put the pieces in play.

"Rake, I want you running surveillance with Dimitri's team. Your humor keeps us going, but right now I need those eyes sharp."

Rake grins, snapping me a salute. "You got it boss."

I turn to Brick. "Brick, you and Angel are on intel. Get in Tane's head, find his soft spots."

Brick's smile is feral, eager. "We'll rip that bastard wide open." Angel cracks her knuckles at his side, hyena-quick and loyal.

My heart pounds with purpose. The stakes are sky-high, but we're ready. Each of us knows the plan. Understands the risk.

Tane's world is about to implode. And we're the ones holding the detonator.

I nod, satisfied that everyone understands their role. The screens behind me flicker to life, displaying maps, documents, photographs-- everything we know about Tane's operation.

"Alright, let's dig into the details," I say, picking up a laser pointer. "Tane has built an extensive network, but it's got vulnerabilities."

I highlight locations on the map—warehouses, distribution hubs, safe houses. "Surveillance will be key. We need eyes on these sites 24/7." I make meaningful eye contact with Rake and Aria's team. They nod, ready to move.

"Beyond locations, we need to leverage our unique strengths. The Snakes have combat and tactical skills." I gesture to them. "The Brixtons bring tech and strategy." My brothers straighten with pride.

"And Aria's crew..." I meet her fiery gaze. "You're our eyes and ears on the ground. The restaurant is the perfect base to coordinate intel and monitor Tane's men."

Aria's lips curl. "We've got this, Aidan." Her men murmur assent, eager to prove their worth.

I feel the mood shifting, determination rising. "It won't be easy," I say gravely. "But if we work together, stay sharp...Tane doesn't stand a chance."

Resolve ripples through the room. We're ready, united. All that's left is to set the wheels in motion. Tane's empire is living on borrowed time. And we're the ones who will collect.

There's an undercurrent of anticipation in the room—we're all ready to move.

I turn to Brick, his hulking frame impossible to miss. "Brick, you'll of course lead the coersion team. Plus, we need you to do your usual thing and find ways to distract Tane's top men."

Brick grins, a slightly unsettling sight. "Don't worry boss, I'll get Tane's men singing like canaries. And he's going to be so distracted he might just forget he's an evil mob boss with a chokehold on these islands." His gravelly voice leaves no doubt that he means business.

My gaze slides to Angel. Her vibrant hair and quick wit belie her ruthless talents. "Angel, you're on extraction. Get our people out safely, if it ever comes to that, by any means necessary." Angel winks, twirling a knife casually. "I'll get it done, Aidan. And I'll make it hurt." Her grin is all teeth, hungry for action.

Damn, she's hot when she's horny for the blood of evil men.

Finally, I look to Slade. His gruff demeanor hides a brilliant mind. "Slade, you're running ops from the restaurant. Keep the intel flowing, and coordinate the teams. You can play with the kitchen equipment during down times, assuming that's okay with Aria, and keep us all fed."

Aria grins, and Slade nods. "Consider it handled." His no-nonsense tone brokers no argument.

I feel the anticipation cresting. My gut twists with nerves, but my voice is steady. "Let's end this. For the Snakes, the Brixtons, the Unknowns. For all of us. And for the people who live on these islands in constant fear. It's time to take Tane down."

A chorus of assent rises around me. We're ready. Tane has no idea what's coming for him.

The tension in the room is palpable as we discuss the potential risks ahead. Tane has resources and manpower on his side, but we've got determination.

"Tane's network runs deep," I say, my voice low but firm. "We have to anticipate anything. Ambushes, double-crosses...this guy fights dirty, and he's no doubt screaming for our blood after last time."

Around the table, jaws clench and eyes harden. They know I'm right.

Josef speaks up, his Russian accent thick. "We've got surprises of our own. Tane won't know what hit him."

Murmurs of agreement sound from all directions. I feel the mood shifting from tense to resolute. We're ready for this fight.

"It's not just about skills, it's about strategy," I continue. "We need to coordinate, work together seamlessly."

Florian nods, his analytical mind already whirring. "The chain is only as strong as its weakest link. We eliminate those weak spots."

The mood turns collaborative as we refine the details.

Angel proposes using her hair salon for discreet meetings.

Slade draws on his culinary skills for creative diversions.

Brick outlines interrogation techniques, his grin turning wolfish.

By the end, the plan is honed to a razor's edge. All the pieces in place, ready to strike. Tane's empire will crumble, and we'll be the ones to do it.

I nod, looking around the room as I reiterate the plan in one final rundown.

Devon speaks up, arms crossed tightly over her chest. "And what about you, Aidan? Where will you be while we're out risking our necks?"

I meet her challenging stare. "I'll be overseeing the entire operation. Making sure everything runs smoothly, adjusting the plan if needed. Tane has eyes everywhere, we can't afford mistakes. Zeke and Skyler and Dimitri will be here with me the whole time."

Devon considers my words, glancing at Zeke and Skyler who nod to let her know they're okay with it. They know I'm the right person to lead the overall group.

"We all have a role," I continue, voice carrying through the bunker. "Alone, we're strong. Together, we're unstoppable. Tane has money and muscle, but we've got heart and brains on our side. And that's what wins wars." I pause, letting that sink in. "We end this, for all of us. No more living in fear, no more looking over our shoulders. It's time to take back these islands."

A fierce energy fills the room. Backs straighten, and eyes blaze with purpose.

"Let's do this," Aria says, steel in her voice.

The rest join in, an impassioned roar. "Let's do this!"

The pieces are set in motion. Very soon, we make our stand.

The energy in the room shifts as everyone begins preparing for their roles. There's a sense of focused intensity, a honing of purpose.

Angel starts gathering surveillance equipment, checking cameras and bugs. Her quick fingers work steadily, betraying none of the nerves I know are coiled inside. She catches my eye and winks, always ready with that sly humor of hers even now.

Nearby, Brick cleans and checks an array of weapons with calm, practiced motions. The giant, hulking man is steady as stone, the eye in the midst of the gathering storm. I know he'll do what needs to be done when the time comes, no questions asked. That ruthless core is exactly why I need him.

Rake leans against a wall, cracking jokes to try and cut the tension. But his smile doesn't reach his eyes, and he fidgets with a knife anxiously. The gangly man hides his fear behind humor, but we all feel it. Fear just means you've got something to lose.

I clap Rake on the shoulder as I pass him. "We've got this, brother. Just stick to the plan."

He nods, jaw tightening. "I know. Doesn't mean I have to like it."

"None of us do. But it ends soon." I meet his eyes meaningfully. We've come too far to fail now.

Slade strides up, his face set in hard lines. He jerks his chin toward the door. "The teams are ready. When exactly are we rolling out?"

I squeeze his shoulder, sensing his tightly leashed energy. My feral wolf, always straining at the leash. "Soon. We'll make Tane bleed for what he's done, I promise you that."

Slade's eyes blaze at the promise of violence. "Good. I'm ready to rip his throat out."

I smile darkly. "All in due time." I turn to survey the room one last time. My soldiers, my family. "So let's make sure we're ready to destroy this fucker for good!"

A chorus of fierce shouts answers me.

Revenge and justice await.

CHAPTER TWENTY-SIX

DIMITRI

The Next Day

I watch Aria from across the room, desire burning through my veins. The curve of her neck, the sway of her hips as she moves around the kitchen—I want to possess every inch of her. This need goes beyond lust. It's primal, and yet somehow still tender.

I step forward into the dim light, the city's glow framing Aria's silhouette. "Come here," I say, my voice low and firm.

Aria doesn't turn, continuing to slice fruit at the counter. "In a minute, Dimitri."

I close the distance between us in three long strides, spinning her around to face me.

Her eyes widen, her gorgeous full lips parting in surprise.

My hands find her waist, pulling her against me. "We need to talk. Now."

I feel Aria tense, her heartbeat quickening against my chest. She searches my eyes, perhaps seeing the raw desire burning behind my usual stoic facade.

"What's going on, Dimitri?" she asks softly.

I bring one hand up to brush her cheek, reveling in the silkiness of her skin. "Things have been...different between us. I know we talked after our argument, and things have been better, but I want to make sure you're okay."

Aria leans into my touch, eyes slipping closed. "I know. I've felt it too." She pauses, biting her lip. "But I'm scared, Dimitri. What if this changes everything? The restaurant, Tane, all of it..."

My thumb caresses her jawline as I tilt her chin up. Our lips are a breath apart. "It already has, Aria. We can't turn back now. The only way is forward."

I kiss her then, slowly at first, then building in urgency. She responds in kind, her hands fisting in my shirt. We come up for air, our foreheads touching, breathing ragged.

"I'm ready, Dimitri," Aria whispers. "I trust you."

I smile, brushing a strand of hair from her face. No more words are needed. Our bodies speak for us now, destined to intertwine in the dim light of the loft. With our bodies entwined, we can work through any conflict.

I pull Aria into my lap, needing her closer. Our kisses deepen as our hands roam and clothes become barriers we desperately want gone. I trail hot, open-mouthed kisses down her neck and she arches into me with a breathy moan.

"Dimitri..." she gasps as I palm her breast, teasing a nipple into a tight peak.

I capture her mouth again, drinking in her sweetness. My desire ramps higher, my body coiled tight. I have to pace myself, take this slow.

Aria deserves reverence, worship.

I lay her back on the couch, my hands skimming her sides, memorizing every curve and valley. Her skin is like warm silk under my calloused touch. I trail kisses down her torso, pausing to swirl my tongue around her navel. She shivers, her fingers tangling in my hair.

"Please..." she begs softly.

I glance up, seeing the naked need in her eyes. I hook my fingers under her panties.

"Tell me what you want, Aria. I need to hear you say it." My voice is rough, strained.

"I want you, Dimitri. All of you. Make me yours."

At her breathless consent, I strip her bare, exposing her fully to me. She is exquisite in the dim light, an angel made of flesh. I kiss back up her legs reverently, ready to worship every inch of her.

We've been here many times before, but tonight... this is different.

I trail a hand up her inner thigh, feeling her tremble with anticipation. When my fingers finally reach her slick heat, she arches into my touch with a sharp cry.

"So wet for me already," I murmur.

I stroke her slowly, well aware of what makes her gasp and moan.

Her fingers dig into my shoulders, her body wound tight as a bowstring.

I circle her clit, applying just enough pressure to make her shudder.

"Please, Dimitri..." she pants. "I need you."

The raw desire in her voice shreds my restraint. I shed my clothes and cover her body with mine, groaning at the skin-on-skin contact.

She wraps her legs around my waist, her heels digging into my back.

I enter her in one long stroke, swallowing her throaty moan with a searing kiss. She feels like heaven around me, hot, slick and impossibly tight. I set a slow pace, pulling almost all the way out before thrusting deep again.

Aria claws at my back, urging me on with breathless pleas.

I quicken my pace, angling to hit that sensitive spot inside her.

She shatters around me with a sharp cry, her inner walls fluttering and clenching.

I follow her over the edge with a guttural groan, emptying myself inside her welcoming heat.

We cling together as the aftershocks fade, our hearts hammering against each other. I brush damp hair from her face and kiss her tenderly.

Now that round one is over, the superficial lust addressed, it's time to put her to the test.

I guide Aria through a series of commands, assessing her willingness to submit. My voice is firm but gentle as I say, "Kneel for me."

She hesitates, uncertainty flashing in her eyes. "Dimitri...this is...different."

"Trust me," I urge. "Do it."

Slowly, she sinks to her knees on the plush carpet. I can see the conflict raging within her—the desire to please warring with her fear of losing control.

"This is hard for me, Dimitri," she says softly, her eyes downcast.

I tip her chin up to meet my gaze. "I know it is. But I need to know we can trust each other completely, even in this."

She takes a shaky breath and nods.

I caress her cheek, my heart swelling with pride at her courage. We still have a way to go, but this first act of submission is a milestone.

Leaning down, I press a gentle kiss to her forehead. "You're doing so well, my darling. I won't take us further than you can handle." In my line of business, I've learned exactly what buttons to press, and—more importantly—when to stop, to slow down, to be guided even when I'm in charge. Especially when I'm in charge.

She smiles tentatively up at me. "I'm trying, for you. Because...I trust you."

I help her stand, wrapping her in a warm embrace. Tonight we explored new territory, and it might not have seemed like much, but ultimately it deepened the bond between us. Trust is more important than ever, and obtaining it in one area of our lives will surely translate into others.

I pull back slightly to look into her eyes, my hands still cradling her face. "This isn't just about power or control, Aria. It's about trust—absolute, unconditional trust."

She nods, understanding dawning. "I do trust you, Dimitri. With everything I am."

"I know," I murmur. "And that means everything to me."

I lean in, capturing her lips in a searing kiss. She responds eagerly, the last of her reservations fading away. It's a perfect moment, two souls meshing, tangled together with want.

When we finally break for air, her cheeks are flushed and her eyes bright. The atmosphere between us has shifted, charged with renewed passion and intimacy.

"What do we do now?" she asks breathlessly.

I grin and sweep her up into my arms, carrying her towards the bedroom. "Now, my love, I intend to show you just how much I appreciate your trust."

The long night ahead will be all about worshipping her body and spirit, reaffirming the unbreakable bond we now share. Her courageous act of submission has forged our souls together at the deepest level. And I plan to spend every moment proving myself worthy of the gift of her trust.

Our lips lock in a heated kiss. I set her down gently near the foot of the massive four-poster bed dominating the room. She laughs happily as I kick the door shut behind us.

My hands trail down her sides, fingering the soft swell of her hips.

She stands before me gloriously nude, moonlight from the window casting a silver glow on her flawless skin and illuminating her gorgeous curves.

I drink in the sight hungrily, desire raging through my veins. I cannot get enough of this woman.

I circle behind her, my fingertips ghosting along her shoulders, down her spine.

She shivers at my touch.

Leaning in close, I brush her hair aside and graze my lips along the graceful curve of her neck.

"So incredibly beautiful," I murmur against her skin. My hands glide around to cup her breasts as I trail open-mouthed kisses down to her shoulder.

A soft gasp escapes her lips.

Turning her in my arms, I capture her mouth again, walking her backwards until her legs hit the bed frame. Gently but firmly, I push her down onto the silken sheets.

I shed my own clothes swiftly before joining her.

Our bodies align in flawless symmetry, skin against skin.

My hands and lips worship every inch of her flesh, drawing out sweet cries of pleasure.

This is only the beginning.

Tonight I will take her to the peaks of ecstasy again and again, our passion burning bright as the city lights outside. Here, tangled together in satin sheets, we let the outside world fade away.

Nothing exists except her body and mine, moving as one.

CHAPTER TWENTY-SEVEN

FLORIAN

The room glows in the candlelight, shadows dancing across the walls. Everything is in place, just as I wanted. My pulse races with anticipation. Tonight, we're going to have some fun.

I light the last candle and glance over the items on the table: silk scarves, a leather crop, ice and hot wax. A shiver runs down my spine as I imagine using them on Aria's soft skin.

My Aria. So beautiful yet untrusting, quick-witted and sharp-tongued. But she loves me, as I love her. Tonight she'll give herself to me completely.

I hear the loft door open and close, followed by the soft pad of bare feet. Aria appears in the doorway, wearing only a silky robe. Her eyes widen at the setup, a mix of heat and uncertainty in her gaze.

"Come in, Aria." My voice is rough with desire. "Tonight, we explore."

She hesitates, biting her lip. I can see the battle in her eyes, longing warring with fear. Aria has been hurt before. She needs to know she can trust me.

I hold out my hand, my heart clenching. "Aria, you know I would never hurt you. But I want to give you pleasure like you've never known."

A smile plays on her lips as she takes my hand. "I know, Florian." Her fingers tighten around mine, pulse racing under my thumb. "Let's see where this takes us."

Joy and heat surge through me as I pull her into my arms.

She melts against me with a sigh, her hands sliding up my chest.

I crush my lips to hers, kissing her with a hunger that has been building for weeks.

Tonight I'll show her how much she is loved, and find new depths of connection. But first, I must make sure she's comfortable.

I reluctantly break the kiss, gazing into her eyes. "Remember, you're in control, Aria. If anything feels too much, just say 'red' and we stop."

Aria smiles, trailing a finger down my cheek. "I trust you, Florian. Now, show me what you have planned."

A growl rises in my chest. The night is still young, but already I can feel the first stirrings of release.

Tonight, there will be no holding back.

I pull Aria close, crushing my lips to hers once more.

She opens to me with a soft moan, her hands sliding into my hair. I kiss her deeply, pouring my love and desire into the embrace.

When we finally break apart, she gazes at me through heavy-lidded eyes. "Florian..." My name is a plea on her lips, filled with need.

Heat surges through me. I take her hand and lead her into the bedroom, my pulse racing.

The room is dimly lit by candles, shadows dancing across the walls. Aria's eyes widen as she takes in the scene, her gaze lingering on the silk ropes laid out on the bed.

I wrap my arms around her from behind, nuzzling her neck. "Do you trust me?" My voice is a rough whisper against her skin.

She tilts her head to the side with a shiver, baring her throat in submission. "Yes."

Triumph and desire roar through me. I kiss along the curve of her neck, grazing her skin with my teeth. "Then surrender to me tonight, Aria."

A soft moan escapes her. She turns in my arms, gazing up at me with eyes dark with need. "I'm yours, Florian."

Those two words ignite my blood. I crush my lips to hers once more, kissing her with a hunger that threatens to consume me. My hands slide under her robe, finding warm flesh.

She gasps into my mouth as I cup her breasts, teasing her nipples into hardened peaks.

Tonight I'll give her pleasure and take my own, exploring new depths to our intimacy. And by the time the sun rises, she'll well and truly trust me. Things have been a little rough lately, and this is exactly what we need to prove our loyalty to each other. Our love for each other.

I slide the silk robe off her shoulders, letting it fall to the floor.

Aria stands bare before me, shadows dancing across her exquisitely smooth skin. Her cheeks flush under my gaze, a mix of shyness and arousal.

"You're so beautiful." I whisper the words like a promise, claiming her mouth in a possessive kiss. My hands roam her body, mapping every curve and hollow.

She trembles against me, soft sounds of pleasure caught in her throat.

When I break the kiss, her lips chase mine for a heartbeat before she catches herself. Her breath comes fast, her eyes dark with desire.

I cradle her face in my hands, thumb tracing the fullness of her lower lip. "On your knees."

Aria sinks to her knees without hesitation, her gaze locked on mine.

I caress her cheek, a surge of pride and tenderness winding through the raging heat of my desire. Her willingness to submit so fully is a gift beyond measure. One I will honor tonight.

I take a step back, my fingers working at the buckle of my belt.

Aria's gaze follows my movements, her lips parting on a soft inhale.

The belt slides free with a whisper of leather on leather. I let it fall to the floor, my eyes never leaving her face.

Her tongue darts out to wet her lips, her cheeks flushing an even deeper shade of pink. But she holds my gaze, waiting with a patience born of trust. My Aria, so beautifully submissive. Tonight I'll push her further than ever before, and she will surrender beautifully.

The thought has arousal pulsing hot in my veins. I cup her chin, tilting her face up to meet my eyes. "Are you ready, my queen?"

She leans into my touch with a soft sound, eyes shining. "Yes."

One word, full of promise. Tonight we explore the depths of our connection, and by the dawn's first light, she will be forever mine.

I release her chin and take a slow step back, fingers working at the buttons of my shirt. Aria's gaze follows my movements, her lips parting on a soft inhale. The shirt slides from my shoulders and falls to the floor.

Her tongue darts out to wet her lips, her cheeks flushing an even deeper shade of pink. But she holds my gaze, waiting with a patience born of trust. Such a gift, her willingness to surrender control.

The thought has arousal pulsing hot in my veins. I unbuckle my belt, sliding it free with a whisper of leather.

Aria sucks in a sharp breath, her eyes darkening. Her reaction feeds my desire, and I have to fight the urge to close the distance between us in a single stride.

No, not yet. I'm going to take this slow for us, so we can both relish it.

I drop the belt, tilting my head with a considering look. "On your hands and knees."

Aria sinks into position without hesitation, head bowed in supplication. The sight of her waiting so beautifully has heat pooling low in my belly, my hard cock straining against the confines of my slacks.

I reach down and cup the back of her neck in a firm grip. "Look at me."

She lifts her head immediately, meeting my gaze. I caress her cheek with my thumb, drinking in the sight of her flushed skin and parted lips. "Such a good girl. Are you ready to continue?"

"Yes," she breathes, her eyes shining with promise.

"Then we shall begin." I release her, stepping back.

I select a slender crop from the table, running the tip down the delicate arch of Aria's spine.

She shivers at the touch, anticipation thrumming through her body in a subtle tremor.

I trail lower, circling the rounded globes of her ass before bringing the crop down in a sharp snap.

Aria gasps, her back arching. I caress the reddening mark left behind, feeling the heat radiating from her skin. "Color?"

"Green," she whispers, the single word conveying her need.

I reward her with another stinging blow, watching in fascination as her body absorbs the sensation, craving more.

The blows come faster now, leaving crisscrossing marks across her ass and thighs. Aria moans with each strike, rocking back to meet my crop.

I can see the effects in the clenching of her hands, the restless roll of her hips, the slickness glistening between her legs. She's losing herself in the rhythm of pain and pleasure, and I'm unraveling along with her.

I toss the crop aside, kneeling behind her to replace it with my hands.

She cries out as I squeeze the tender flesh, massaging deep. I bend forward, licking a hot trail over the marks I've left behind, tasting salt and spice on my tongue.

Aria is panting hard, pushing back against my mouth with desperation.

I slide one hand between her legs, groaning at the wet heat that greets my fingers. She's soaked, her inner muscles clenching around nothing as she seeks relief. But not yet. We have farther to go before she's allowed release.

I withdraw my hands, ignoring her whimper of protest. "On your back. Now."

Aria immediately flips over, gazing up at me with eyes glazed by desire. Her body is flushed, nipples tight and rosy peaks. She has never looked more beautiful.

I settle between her spread thighs, pinning her in place with the weight of my body.

Aria wraps her legs around my waist, pulling me close as our lips meet in a searing kiss. In this moment, we're bound by more than desire. We are connected by trust and love.

I break the kiss, gazing down at Aria with a mix of passion and tenderness. Her hair is a tangled halo around her head, lips swollen from our kisses. She looks thoroughly ravished, and I feel a surge of primal satisfaction at the sight.

"How do you feel, Aria?" My voice is rough with desire.

She smiles up at me, her eyes shining in the candlelight. "Incredible. Thank you for taking me there."

Her words ignite a blaze of warmth in my chest. I cup her cheek, stroking my thumb over her cheekbone.

"You're welcome, my love. Tonight, we pushed boundaries and found new depths in our connection. This is only the beginning of our exploration."

Aria's smile widens. "I'm ready to explore wherever this takes us."

I kiss her again, pouring all the love and devotion I feel for this woman into the embrace.

When we part, I rearrange the blankets around us and draw her close against my side.

Aria rests her head on my shoulder with a contented sigh.

I stroke her hair, basking in the afterglow of our intimacy. The night is still young, but for now we rest, our hearts and bodies sated. The secrets and desires we discovered tonight have only strengthened the bonds between us. This is what I have always craved: connection, trust, love.

So many people cling to me in an attempt to get closer, not to me, but to my fame. They long to be part of my entourage, many of them willing to sacrifice their bodies to me as tribute. It used to delight me, to fulfill my desires, but now it just leaves me hollow.

I didn't know I could ever reach those peaks of pleasure again that I enjoyed right at the start of my fame, when I was blissfully unaware of why lust and desire came so easily. I'm an attractive guy by conventional standards, sure, but I'd be an absolute idiot if I thought my looks were the reason women literally post their used panties to me in the mail.

But with Aria, it's different. She couldn't care less what I do when I'm not with her. She's supportive of my music career, sure, but in the same way someone might be supportive of an accountant or a mechanic—there to listen to the stories about my day, and asking about the moment she knows matter. Okay okay, I guess my job is a little more exciting than most, and she does enjoy being backstage at my concerts.

But it's the real me she sees inside, that she craves. That she would do anything for.

And I feel the same way about her. Aria, my stunning queen.

With Aria, I have finally found a home.

CHAPTER TWENTY-EIGHT

AIDAN

I stand in the shadows, the glow of computer monitors barely illuminating the dark command center. My eyes scan the screens, digesting the intel displayed before me. Tane's network has been laid bare through surveillance footage and intercepted communications.

The tension in the air is palpable as my team gathers around, their faces etched with determination and focus. We're making significant progress, and it's almost time to strike.

I turn to face them, their eyes locked on me, awaiting my command. "Alright team, here's the situation. Tane's reach is vast, but he's not invulnerable."

I click a remote, bringing up a map on the central monitor. "What we've found over the last few days is communication lines here and here are lightly guarded." I gesture at two weak points on the map. "Surveillance indicates gaps in security shift changes near his downtown warehouse." I pause, and everyone nods. "What's come to my attention, however, is Tane is apparently extra paranoid at the moment. It's fairly understandable based on what we did to him on the other island, combined with the fact he's incredibly unhinged."

Angel cracks her knuckles, adrenaline already pumping through her veins.

Brick's stare darkens, his mind turning over the possibilities. "I love exploiting paranoia," he growls. "It's one of my favorite hobbies."

"Yes, exactly," I continue, my voice steady and commanding. "We need to use this information to insert ourselves seamlessly into his operations."

This is it. The moment we've trained for. Failure is not an option. Tane's empire will fall, and we will be the ones to topple it. I feel the weight of my team's trust, their lives in my hands. But I know they are ready. We all are.

Time to execute the plan. No turning back now. I take a deep breath and give the order. "Let's do this."

I nod to my team, their fierce determination mirroring my own. "You all know your roles." I glance at Brick. "You're sure you're ready for stage one?"

Brick grins, a twisted glint in his eyes. "Don't worry, I have my methods."

I know Brick's talents run dark, and we need that wicked edge. "Stay sharp and stick to the plan." I finish, looking at each of them. "Let's finish this once and for all."

They nod, determination etched on their faces.

The time has come to tear down Tane's empire, and it's now or never. The thought of failure is terrifying, but as I watch my team prepare, I know we're as ready as we're ever going to be. If all goes to plan, Tane won't see us coming until it's too late.

I take a deep breath as I look over the team, the weight of this mission settling on my shoulders. So much planning and preparation has led us here, to this pivotal moment. It's time to put our skills to the test.

I unfurl the building schematics across the central table, the team gathering around. "Here's the layout of Tane's headquarters. He has warehouses which are more vulnerable, but he's rarely there. Intel shows he keeps his private office on the top floor."

I point to the fortified location, our target for planting surveillance devices. "Access is restricted, so we'll need to stealthily bypass security."

Dom cracks a smile. "Leave that to me. We'll be ghosts."

I nod, knowing I can count on his skills. "Once inside, we split up. Skyler, your team heads to the server room to tap their network."

Skyler adjusts his glasses as he studies the map. "Just point me to the tech."

"Brick, take your team to sweep for any prisoners Tane may be keeping on site. See if you can get any intel out of them."

Brick pounds a fist into his palm. "Oh, they'll talk."

His enthusiasm is unsettling but necessary.

"The rest will hit Tane's office with me to plant the surveillance gear. In and out, quick and clean."

I make eye contact with each of them. "Watch each other's backs. At the first sign of trouble, we vanish like ghosts. No unnecessary risks. But, if the opportunity strikes to take him down while we're there, I trust your judgement to act."

They give curt nods. My team knows the stakes, how critical this mission is in our ongoing war against Tane. We have to succeed.

I roll up the schematics, the plan now finalized and clear. "Let's move out and end this, once and for all."

Resolute, we head into the night, ready to infiltrate Tane's stronghold. The darkness will conceal us as we position for the final strike against our enemy. Tane's reign ends tonight.

"No room for mistakes, people. We have one shot to cripple Tane's operation." I meet each of their eyes, seeing my own steely resolve reflected back. "When we walk out that door, we do this right. Failure is not an option."

Brick slams a fist into his palm. Skyler cracks his knuckles. Dom checks his weapon one last time.

I take a deep breath. "This is it. Let's go bust this place wide open."

We get ready to infiltrate. The hunt is on, and Tane has no idea what's coming for him. My team is prepared to end this, no matter the cost. The time has come to strike.

I take a moment to myself in the quiet command room, the only light coming from the glowing monitors that display our intel on Tane's operation. We've spent countless hours here, planning and preparing for this day. Now it's arrived.

So much is riding on this mission. Not just taking down a dangerous criminal, but proving we have what it takes to outsmart someone with endless resources. If we fail, it could unravel everything we've worked for.

I close my eyes, visualizing the route, rehearsing the plan step-by-step. We will get this right. There is no other option. Too many are depending on us.

I gather the team one last time before we head out into the night. I can see the anticipation in their eyes, feel the energy humming through them. Time for a final push.

"I know tensions are high, but stay focused. We've trained relentlessly to get to this moment. Tane has no idea what's coming. We're a highly skilled team with one purpose—taking him down. It won't happen in one evening, but today's efforts will get us that much closer." I make eye contact with each of them. "Trust the plan. Trust each other. We go in clean and precise. Get ready to watch this empire crumble."

They pound fists, slam guns, shout affirmations. We're amped and ready.

"Let's do this." We move toward the doors, determination burning through our veins. The hunt has almost reached its apex. Tane's reign ends soon.

CHAPTER TWENTY-NINE

SKYLER

The neon lights of the city blur beneath me as I perch on the rooftop, dressed in black with night vision goggles tight over my eyes. My heart thrums against my ribs, the thrill of the hunt pulsing through me.

"Four guards on rotation at the gate," I mutter, peering through binoculars at the fortress below. "Cameras on all corners. You're not keeping me out, Tane."

I won't let him kidnap anyone this time. Not anymore. Or at least I'll do my fucking best. Every minute anyone spends trapped in one of Tane's compounds, their light grows dimmer. Their creative spirits smothered, their fire dampened by Tane's cruelty. Plus, Devon and Angel have been kidnapped more than enough at this point. I don't know if either of them could survive another time. Hell, I don't know if I could survive another time.

My jaw clenches. The thought of my Valkyrie down there, collared and leashed, ignites a rage in my core. Left alone with hordes of Tane's creepy ass henchmen. She deserves so much more. Freedom. Passion. Adventure. I can't let that happen to her again.

I creep along the rooftop's edge, my boots silent on the gravel. At the rear corner, I anchor my rappelling line and hook my harness.

A breath to steady my nerves. Then I'm over the side, suspended in open air. The ground spins dizzily below as I descend, swallowed by shadows.

I'm coming for your information, Tane. I'm coming. And that's just one near-final step before we put your cruel reign to an end. Put you to an end.

I touch down in the alley, gravel crunching softly beneath my boots. Crouched low, I scan the perimeter, mapping my infiltration in my mind.

There—a gap in the camera coverage near the loading dock, just like Aidan showed us on the schematics. My pulse quickens.

"Almost there, Taney-tane," I whisper into the night. "Stay distracted for me."

I slip from shadow to shadow, all of my senses heightened.

The guards pace obliviously, assault rifles slack in their hands. Fools. They have no idea what's coming.

At the loading dock, I pull out my decryption device and get to work hacking the keypad. 30 seconds and I'm in. The door clicks open.

My lips curl in a smile. "Let's see what secrets you're hiding, Tane."

I ghost through the sterile halls, a specter in the darkness. Each step brings me closer to the answers we seek. I won't leave here without them. There is no room for mistakes this time.

Voices sound ahead, deep in conversation about something they saw on TikTok. I press myself flat against the wall, scarcely breathing as two guards pass. Oblivious, thankfully sucked into the latest clickbait rather than noticing little old me breaking in to their maximum security stronghold. My hand slides to the knife at my hip, hungering for violence, but I resist the urge. Not yet.

It's almost a shame they're terrible at their jobs and making this easy for me, removing the need for violence. But I know that time will come soon enough.

I find the main office and slip inside. My pulse thunders as I slot my flash drive into the computer. "Come on, come on," I urge through gritted teeth. The download commences, my eyes darting between door and screen.

Almost there. I'm almost—

Footsteps in the hall. I dart beneath the desk, forcing my breathing to steady. Just a guard's routine patrol. He'll pass soon enough.

And then Tane's secrets will be ours.

The guard's heavy footsteps grow louder as he approaches the office door. It's thankfully a large desk, but even so I'm awkwardly crunched underneath it. I hold perfectly still beneath the desk, my muscles tensed and ready to react. Obviously, I'd prefer not to draw attention to myself and therefore our plan, but sometimes you've gotta do what you've gotta do.

The door creaks open. I see the guard's boots enter, and hear him shuffling around the room. Checking things casually, he has no idea I'm here. After a few agonizing moments, he turns and leaves, the door clicking shut behind him.

I let out a silent breath of relief, not that I didn't get to hurt the asshole, but because he didn't cause a delay in our plans. The download finishes, and I pocket the flash drive. Time to get out of here.

I crack the door open, peeking out. All clear. I slip into the hallway, moving swift and silent through the corridors. Almost to the exit.

Suddenly, there's a shout from behind—I've been spotted. Fuck! No time for stealth now.

I break into a sprint, my boots pounding the concrete floor. More yelling, and then gunshots, bullets ricocheting off the walls around me. Adrenaline surges through my veins as I barrel toward the exit.

I burst out into the night air, my pulse roaring in my ears. The guards are close behind, still shooting. I weave and dodge, making for the shadows of the alley ahead.

A bullet grazes my shoulder but I keep going, fueled by determination, ignoring the searing pain that shoots through my shoulder and upper arm.

I lose them in the dark maze of alleys, scrambling up a fire escape to the rooftops.

Only when I'm a safe distance away, lost in the glittering sea of the island city, do I finally stop to catch my breath. I made it.

And now Tane's secrets are ours.

I glance down at my shoulder, seeing the tear in my shirt and the blood seeping through. Just a graze, but it stings something fierce. No time to tend to it now though. I've got what I came for.

I make my way across the rooftops, using the skills Rake taught me to leap silently between buildings. Parkour basically makes everything a giant playground and I'm fucking here for it. The city spreads out below me, neon and headlights twinkling in the night. Silhouettes of palm trees flicker, and the ocean spreads out into forever, dark and dangerous. Up here, everything almost looks beautiful, hiding its dark underbelly.

My thoughts go to Devon, hoping she's holding up okay while I'm gone. This info could be the key to taking Tane down for good. To finally getting our lives back. She's been so strong through it all, but I know it wears on her. That every time Tane's name is mentioned, her memories of her father's actions, and how this all started, come flooding back.

As I reach the rendezvous point, Zeke comes into view, pacing anxiously. His head snaps up when he hears me, relief flooding his face. "Skyler! You made it. Are you alright?" His brow furrows at the blood on my shoulder.

"Just a scratch," I say, tapping the flashdrive in my pocket and then yanking my hoodie off my head and running my fingers through my hair. "But I got it. Let's get out of here."

He nods, all business again. We descend the fire escape and load into the idling car below.

Dom is at the wheel, his face grim. But he cracks a smile when he sees me. "Welcome back, killer."

I grin wearily back at him. It's good to see my family again.

Dom taps me on the shoulder supportively as we speed off into the night, our mission complete. For now.

I give Zeke and Dom a quick rundown of the mission as Dom expertly navigates the dark streets. How I infiltrated the compound, avoiding the patrols. Swiping the intel from Tane's office. My narrow escape when the guard showed up.

"You took a big risk going in there solo," Zeke says, concern in his eyes. "But it paid off. This intel could expose all of Tane's operations."

I nod. "It was worth it. That bastard's done too much damage already."

"Do you think he'll figure out it was us?"

I shrug. "I don't think anyone saw my face, with my hoodie pulled down like that. But I'm sure he'll have suspicions he's unable to prove."

Dom's tattooed knuckles whiten on the steering wheel, and he lifts a hand to crack his fingers. "When do we take the fight to him? I'm done waiting around. Sneaking around has its uses, but I'm ready for these knuckles to come into contact with some skulls."

"Soon," Zeke assures him. "We just need to decipher these files, and find his weak spots."

Dom grunts unhappily but doesn't say anything further. He knows this plan is right, as frustrating as waiting may be.

We pull into the hidden garage of our command center. Home sweet home.

Devon and Rake are waiting for us inside, pacing anxiously. They rush over when they see us. "Well?" Rake asks impatiently.

"We got what we needed." I hold up the flash drive triumphantly.

He grins. "Well done, man." He slaps me on the shoulder and pain surges down my arm. I wince.

Devon shakes her head, her eyes fiery. "It's not worth losing you. None of this. I'm so glad you're safe." She gestures at my injury. "What happened to you, Sky?"

"Just a little gunshot," I shrug, and wince at the pain the action causes. "Nothing serious."

Her mouth flies open. "A gunshot? And you're playing it off like it was nothing? Clearly you're in pain."

"Hey, it was a graze. And it'll take more than that to kill me," I say lightly, though her concern warms me.

Devon squeezes my other shoulder.

Zeke nods. "Okay, let's debrief so we can start analyzing this intel with the rest of the team. We don't have any time to waste."

I take a deep breath and nod. Mission accomplished, but the real work is just beginning.

I follow Devon into a large open room filled with computer stations and monitors. The rest of the team is already gathered. They look up expectantly as I enter.

I toss the flash drive to Zeke. "Let's see what secrets this holds."

He plugs it into the main computer and gets to work decoding the encrypted files. Screens fill with data—financial records, communications, shipment manifests.

"Jackpot," Zeke murmurs. "This is just about everything we need to take down his operation."

I feel a fierce surge of satisfaction. After everything Tane has done to us, all the pain he's caused, we finally have him.

Satisfied with what he sees on his many screens, Zeke stands and approaches. He squeezes my shoulder, pride in his usually stern eyes. "You did good, man."

Zeke's opinion always carries extra weight with me, and I feel a little smile threatening to break out.

"Hell yeah he did!" Rake crows. "Now let's use this to make Tane sorry he ever messed with us."

I meet Devon's gaze across the room. In that moment, an unspoken promise passes between us. We're going to tear Tane's empire down, piece by piece, until there's nothing left. This ends so soon I can taste it. Aria's up next, her role filling in one more piece in Tane's evil puzzle.

My heart pounds with anticipation.

Tane took everything from us, but now we're taking it back.

And this time, we won't stop until the job is done.

CHAPTER THIRTY

ARIA

The throbbing bass pounds in my chest as I step into the club's smoky interior, the smell of expensive liquor and designer perfume hanging thick in the air. My heels click on the polished floor, and I feel dozens of eyes turn to appraise me.

Part of me immediately assumes the stares are because I look awkward, and I almost fall for it to stop and smooth my dress. But I remember just in time that I'm not here to be Aria, the self-conscious girl who doesn't think she's good enough. No, tonight I'm a stunning enigma. Someone who wants to be seen for all the right reasons.

I slide through the crowds, forcing myself to exude an air of aloof confidence despite the anxious hammering of my heart. These people reek of old money and privilege. I'm an imposter among pedigreed wolves. But what they think of me is not my business, and I have a job to do.

"Invitation?" the bouncer rumbles, massive arms crossed over his broad chest. I offer him the forged paper with a coy smile, channeling all my nerves into the deception. With Skyler's recent finds, it didn't take Aidan and Zeke long at all to create a replica invitation that would enable me to slip inside this event. His eyes linger on my curves poured into the slinky black dress before he nods, stepping aside.

I may have made it past the gatekeeper, but I'm far from safe. I weave between socialites and tycoons, their laughter too loud, their smiles too wide from champagne and pills. I catch snippets of conversation about yachts in St Lucia and skiing in Aspen. A glittering facade over a rotting core.

I spot the door hidden behind velvet drapes, and the hulking guard watching the entrance. Showtime. I sashay over, lowering my voice to a sultry purr.

"I heard this is where the real party is," I say, trailing a suggestive nail down his chest. He smirks, leaning in close. The game is on.

His hot breath caresses my ear as he whispers, "What's the password, sweetheart?"

I suppress a shudder, forcing myself to meet his leering gaze. "Frangipani clusterfuck," I reply, resisting the urge to giggle and infusing the words with as much sinful promise as I can muster.

He notices my lip twitch at the corner, and for a moment I think I'm toast. But then he steps back and pulls the curtain aside, revealing the spiral staircase descending into darkness. "Enjoy," he says with a wink. "Glad you like the password. I made it up myself."

I take a deep breath and make my way down, one precarious step after another. The temperature drops and flickering candlelight casts twisting shadows on the stone walls. It feels like I'm descending into the bowels of some gothic castle, not an exclusive club.

I'm really not sure what to expect. All I know is this is where I'm meant to be, if we want to get the real tea on Tane.

At the bottom, I'm greeted by a scene from my darkest nightmares. Grotesque taxidermy and strange occult artifacts line the room. In the center, a group of elites are gathered around a table, money and white powder changing hands as they engage in depraved games.

It's then that I spy the pool table. I was expecting something dark based on Angel and Devon's recounting of Tane's weird torture display in his vacation mansion, but not even hearing about bodies in display cases could have quite prepared me for this.

I didn't notice it at first because several men are partaking in a game, pool cues in hand. It's the pool balls that intrigue and horrify me. Each of them, transparent, made out of some type of thick material. Encasing what are clearly human body parts. Inside several, I notice vertebrae. Another seems to house a human heart.

My stomach roils as one of the men sends the white pool ball thwacking into what can only be a pair of human eyeballs housed within yet another translucent pool ball. The other men laugh heartily as they watch the eyeballs go around and around before the ball finally plunks into a corner pocket. The perverse joys of the super wealthy never cease to freak me out, and I shudder, not so much at the eyeballs as at them. The ones enjoying this.

A familiar ding-ding-ding noise starts up in the corner. Pinball. I glance over, and to my shock—although I really need to start expecting things like this—several people are gathered around what appears to be a vintage game. But, instead of the little metal balls I'm accustomed to, the group appears to be playing with shriveled human testicles. The flapper things at the bottom of the game resemble human fingers. Jesus.

I get the part where Tane is an evil mob boss who takes pleasure from hurting people to get his way. And I get the part where he's focused on money and power. But to have custom-made games out of body parts suggests Tane's enjoyment from his activities goes way farther than simply 'being insanely rich'.

My eyes dart around the room. There's more. There's always more, when it comes to people like Tane. The hides on the wall, human. One I even recognize in jacket form. Wow, the guys thought they were sending a dark message to Tane when they sent him Denzo's tattooed skin in leather jacket form, but Tane just added it to his collection. There it is, framed and displayed in all its glory.

I try my best not to puke as I notice little details in the furniture. Leather upholstery accented with what can only be human teeth. Lamps with spines as the stands that hold up the lightbulbs. Jesus. The other girls weren't lying when they said Tane is a depraved lunatic, and that I should be prepared for anything, coming here.

Focus, Aria, I scold myself. I'm not here to inventory and judge Tane's interior design choices, as distracting as they may be.

I discreetly take in the appearances of everyone in the room. Most, but not all of them, men. Some familiar, known for running prominent businesses on the island. Ensnared in Tane's debauched business interests, no doubt. I mentally catalog each of them, eager to take these details back to the team. Each identified individual a potential weak spot in Tane's formidable armor.

It's hard for my eyes to stop trailing away from the boring businessmen trying to big-note themselves, and focus on this room of horrors.

But before I can take in any more of the atrocities before me, a petite blonde in a lacy black dress notices me staring, her heavily lined eyes narrowing. "Who the hell are you?" Her question draws the attention of the others. "And why are you staring at everything? This is meant to be discreet, exclusive. Are you some kind of influencer? Are you going to put this on a live stream? Mind your business."

I force myself to exude uncaring boredom, despite the horror of the things I've just observed. "I'm looking for a real party. This looks a bit...tame." Their expressions range from annoyance to intrigue. Time to make an exit before my luck runs out.

I turn and saunter back up the stairs, my pulse racing. I think I got what I came for, but I can still feel their eyes crawling over me. I did what I came here to do, my virgin surveillance mission of this type. Now to get this intel back to the team.

I emerge back into the main club, the pulsating music and chatter washing over me. For a moment, I'm disoriented by the normalcy of it all compared to the depravity downstairs. Anyone would think it was a typical nightspot where tourists can blow off some steam. I take a steadying breath.

Blending in with the crowd once more, and keeping my head down, I swiftly traverse the dance floor, avoiding being groped by drunken men whose hooded eyes attempt to devour my body. The thumping music and press of bodies conceal me as I weave toward the exit. Eventually, I make it through to the other side. The sense of relief is overwhelming. I made it out, but the images of that basement will haunt me for as long as I have a memory. Almost there. Just a few more steps and I'll be free.

Right as I get to the door, a large hand clamps down on my shoulder, rooting me in place. My heart leaps into my throat as I turn.

"Leaving so soon, beautiful?" The bouncer leers, tightening his grip. It's the one who was so proud of his ridiculous password. Behind him, I spot two of Tane's men scanning the crowd, clearly looking for me.

"I got what I came for," I reply cryptically. His eyes gleam with interest.

"Pity. I was hoping we could get better acquainted. Seeing you appreciated my sense of humor and all."

I force a laugh. "Another time, perhaps." Before he can respond, I slip out the door into the cool night air, letting out a shaky breath. I did it. Now to get this intel back to Aidan and the others. We're one step closer to taking Tane down.

The damp air kisses my skin as I hurry down the street, the chill of the night a relief after the suffocating atmosphere of the club. I hurry down the sidewalk, my heels clicking on the pavement, not stopping until I'm blocks away. Only then do I release the breath I'd been holding. Made it.

But those twisted images still claw at me, threatening to drag me back down into the dark. I have to get this intel to the team. We have to make this right, get the victim's remains back to their families, even if their body parts are now inside pool balls or used to construct pieces of furniture. But that will have to wait.

Glancing over my shoulder, I spot a sleek black car idling across the street. The windows are tinted but I can feel eyes on me. Have I been made? My pulse quickens.

Casually, I hail a taxi and give the driver an address a few blocks from our safehouse. "Step on it," I urge. Once we pull away, I risk another look back. The black car is following.

Damn it. I was careless. I sink lower in my seat, mind racing. How did they figure me out so quickly? What do I do now? Lead them right to the others?

"Change of plans," I tell the driver. "Lose the car behind us first. I feel like we're being followed."

He nods and hits the gas, weaving expertly through traffic. But the black car stays right on us. I rack my brain, trying to come up with an alternate plan. "Jeez, I thought you were some paranoid drunk bitch. But you're right, this car does not want to let us out of its sight."

Up ahead, I spot a busy shopping plaza. "Pull in there," I direct the driver. He shrugs and follows my instructions. As soon as we stop, I toss cash over the seat and bolt from the cab, disappearing into the crowds. The black car won't be able to follow me on foot.

I need to lay low and make my way back carefully. Lives are depending on the intel I gathered tonight. Failure is not an option.

I weave through the plaza, merging with groups of late night shoppers to stay hidden. Thank god for capitalism making people feel obligated to rush around late at night in the leadup to the holidays, making people feel obligated to spend money they don't have on things they don't need.

I almost twist my ankle at one point, but I don't dare stop. At a fountain, I slip off my shoes and stash them behind a planter. I'll attract less attention in bare feet. Heels are essential sometimes, and often pretty, but they sure do make me less efficient.

Checking over my shoulder, I don't see any signs of pursuit. But I can't let my guard down yet. I head towards the rear of the plaza, scanning for an exit that won't leave me exposed.

There—a service corridor used for deliveries. I glance around before slipping inside, finding myself in a dim passage lined with doors leading to the shops' backrooms. The smell of garbage hangs heavy, a contrast with my elegant attire.

I move swiftly but silently, listening for any sounds of footsteps other than my own. At last, I reach a metal door leading outside to an alley. Freedom.

As soon as I step out, rough hands grab me from behind. One clamps over my mouth before I can scream, the other locks around my waist. I'm dragged backwards, my heels digging into trash-strewn pavement.

A raspy voice hisses in my ear. "Thought you could run, little lady?" My blood turns to ice. It's one of Tane's men. One from the club basement. How did he find me so fast?

My mind blanks with panic. I thrash with all my strength, but his grip only tightens. He starts to drag me towards a waiting car, my worst fears realized. Once I'm in there, I'm as good as dead.

Angel and Devon's recounting of their kidnapping experiences run through my mind. The way they were treated, and the way they almost lost their lives so many times. I can't let that happen to me. To any of us, ever again.

Adrenaline surges through me. It's now or never. I stop resisting and go limp, catching him off guard. The second his grasp loosens, I make my move...

I drop all my weight while simultaneously driving my elbow back into his gut. He doubles over with a choked grunt, and I slip from his grasp. Without looking back, I bolt down the alley, barefoot, ignoring the pain of gravel under my feet.

I can hear him recovering and giving chase. My lungs are on fire but I push harder. Just a little farther to the next street, where I can hopefully lose him or find help.

Suddenly, headlights flash at the end of the alley, blinding me. A sleek black car peels around the corner, engine revving. It's barreling straight for me, ready to cut off my escape.

I'm trapped. Nowhere to run or hide in this narrow passage. The car is almost on me when my survival instincts kick in. At the last second, I hurl myself sideways, hitting the ground and rolling hard beneath a metal staircase. The car screeches past, unable to stop in time.

I lay stunned for a second, scraped and bruised but alive. My pursuer's footsteps close in. This is it. I'm out of options. I squeeze my eyes shut and brace for the end.

Suddenly, a new set of footsteps join the first. There's a scuffle, a pained yell, then silence. I crack open one eye. A familiar figure looms over me, a large and tattooed hand extended.

"Need some help, princess?"

Relief floods through me. "Dimitri!" I let him pull me to my feet. He came through for me, like he always does. I'm safe. For now.

"Tane's got more than just a criminal operation. He's running a house of horrors. We need to shut it down," I say, my voice hard with conviction.

We drive back to the Brixton's compound in silence, Dimitri using his free hand to squeeze my thigh reassuringly a few times on the way.

As soon as we get back to the main operations room and I recount what I saw, I see my own anger and disgust reflected in their faces.

Devon's jaw tightens, fury smoldering in her eyes. "Good work, Aria. This gives us the leverage we need."

Brick slams a fist on the table. "His behavior is escalating. Let's take him down."

The others nod, determination steeling their features.

I know we won't stop until Tane and his sadistic empire are burned to the ground.

This ends now.

CHAPTER THIRTY-ONE

DOM

The sun beats down on my back as I kneel in the dirt, the rich scent of earth filling my nose. My hands are stained with soil as I gently pack it around the tomato seedlings, nurturing their fragile stems. What started out as a hobby in tiny pots in the living room at our old house has developed into a full-blown garden, my sanctuary from the chaos that surrounds us.

The creak of the gate draws my gaze upward. Brick's hulking frame casts a shadow across the vibrant petals as he steps inside. His usual intensity is tempered today, his dark eyes more curious than menacing.

"Hey, Dom. Mind if I join you?" His gravelly voice is unexpectedly soft.

I gesture to the tools lying nearby. "Not at all. Grab a trowel if you feel like getting your hands dirty."

"Always," he grins, and I know he means it. Brick is always ready for whatever the universe throws his way, the crazier the better.

Brick settles on the ground beside me, dwarfing the delicate trowel in his massive grip. His brow is furrowed in concentration as he mimics my movements, clumsily patting soil around the tender shoots. It's like watching a giant befriend baby chickens—cute but awkward as fuck.

I study his chiseled profile, a glint of admiration warming my core. Beneath the ruthless exterior lies a gentle soul, seeking connection amidst the violence that consumes us. In this moment, we aren't two enforcers who spend our time inflicting pain, but two kindred spirits finding solace in the simple act of nurturing life.

Even monsters can grow plants if they try hard enough.

Brick's questions come slowly at first, his gruff voice hesitant. "How do you keep all this alive? Seems like a lot of work."

I wipe a smudge of dirt from my cheek, gazing out at the riot of colors surrounding us. "It's all about balance. Too much sun will scorch the leaves. Too little water and the roots shrivel." I meet his thoughtful eyes. "Each plant needs different care, just like people."

Brick nods, his fingers trailing over the velvety petals of a nearby rose. I've never seen him so gentle. There's more to this man than I realized. I'm so used to his wild schemes and random obsessions that I haven't really stopped to consider the guy behind it all.

His attention is drawn to the large wooden box in the corner, curiosity glinting in his eyes. He peers inside, watching the wriggling mass of worms churning the waste into fertile soil.

"What's this? Some kind of worm party?" His lips quirk into a crooked grin.

I chuckle at his choice of words. "It's a worm farm. The worms break down organic material into nutrient-rich fertilizer. Nature's way of recycling."

Brick studies the writhing creatures, lost in contemplation. "So they take something useless and turn it into something valuable."

I nod, sensing the deeper meaning behind his words. We too take society's chaos and try to cultivate something good from it, although we might create some trouble in the process. The worms are a metaphor for our own special form of transformation.

Brick falls silent, gazing out at the vibrant life surrounding us. In this moment, we're not predators, but total plant daddies. And perhaps from even the darkest places, beauty can grow.

I scoop up a handful of the dark, crumbly compost from the worm farm and hold it out to Brick.

"Here, feel this. The worms break down waste and excrete these castings which are full of nutrients for the plants."

Brick takes the compost, rubbing it between his calloused fingers. His brows lift in surprise. "It's so soft and rich. The worms made this?"

I nod, pleased by his curiosity. "Their digestion process breaks down organic material into the perfect plant food. It's nature's way of recycling waste into something valuable."

Brick looks thoughtful, his gaze drifting over the vibrant garden. "So the worms take useless crap and transform it into life. They find balance and purpose in the waste."

"Exactly," I reply. "With proper care, the worms thrive, creating nourishment from scraps. But it's a delicate balance—too much waste at once can throw things off."

Brick considers this, his eyes clouded. I wonder if he's thinking of our own violent world, and the challenge of finding equilibrium amidst the chaos. "Okay, got it. Don't cover the worms in a giant pile of shit. Makes sense." He pauses. "How do you keep the worm population from getting out of control?"

I explain the techniques for maintaining ideal conditions—monitoring temperature and moisture, rotating waste inputs, and harvesting castings. Brick listens intently, absorbing every word like a sponge.

I nod slowly, seeing the deeper meaning take root in Brick's mind. Our lives have become unbalanced, overflowing with cruelty and death. We desperately need the wisdom of the worms—taking the rot around us, of which there is plenty, and patiently transforming it into something good. Something we can believe in. A bit like the girls are doing with their clothing line, now that I think about it.

"Kind of like us, right?" I say. "We take the chaos around us and try to turn it into something good."

Brick meets my gaze, his eyes glinting. "Yeah, I see what you mean. It's about finding balance in the middle of all the mess."

He falls silent then, staring down at the compost-filled box, lost in contemplation. I know that look on his rugged face. Brick is churning over an idea, one he's not ready to give voice to yet.

"You've got that look, Brick," I prod gently. "What's going on in that warped mind of yours?"

Brick glances up, a hint of a smile on his lips. "Just thinking...sometimes the simplest solutions are right in front of us."

He leaves it at that, but I can see the spark of inspiration in his eyes. Brick has been moved by the humble worms, their quiet power to transform death into new life. And I know that he'll take this lesson and make it into something entirely of his own creation.

The sun sinks lower in the sky, casting the garden in a warm, golden glow as we finish up. I stand, brushing the dirt from my hands, and take a moment to admire our efforts.

"The garden looks great, Brick. Thanks for your help."

Brick straightens up beside me, gazing around appreciatively. "Anytime, Dom. I actually enjoyed getting my hands dirty in a new way. Might have to take up gardening myself."

I smile at the thought of this hulking, tattooed man delicately tending his own vegetable patch.

Brick notices my amusement and shrugs. "Hey, I'm full of surprises."

We share a laugh, the first real one in a long while. It feels good, like a tiny weight lifted from the constant pressure upon us.

Brick heads back inside, no doubt to turn whatever idea sparked in his head into something tangible and wild. I remain a while longer, sitting amidst the herbs and watching the worms tirelessly churning waste into fertile soil.

This garden is my sanctuary from the madness outside. A place where life springs eternal, if nurtured with care. My garden doesn't see the giant, broken man who has been through so much. It only sees my gentle, tender side. The patient giant who takes his time making sure each sprout, each fresh green shoot, lives its best life here in my garden. And okay, maybe once in a while I speak to them as if they're long lost friends. The kind that see my every flaw and accept me anyways.

Perhaps Brick is right, and the key to overcoming the darkness is simpler than we realize.

Patience, balance, transforming decay into new growth—this is the wisdom we must cultivate within ourselves.

With time and persistence, and the help of busy worms, even the most damaged soil can thrive again.

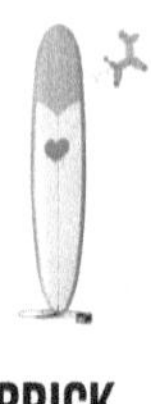

CHAPTER THIRTY-TWO

BRICK

L ater that evening

The monitors glow against my skin, casting the room in an eerie blue light. Surveillance duty isn't glamorous or particularly fun, but it's crucial. Tonight, Tane's men face a test they won't forget.

He's been so obsessed with his men proving their unquestioning loyalty to him, and his paranoia is only getting worse. Test after test, so I'm sure this one feels no different.

The instructions were cryptic, but every communication with Tane is getting to be that way. Barely an eyebrow was raised when his men received their invites on their phones, their contact information craftily downloaded by Skyler when he snuck into the compound the other night.

My eyes flick between screens, watching the convoy roll up. Tane's foot soldiers exit the vehicles, tense and alert. They march towards the entrance, oblivious to what awaits inside.

I zoom in on their faces—hardened, yet apprehensive. They know something big is coming, though not what. My pulse quickens. This is going to be interesting.

The men disappear inside. I switch cameras, tracking them through the shop's exotic decor. Incense burns, mingling with the humming equipment. I lick my lips in anticipation. The real show is about to start.

They gather in the back room, eyeing each other uneasily. The tracker devices glint under the light—an ominous promise of what's to come. Their defiance wars with resignation. They don't like this, but they've got no choice.

One by one they step forward, nerves and submission etched on their faces as the little black cylinders are inserted by a bespectacled man wearing a white lab coat. To a layperson, he's a typical doctor trained in outpatient medical procedures like this one. Nobody needs to know he's my cousin, a traveling vet who was more than willing to do me a favor.

A few of Tane's henchmen give the small cylinders a strange look, but luckily, loyalty in this context means you don't ask questions.

Marked. Owned. Controlled. Soon it will be complete.

Tane's lieutenant takes the lead, his jaw set in a hard line. "Let's move out. We've got our orders. And remember, our loyalty is now beyond doubt."

I zoom out, watching them head towards the exit. My eyes remain glued to the screen as the men file out of the back room, some rubbing their arms where the device was inserted. There's an uneasy energy in the air as they process what just transpired.

Most look pissed off, a few seem resigned. But none are happy about the items now embedded under their skin.

One man speaks up, frowning. "Those chips seemed kind of big, didn't they? I thought they were only meant to be tiny things."

Another of the guys shrugs. "Yeah, I suppose they are bigger than I thought they'd be. But it's always state of the art stuff with Tane, remember? I bet these have features we can't even imagine. We just need to go with it. Asking questions would just be our downfall..and you know Tane is just waiting to make an example of anyone who questions him these days."

The others fall in line without argument, expressions ranging from stoic to simmering. I can tell the defiance in them hasn't been fully stamped out yet. Good—it will make breaking them all the sweeter. And, it will make Tane even more angry, which is just icing on the cake.

As they exit the shop, their postures are rigid, their movements sharp and tactical. Tension radiates from them. They're on high alert now, wary of any other surprises coming their way.

My pulse quickens watching them on the monitors. I lick my lips again, already planning our next move. This test was just the beginning, a mere foreshock before the real earthquake hits.

We'll give them some time, let them get comfortable with those chips nestled under their skin. Then when they least expect it, we'll unleash the next exquisite torment. Something to truly test their loyalty and shake them to their core.

I smile darkly, thinking about what we could do next. The possibilities are deliciously endless when you don't play by the rules. I can hardly wait to see how far we can push them before they break.

Just as the last man exits, two strangers saunter in. Even through the grainy camera feed I can tell these guys are trouble. They move with a cocky swagger that sets my teeth on edge.

My pulse kicks up a notch. This wasn't part of the plan. I didn't think we needed to close the whole shop down to get this done, and I figured at worst we'd see a few hippie woo-woo types scouring the little woven baskets for their next chunk of rose quartz.

The men fan out, casually glancing at the weird assortment of crystals and incense around the shop. But their movements are too calculated, their eyes constantly scanning and assessing. These aren't mystical crystal enthusiasts.

Tane's lieutenant notices them immediately, his expression going hard. "Who the hell are you?" he barks out. "This is private business."

The taller stranger just smirks. "We're just browsing, friend. Crystals and whatnot." He gestures at the myriad crystals before him. "Didn't know we needed an invitation." His tone is relaxed but there's an unmistakable challenge in his words.

The shop owner tries to diffuse the situation but I can tell this is a powder keg ready to blow. One wrong move and this whole place could erupt into violence.

I debate whether to intervene, my muscles tensing. Whoever these guys are, they're not part of the plan. But, just as quickly, the tension recedes as the owner firmly escorts the two men out. "This is a place for positive vibes, man. If you guys want to come in here, you need to be chill. And perhaps you could come back later when we're not already at maximum capacity, ya dig?"

The two men glance at each other, shrug, and walk off.

The shop owner remains chill on the surface as he watches them leave, but I notice his shoulders lower in relief that things have, in fact, remained copacetic.

Crisis averted, for now. But those strangers seemed way too interested in Tane's business. There's no way they stumbled into the store by accident. Something feels off. I take a screenshot when they're in clear view of the camera, and make a mental note to look into them later.

Excitement coils within me as Tane's men leave, the devices now embedded under their skin. Anticipation brews within me as I watch them exit the store and clamber into their sleek SUVs. They're probably wondering what the hell Tane has in store next, seeing now they think he's tracking them more closely than ever before.

I sit back, adrenaline still coursing through me as I review the footage. Seeing those hard, proud men forced to submit awakens something primal in me. Sitting here, conducting the situation as if I were commanding an orchestra, a puppet master pulling all the strings. Power is such an aphrodisiac.

This is far from over. I sense it in my bones, the darkness in me thrilled by the promise of what will happen next. I want to see it go down immediately, but of course it has to wait. Patience is the most difficult part of elaborate plans like this one.

A shiver runs down my spine at the thought. I live for this—the chase, the thrill. And I won't stop until Tane and his empire are ours.

Eyes glowing with anticipation, I can't wait to tell Angel, my sweet depraved Valkyrie. We have plans to make, new ways to toy with our prey. There's much still to do, and she's going to love every minute of it.

I lean back in my chair, my eyes fixed on the monitors.

They act tough, but the balance has shifted. With those trackers embedded under their skin, they're marked and bound to us now, and not in the way one might think. Things will never be the same once this plan roars into action.

I lick my lips, already thirsting for more. What other exquisite torments will we devise to truly test their dedication? To break them? The darkness in me hungers to find out.

I can't help but grin. It's a deliciously ruthless move, if I do say so myself.

Adrenaline and anticipation course hotly through my veins. I'm ready. Let the games begin.

Their loyalty to Tane is now sealed beneath their skin, as far as they're concerned. No going back now.

But I imagine for some it was a case of going through the motions. Not everybody loves Tane, despite the fact he could provide them with untold wealth. Some of them work for him out of necessity, not because they think he's a good guy. Putting a chip in their arms doesn't change what's in their hearts.

As the convoy of black SUVs pulls away down the street, I turn back to the monitor, rewinding and pausing on the faces of the two strangers.

Who are they? Why crash the party now? My instincts scream that they're connected to Tane, some kind of random countersurveillance to soothe his growing paranoia. But, more likely, they're part of a rival group vying for Tane's power, just like we are.

A goal I entirely understand, but these guys have come out of left field and they certainly aren't part of our team.

I reach for my phone to call Aidan, my finger hovering over his name. He needs to know what went down tonight. To have the confidence to enter a building with so many of Tane's strongest guys takes confidence, and that suggests to me that these guys have a plan they're ready to put in motion.

The game just changed, the timeline shortened. I press call and wait for his smooth voice to answer, ready to lay out the pieces of a puzzle we're only beginning to unravel.

Whatever happens next, we'll handle it together. But one thing's for sure—it won't be dull.

I nod to myself as I end the call with Aidan, already feeling calmer and more focused. His quiet confidence has that effect on me.

As I head back to the main compound, Angel looks up from cleaning her knives, her piercings glinting in the low light. She can strip a man to his soul with those eyes of hers. "How'd it go?" she asks.

"Pretty successful, actually. Definitely could've been worse. But we've got new players in town." I outline what happened with the strangers at the shop.

Slade emerges from the shadows, his face unreadable as always. "I'll put some feelers out, see what the streets have to say."

I turn to Aidan and Roman. "Keep our surveillance team close to Tane's men. If those two show their faces again, I want to know immediately." They nod, eager for action.

Finally, my gaze lands on her again. My Valkyrie. An angel of death in a sinner's body. Just looking at her makes my blood burn. There's darkness behind her eyes that calls to the darkness in me.

"It's going to get messy," I warn her.

A wicked smile curves her lips. "Good."

Messy is just how we like it.

CHAPTER THIRTY-THREE

ARIA

I take a deep breath and smooth my dress, surveying the scene before me. Aria's is buzzing with activity, every table filled with potential investors sampling hors d'oeuvres and sipping mocktails. Soft music drifts through the open windows, mingling with the sound of waves crashing on the beach just outside.

I weave through the crowd, pausing to chat and joke with guests, encouraging them to try the booze-free feature of the day, my own special concoction called the Tropical Breeze. It's a blend of mango, pineapple, coconut water and mint, topped with a hibiscus flower. The reactions are all positive so far, with many going back for seconds.

Out of the corner of my eye, I notice one man frowning into his untouched glass. I make my way over and introduce myself. "Hi there, I'm Aria. Are you enjoying the Tropical Breeze?"

The man scoffs. "Mocktails. Are they really a thing? I wouldn't think there'd be much business for something like that."

I laugh lightly. "You'd be surprised. People are looking for healthier options these days. And the great thing about these is they can be just as fun and flavorful as traditional cocktails, without the alcohol. We want every guest, no matter what they choose to drink, to feel welcome and valued here."

I can tell he's still skeptical. Time to turn on the charm. I gesture to the woman beside him. "This must be your lovely wife. She's vegetarian, right?"

"Pesky is more like it," the man grumbles.

"Pescatarian, dear," his wife corrects gently. "I do still eat fish."

"That's right, my mistake." I flash an understanding smile at the wife before turning back to the stubborn potential investor. "Well, think of it like this. Imagine taking your wife out to a nice restaurant, but the only veggie option is some sad side salad or rubbery tofu. Meanwhile, your steak and potatoes looks amazing. She'd feel pretty overlooked, right?"

The man nods slowly. "Yeah, okay, I get your point. She'd hate that." He glances at her. "In fact, I'd never hear the fucking end of it."

She slaps him on the arm. "Oh, Steven. Don't be an asshole in front of company. Save that for when we're home by ourselves."

I try to avoid their awkward banter, pretending I didn't hear it. "Exactly. Here at Aria's, we want to make every guest feel special and accounted for. That's how you provide a true oasis from the stresses of everyday life." I lift my glass. "So give the mocktail another try. I think you'll be pleasantly surprised."

The man sniffs his drink and takes a tentative sip. His eyebrows raise in surprise. "Huh. That's actually pretty damn good." He takes a longer draw from the straw, nodding in satisfaction. "In fact, I wouldn't mind having something like this instead of a stiff drink after work once in a while."

I grin and wink at Devon and Dom who are seated at the bar and saw the whole interaction go down. Their smiles tell me they knew I could win him over. With the right balance of charm, wit and understanding, even the toughest critics can be swayed... one opinionated asshole at a time. And that personal touch is what will make Aria's a smashing success.

I make my way through the mingling guests, checking on the passed hors d'oeuvres and mocktails. So far everything seems to be going smoothly. The servers are gracious and attentive, the food delicious and artfully presented. Twinkling lights and tiki torches cast a warm glow over the scene. I breathe in the heady sea air, taking a moment to soak it all in.

This dream made real—my very own restaurant and oasis by the sea. All the years of hard work and sacrifice have led me here. Whatever happens with the investors tonight, I'm proud of what I've built. I don't need them, per se—I've saved enough to be able to make this one hundred percent mine. But my ambition means an injection of cash from investors would help me make my dreams come true at a faster rate.

A commotion from the kitchen area catches my attention. Raised voices filter out from the back. I hurry over, a knot forming in my stomach.

Pushing through the doors, I'm met with a shocking sight. Two of my newest hires, tipsy and half undressed, are making out in the walk-in cooler. Bottles and trays are knocked over, my meticulously prepared food strewn on the floor.

Rage wells up inside me. How could they sabotage this important night with their carelessness? I storm over and yank them apart.

"What the hell do you think you're doing?" I yell. They stare back sheepishly. "The guests out there have entrusted me with an important decision tonight. Your actions could ruin everything!"

I point angrily at the back door. "You're done here. I'm calling you an Uber. Go home and sober up before you cause any more problems."

They scurry out, their heads hung in shame. I start cleaning up their mess, my blood boiling. It's hard to find good help these days when it comes to hospitality workers, and this behavior is nothing new. I'll deal with them later. For now, the night must go on.

With the kitchen chaos handled, I take a deep breath to collect myself before heading back out to the dining area. The investors are sequestered in the restaurant's private dining room to discuss their verdict on funding my business.

I pace back and forth, my nerves fraying as the minutes tick by. If they don't enjoy their experience, even though I might not technically need their financing, these people are exceptionally well connnected in the hospitality community, and their word of mouth could do untold damage.

Trying to stay calm, I run through possible scenarios in my head. Maybe they want me to tweak the concept or menu before committing. I could work with that. As long as they believe in me enough to invest in some capacity.

The door opens and the investors file back into the main dining room. I hold my breath, bracing for their response.

The head investor steps forward, face unreadable. "We've reached a decision," he announces. "We need to face that the market here is saturated. Not many restaurants are able to withstand the competition or the constraints of doing business on an island with the associated food costs."

My heart sinks, but before I give up entirely with my dreams shattered, the man continues. "However, we see real potential in you and this concept. Gone are the days when tourists are satisfied with a chain restaurant being replicated from the mainland. People visiting these islands want something different, new, exciting—without pushing it too far."

Hope flares in my chest, my stomach un-contorting itself.

"We want to move forward with a substantial investment. One that will allow you to grow this business faster than you imagined."

Relief washes over me. We did it! My team exchanges excited looks as I shake hands with the investors. The future is bright for my little oasis by the sea.

I'm floating on a wave of euphoria when a worrying thought hits me—what if the investors want creative control? My concept is deeply personal. The menu carefully crafted. I can't let anyone compromise that. There must be a catch.

As the investors discuss logistics, I interrupt. "Before this goes further, I need to know I'll retain full creative control. The concept, the menu— that's non-negotiable."

The head investor looks surprised, then laughs. "Of course! We're just here to support you financially. This is your vision—we'd never dream of stifling that."

I exhale in relief. We're on the same page.

"I can't wait to see what you dream up next," he continues with a wink. "Just save a table for us—this place is going to be the hottest spot in town, and just like you, we need a fantastic venue because we have our own investors to impress! Although, from what you've showed us tonight, they'll all be thrilled that this establishment is part of our portfolio."

The investors depart in high spirits, leaving me to debrief with my team. We did it. The future is ours. With the shrewd business sense I've honed over the years, and the unwavering support of my men behind the scenes, success is inevitable.

My oasis will flourish. A haven by the sea for all who need an escape. And the perfect cover for all our other 'business ventures' in this town.

The thrill of victory courses through me.

I gather Florian, Dimitri, and Josef in my office after the investors depart. We're all still riding the high of success.

"We did it!" I exclaim, pulling them in for a celebratory embrace. Their strong arms wrap around me, enveloping me in their warmth.

"You were amazing out there," Florian says, pride in his voice. "They didn't stand a chance against your charm and wit."

"Couldn't have done it without you three backing me up," I reply. "You give me the strength I need."

Dimitri grins wolfishly. "Soon this whole city will be ours. The restaurant is the perfect front for our other operations."

Josef nods in agreement. "With these investors on board, we'll have the capital to expand quickly."

I smile, reveling in our shared anticipation. The thrill of gaining power and influence here energizes me.

"It's nice to know we have them on our side, but that we don't truly need them," I say. "For once, we have the upper hand. And we intend to use it wisely...in more ways than one."

My men's eyes darken with desire at the promise in my words.

The night is still young, and we have much to celebrate.

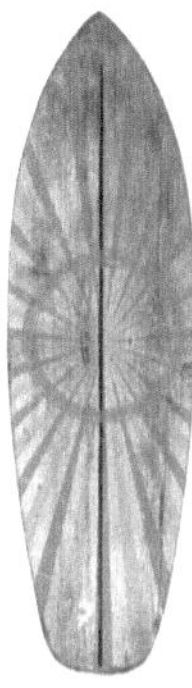

CHAPTER THIRTY-FOUR

RAKE

The sun glints off the waves as Brick and I stroll along the beach. I take a deep breath of the salty air, letting it fill my lungs.

"Remember that time on the other island when we tried to protect the girls without them knowing we were there?" Brick grins. "Man, that did not go as planned."

I chuckle. "Didn't we think about trying to pose as pool cleaners to get inside? But we settled on old-school trenchcoats and hiding behind large potplants."

"Yep. Ordered those fake mustaches and everything." Brick shakes his head. "We looked ridiculous."

"Hey, I would have made a very sexy pool boy!" I nudge him playfully.

We're quiet for a moment, listening to the rush of the surf. I know we're both thinking about the fight ahead.

"Alright, enough moping and enough nostalgia about pool boy dreams that never happened," Brick finally says. "We need a new strategy to take down Tane's goons. A foolproof plan."

"We could start with low-level intimidation tactics," I suggest. "Like leaving disturbing balloon animals at their targets' homes, or popping up in their rear-view mirrors during late-night drives. But as the pressure mounted, we'd escalate things. Arson, kidnappings, selective amputations—nothing would be off-limits."

"We'll be like a pack of demented leprechauns," Brick said, his eyes alight with twisted glee. "But that sounds like it will take a while to ramp up to the stage we need... we need Tane gone, like... yesterday."

I rub my hands together. "Ooh, I've got one. Hear me out: we send them all free passes for hot yoga classes..."

Brick bursts out laughing. "Hot yoga? For Tane's meathead mobsters?"

"Just imagine it!" I continue, grinning. "We get them in their little spandex shorts, all contorted into wild poses. Then—BAM!" I slam my fist into my palm. "We ambush them mid-downward dog!"

Brick is doubled over, wheezing with laughter. "I'd pay money to see that. Tane's top hitman wobbling in tree pose."

"Right? They won't know what hit them!" I'm on a roll now. "I bet we could convince them it's some kind of mandatory fitness training. A Pilates Day of Reckoning!"

Brick wipes his eyes, still chuckling. "As appealing as that mental image is, I don't think yoga is our best bet. We need something they can't resist..."

I nod, ideas churning. We walk further down the beach, scheming. The sun glints off the waves, but my mind is sparking even brighter. Brick and I will come up with the perfect plan to take Tane down—no matter how ridiculous we have to get

Brick's eyes light up. "I've got it. We send them an invitation for an exclusive whiskey tasting."

I raise my eyebrows, intrigued. "Go on..."

"We tell them it's some super rare, small-batch whiskey from like, I dunno, a monastery in Tibet or something." Brick warms to the idea. "We hype it up as the smoothest, most luxurious whiskey ever to touch their lips. The kind of whiskey kings would kill for."

I nod along, seeing where he's going with this.

"So of course, they all show up, ready to sample this mythical liquor." Brick pauses for dramatic effect. "But little do they know, the whiskey is spiked with a powerful sedative."

He mimes someone passing out. "Nighty night, Tane's thugs. They'll be out cold before they can say '12-year single malt.'"

I laugh, clapping Brick on the back. "I love it! Operation Whiskey Down, let's call it. We'll toast to it!" I pretend to clink glasses with him.

Brick grins. "Here's to taking down Tane with creativity and style."

We walk along the beach tossing ideas back and forth, each one more ridiculous than the last. But with Brick by my side, I know we'll hatch the perfect scheme soon enough. Tane won't know what hit him.

Brick's eyes light up as another idea comes to him. "Okay, get this. We send each of Tane's main guys a gift basket."

I raise an eyebrow, intrigued. "What's in these mystery baskets?"

He rubs his hands together gleefully. "Nothing but the finest bath bombs and scented candles. Maybe a nice loofah or two."

I burst out laughing at the image. "Can you imagine those muscle-bound goons soaking in a tub surrounded by candles and bath bombs? Their massive arms covered in suds?"

Brick joins in my laughter. "Right? Have you seen *me* in a bathtub?"

I'm doubled over by this point, the image of Brick splashing around in the tub with a rubber ducky.

We include a card saying it's a 'relaxation package' from an anonymous admirer."

"They'll be so confused but won't be able to resist trying it all out," I chuckle. "And their egos will be so puffed up they won't dare tell each other about it."

"Exactly! Then when they're all pruney and smelling of lavender, we make our move." Brick mimes kicking down a door.

"Operation Bubble Bath Blitz!" I proclaim. We high five at the ridiculous yet brilliant plan.

As the sun sinks lower, our schemes grow wilder. No idea too absurd or impractical. Laughter and camaraderie carry us through the evening.

"Wait, I've got it!" he exclaims at one point. "This plan is so simple in its insanity, we can't fail!"

"Oh yeah? Now I need to hear this one," I laugh and shake my head.

"So...we dress up as a group of deranged clowns straight out of a Stephen King novel and start terrorizing the streets. We'll target Tane's men, of course, but also the people closest to them. Wives, kids, dogs, no one would be safe. The goal would be to shatter the illusion that Tane Brown is invincible, and replace it with fear—gnawing, all-consuming fear."

"That's a great plan, but it would take far too long. Fear takes a while to build, even when there are killer clowns involved."

Brick considers my opinion for a moment, his lip twitching. For a second, I worry I've offended him with my quick dismissal of his crazy plan. But just as quickly, he nods and shrugs. "You're right. But let's keep that up our sleeves for a rainy day. I might order a psycho clown outfit for each of us in the meantime... just in case."

His plans may seem like straight-up lunacy to the untrained, but underneath the jokes, I sense Brick's brilliant strategic mind at work. He's a master at understanding people's weaknesses and using them to his advantage. His plans aren't just physical, they're intensely psychological as well. This is all part of his planning process, and Tane doesn't stand a chance against his brilliance. Because underneath his comedy, Brick knows that Tane and his army are some of the most evil imaginable.

I laugh, recalling the near-death experience we barely survived on the other island. "Man, we thought we were so slick, like a pair of sexy, dark knights." I pause. "But for real. We need to take that bastard down, Brick. He's got the whole island chain under his thumb, and I'm sick of it." I clench my fists, the desire for retribution burning in my blood.

Brick nods, running a hand through his shaggy surfer hair. Usually it's tied up in a man bun, but today it runs wild and free. His 'brainstorming hair', he calls it. "I'm thinking... maybe we take them out one by one, and see how long he lasts. Seeing his precious goons get picked off like that would have to fuck with his head."

I double over with sadistic glee, which I assume looks comical given my gangly frame. "Oh, I've got some ideas, Brick. Gruesome, twisted, and oh-so-sweet. Can we start with that one bastard, the one with the gold tooth?"

"Wesley, I think his name is? Denzo's replacement?" Brick asks, a devious smirk curling his lips. "The one who tried to salsa on Aria's Oasis's dance floor, thinking he's Casanova? Oh, I've got a plan for him. Do you know how much I love my veggies?"

My eyes widen, a sick grin spreading across my face. "You're sick, Brick. You know that, right?"

"Dark, twisted, and absolutely delicious," Brick growls. "We'll lure him to a quiet spot, and then I'll show him the true meaning of being a side dish."

I choke on laughter, nearly doubling over. "You're a sick f**k, but I love it. Next? What about the one with the little... complex?"

I can just about see Brick's mind spin, gears turning as I consider their next victim. "Ah, I know just the thing. We'll invite him to Aria's, pour on the charm, and then we'll introduce him to my 'special' squeeze."

"Oh, no," I whimper. "Please, Brick, not the ball vise again!"

"Oh, yes, my dear friend. And this time, we'll make sure there's no escape. We'll show Tane and his men once and for all that they've picked the wrong crew to mess with."

"Sure," I shrug, "But what about Tane himself? I've got a score to settle with that fucker. We all do. He thinks he can just keep screwing people over and hurting innocent people? Fuck that. He needs the best of the worst... the worst of the best... you know what I mean!"

Brick's eyes gleam, the fire in his eyes sending a chill down my spine. "Don't you worry, my friend. I've been saving the best for last. We're gonna take him down in a way he never saw coming. We'll lure him to Aria's, and we'll make it a night he'll never fucking forget."

I tilt my head, observing the dangerous glint in Brick's eyes. His psychotic creativity energizes me. "Do tell, Brick. I love it when you get... extra creative."

Brick takes a deep breath, his voice taking on a low, sinister cadence. "We'll invite him to the restaurant, maybe even make him think we're ready to back down. I haven't decided whether we'll stay anonymous at this point. Either way, when he least expects it, we'll strike. I've got a little surprise for him, courtesy of my new... friend."

My eyes widen as understanding dawns on me. "You mean..."

Brick grins, his teeth shining in the dim light. "Yes, my friend. We're going to give Tane Brown a taste of his own medicine, literally." He cackles, the sound sending a shiver down my spine.

"Well, I'll be damned," I let out a low whistle. "I never thought I'd say this, but I'm actually starting to look forward to this war."

And with that, we start making our way back from the beach, our footsteps echoing with the promise of destruction and retribution. Tane and his men may have underestimated the Snakes and the Brixtons, but they're about to learn that this island's underbelly has a bite far deadlier than its bark.

"I can't believe you vetoed 'Killer Clownage'," Brick shakes his head. "Or the Terrifying Titty Twister," he says, referring to a plan he randomly blurted out the other day over coffee.

As the sun begins to set over the water, a chill wind picks up, carrying with it the scent of blood and betrayal. Very soon, the tides will turn.

In only a matter of days, Tane Brown will discover that it was one thing to start a war with the Snakes and the Brixtons... but it's an entirely different game to try and finish it.

We have a solid, although unconventional, plan.

And as the bodies pile up, and Tane's grip on power—and his sanity—starts to slip, we'll be ready to make our move.

We'll infiltrate his inner circle and inflict maximum pain before dealing the final blow.

CHAPTER THIRTY-FIVE

SLADE

We're at Aria's again. It's become our new hangout spot while Aria gets the team trained—she has to be there, and we need a place to be, so it works out. To be honest, I much prefer it to the hustle and bustle of any of the other options around here, because they're inevitably full of annoying tourists who flock to the area. For now, this is our quiet reprieve, although of course, it won't permanently be this way.

Rake and Brick enter and everyone turns to stare—Rake, the gangly fucker next to the brick wall that is, well.... Brick. They make a ridiculous fucking pair, and they both seem to be energized by that. I roll my eyes and groan, turning to face Josef and Florian and Dimitri who are sitting just down from me.

"So what do you guys actually do? I just realized we don't know much about you for people who are our partners." I've been suspicious of this lot since we first met, and not being aware of something as simple as their day-to-day activities is creeping me out. When Aidan told us about Dimitri owning a string of sex clubs, I wasn't surprised. Of course that man would have a sex club. "Other than Dimitri's business, which, of course, we now all know about..."

"Damn, Slade. Your voice is dripping with judgement right now," Angel taps me on the shoulder.

"That's not judgement, it's just my regular voice." Which is always dripping with judgement, but I would never admit it.

She smirks. "Oh, so resting Slade face now has a voice equivalent? Gotcha!"

I feel my cheeks redden slightly. She understands me more than most, but it doesn't mean I escape her teasing me about my gruff exterior. It's hard to be a grump, some days.

"Why? You have a problem with sex clubs?" Florian raises an eyebrow at me. "You don't like that kind of thing?"

"No, I just... haven't been to one." I shrug. "It's not something I've really thought about."

"I bet Roman has." Angel rolls her eyes and glances in his direction.

Roman smirks. "There may have been a piece of equipment named after me... maybe more than one."

"Oh god, really? Like what?" Angel quirks a brow. "I was joking, but I shouldn't have said anything. Once you get Roman started on a topic like this..."

"...one where he's the center of attention, which is his favorite place to be..." I add, glad for the distraction away from me.

"That's a story for another day," says Roman, enigmatically.

"And the rest of you?" I push, my mouth on some struggle bus between a scowl and a neutral expression.

"Well, Florian is a musician," says Josef. "He's got quite a following, in fact."

"Seriously?" There is something about Florian, I have to admit. A certain kind of charisma. Although I wouldn't say he's a flashy guy... he's one of those people who just seems to have something up their sleeves at all time, even when they're not wearing any. Grr, I hate that type. So self-assured, so put-together.

"Yeah! I knew he looked familiar!" Angel tugs on my sleeve, her eyes growing large with excitement. "Remember me saying?"

Devon looks up his band on Instagram. "Oh my god. You have... *millions* of followers!"

He shrugs, the picture of humility. Gross. "Some of them are the same person with a bunch of accounts. But yes, I guess you could say we've been pretty successful over the past few years."

"Wow! And you, Josef?" Angel quirks a brow in his direction.

He shrugs and almost imperceptibly shrinks into himself. "I tend to stick to myself a bit more. Spend time in the garden. You know, that type of thing."

"He's very modest," Aria says as she strolls by with drinks in hand. "Josef is actually a really talented writer. And he also dabbles in photography on the side. That's actually how the two of us met."

I hadn't realized what an introvert he is, having not spent a lot of time with him. But it all comes together as I take a closer look at the guy. The edgy glasses, his long, elegant fingers. Giving off the 'quirky intellectual' hipster vibes that belong in an open mic night at a community-owned produce market. He's quiet, constantly thinking. A bit like me but without the perpetual scowl.

"Yeah, Dimitri called me in for an.... interesting project. And things went from there, I guess you could say," he says, smiling at Aria.

"He totally took all the pictures for my club's website," says Dimitri. "That was his first taste of being my partner in crime, and he's never left my side since."

Josef smirks. "It is what it is, I guess."

"So do you perform regularly?" Angel asks Florian, before turning to Josef. "And what type of books do you write? Where can I get them? I need to check these out!"

"Me too!" exclaims Devon, taking a moment away from her phone.

"Yes, fairly regularly," says Florian. "Occasionally I'll head to the mainland, but we're establishing a bit of a fan base here which has been nice. And so much is virtual these days, even with music."

"And my books are available all over the place," adds Josef. "You can find me on the main online stores. I'm trying to get them on bookshelves here locally, but haven't had a chance to drive around door-to-door like some weirdo book salesman. My latest is a spicy thriller called "The Goodreads Murders.""

Devon gasps. "Oh my god, I *love* that title. Adding to the top of my TBR." She grabs Josef by the shoulder and shakes him slightly in her excitement. "This is the most exciting news I've heard all day!" She pauses and glances apologetically at Florian. "No offense... music is cool and all, but... I need a link! I need this book immediately!"

Florian smirks. "It's okay, truly. It's actually nice not being the center of attention for once."

Angel laughs. "And we have Amazon and TikTok accounts, Dev. I'm sure we can figure it out. And, if not, the online book groups will point us in the right direction."

"Okay, well I wasn't counting on you two being a couple of fame whores," I grumble. "Just what we needed when we're trying to stay undercover. Might as well just get a bunch of flashing lights and have people follow us around with sparklers."

"Who's a fame whore?" asks Roman. "These guys are just sitting here chilling while the girls pepper them with questions."

"Oh that's right. The fame whore is you." I roll my eyes, and Roman wiggles his shoulders, only serving to infuriate me more.

"Okay, grumpy," Roman smirks. "If that's what you want to believe."

This whole conversation is annoying.

I'm so glad we have a mission to focus on.

CHAPTER THIRTY-SIX

ARIA

The crashing waves echo in my ears, blending with the pounding of my heart as I stare out at the endless blue horizon. I take a slow sip of my faux mojito, letting the cool mint dance over my tongue.

"So it's crazy that we've found each other like this," Devon says, "each in our own unconventional relationship situation." Her eyes are bright with excitement. "I mean, finding just one other person in a relationship like ours is so rare. When Angel and I connected, I thought it was a total fluke."

Angel nods, her vibrant purple hair bouncing with the movement. "Seriously! And then here you come, making lightning strike twice."

I can't help but laugh. "If you told me a year ago I'd be sitting here, in this kind of relationship—one woman and several men, living together in romantically, I would've thought you were insane. I'd thought it was something that only happens in books." I take another sip of my icy beverage, and it's bold flavors help ground me as I delve into this new dynamic. "I never imagined finding one man I was compatible with, let alone three. But Dimitri, Josef and Florian just work. As bizarre as it sounds, we balance each other out."

Sharing this makes my heart swell with gratitude and pride. The road that led me here was long and painful, full of men who claimed to love me but tried to tear me down. Their scars still ache within me, and I'd be lying if I said there weren't still times I wake up in the middle of the night, my heart pounding, or find myself stuck in a dream where I can't run or scream, and they're chasing me.

Some things just don't heal overnight, and maybe some things never heal at all. Yet, somehow I've found partners who lift me up and push me to become my best self.

Angel and Devon are the first people I've found—other than the guys of course—who truly understand. Their smiles radiate warmth and acceptance as I bare pieces of my soul. For once, I don't feel alone, and it's refreshing being able to share my journey with them, openly and honestly.

I take a deep breath before continuing my story, comforted by the compassion in their eyes.

"For years, I was trapped in a relationship that slowly destroyed me. He isolated me from friends and family, insulted me, gaslit me until I doubted my own sanity." The words pour out in a torrent, releasing pain long-buried. "We'd argue often, and I didn't know how he did it at the time, but I always ended up looking like the crazy one. I felt like I was losing my mind. Therapy has shown me that he had traits of narcissism, and making people feel like that is really common. Someone like him actually has the power to make you lose your mind, and lose yourself."

Angel reaches out and squeezes my hand. The simple gesture of support nearly brings me to tears.

"The manipulation took a toll on my self-esteem," I continue. "I stopped doing things I loved—writing, cooking, dreaming. I was just focused on survival."

"So how did you get out?" Devon asks, her voice gentle.

"Leaving was the hardest thing I've ever done," I shrug. "I had to claw my way out of that pit of despair and learn to love myself again. Go to therapy, set boundaries, rediscover my passions." I meet their gazes, my vision blurry with tears but also pride. "It's a constant struggle, but I'm getting there. And finding Dimitri, Josef and Florian has shown me what real love can be. All three of them encourage me to shine, not snuff out my light."

Devon nods, her eyes glistening. "You're so strong, Aria. We've got your back now—all of us misfits have to stick together."

Their faith in me ignites a fire in my spirit. With friends like these, I know I'll make it through. I'm just so grateful we crossed paths.

I take a deep breath and smile, the heavy emotions of the past fading as I focus on the present.

"Enough dwelling on the darkness. I want to celebrate the good in my life now!" I say brightly.

Angel and Devon's faces light up at my enthusiasm.

"Like my new restaurant! It's been my dream forever to run my own place." I clap my hands together, barely able to contain my excitement.

The others respond with claps of their own, beaming at me.

Their enthusiasm makes me feel really good, validated somehow I suppose, and I continue. "Dimitri's helping me with the business side of things—you know, paperwork, licenses, all that official stuff that requires you to sit down and focus on details and take things step-by-step." I shudder at the thought.

Devon chuckles knowingly. "Gotta have someone organized to balance out your creative spirit."

I laugh. "Right? And Josef designed the interior. I gave him the overall concept, and then he wanted it to have an airy, relaxed vibe that could be amped up with lighting to change the atmosphere a bit. And lots of plants to bring the outside in!"

"Oooh, I love that earthy look combined with tropical elements," Angel says.

"Me too. It'll be perfect for a beachfront bistro." I sigh happily, picturing my little slice of paradise.

"And Florian offered to write a jingle for the restaurant! He's so talented." I shake my head in amazement. "I don't know how I got so lucky finding these three. It's like..."

"Fate brought you all together," Devon finishes with a smile.

I grin back. "Exactly."

With the support of my lovers and friends like Devon and Angel, I know I'll make my dream a reality. The past, and our ongoing war with Tane, can't hold me back anymore—I'm ready to soar.

"You're going to do amazing things, Aria," Angel says warmly. "I just know it."

"Thanks, I really hope so." I take a deep breath as I look out at the sunset painting the ocean in dazzling hues of orange and pink. "It already feels like my dreams are starting to come true."

"Well, I think this calls for a toast, don't you?" Devon raises her glass with a playful smile.

Angel and I lift our drinks. "Absolutely!"

"To finding family on our terms," Devon proclaims, "and choosing relationships that help make us into better people."

"To embracing the beauty in ourselves and in each other," Angel adds softly.

"To new beginnings," I finish, feeling a swell of gratitude.

Our glasses clink together musically. As we sip our drinks, a sense of contentment washes over me. Here, surrounded by the hush of the waves and the company of new friends who truly understand me, I feel at peace.

We chat lightly as the sunset fades to twilight and the first stars emerge in the dusky sky. A warm breeze rustles the palm fronds overhead. In this perfect moment, the past seems far away.

All I can think about is the bright future unfolding before me, full of joy and possibility. And two new friends

CHAPTER THIRTY-SEVEN

ANGEL

The moon hangs low over the darkened sea, its reflection rippling in the gentle waves. I sit alone at the bar, nursing the remnants of my cocktail, the bittersweet taste lingering on my tongue.

Aria and Devon already headed out after finishing their drinks, but I needed a moment to think. To process Aria's story about her string of toxic relationships. How men had bruised her heart again and again before she wised up.

I know that pain all too well.

Haven't we all been there? Haven't we all let the wrong people into our lives, into our beds, into our hearts? Believing their pretty words and ignoring the red flags waving wildly right before our eyes?

I stare out at the endless ocean, remembering my own parade of losers and users over the years. The manipulators. The liars. The ones who treated me like an object. A means to an end. And of course, my stalker. The one who groomed me, and built me up over and over, only to cruelly tear me down. Who made me do awful things that made me almost not recognize myself. The man who very nearly destroyed me, and in some ways did.

Back then, I thought that was just how things were. How men were. I didn't know any better.

But now...now I've seen the light. Experienced real respect, real care, real love. It took four very special men to open my eyes to that, to show me I deserved more. Deserved better. I'll always treasure them for that gift.

Devon clearly went through the same learning curve with the Snakes, who hold her up with a reverence like she's their queen... but who are also willing to put her in her place when she's being a sassy brat.

And Aria—so strong, so wise now after weathering her own storms. I admire that strength, that wisdom, even if it came with battle scars.

Maybe that's the key. Learning from our mistakes. Using them to grow. To become the people we were meant to be all along.

I breathe in the briny air, feeling at peace. The past can't hurt me anymore. I have my true friends now. Four incredible men who love me and who would burn the world down or hand me my own matches and a tank of fuel. And the future's still unwritten.

The waves continue their endless dance as I sit alone at the bar, lost in thought. Aria's words keep playing through my mind, her stories of heartbreak and betrayal resonating deep within me.

I let my mind wander back to when Devon and I first met and started to form a friendship.

We came from such different worlds. But we were kindred spirits in a way, even though we didn't know it at the time. Both searching for something more beyond the cards life had dealt us. Both somehow ending up here, on these islands, as if they called to us to pull us out of the partial lives we'd been living.

I remember joking with her about what it would be like to live the lives we were brought up to think we should want. Devon always imagined a little house with a wraparound porch. "Somewhere quiet," she'd said with a wistful look in her eye, "with a big yard where I could plant a garden and host tea parties where we all wore flowery dresses and big sunhats."

Me, I'd envisioned something more fanciful—the picture perfect life you'd see on TV. "A handsome husband with a boring day job...maybe an actuary or something like that. Two kids, a dog, a designer cat... a position on the PTA, a minivan, a picket fence..." I'd trail off, giggling.

I take another sip, sighing as I watch the waves. Those dreams most certainly faded with time, as I realized it was my lot to take a different road, but the bond between me and Devon never will. She's family now. And I know she'll always be by my side.

I swirl the little umbrella around my drink, lost in thought. On social media, everyone seems so happy—perfect families, dream vacations, success after success. But how much of it is real? How much is just a carefully curated façade?

I think about my own life experiences. The highs and lows, the adventures and misadventures. It hasn't been perfect, but it's been mine. Authentic.

Sure, I don't have a Pinterest-worthy lifestyle. My relationships have been...complicated. And there are still chapters left unwritten. But that's okay.

Happiness isn't something you achieve and then you're done. It's not some finish line to cross. Real happiness is found in the imperfect moments—in the connections we forge, the lessons we learn, the memories we make.

Maybe true joy is about embracing the full spectrum of life. Seeing the beauty even in the darkness. Finding meaning in the chaos. And being grateful for this crazy, messy, wonderful ride.

I lift my glass in a silent toast, both to the waves and to myself. Here's to living authentically.

I drain the last sip of my drink, savoring the bittersweet taste. As I set the empty glass on the bar, a sense of calm washes over me. For the first time in a long while, I feel at peace.

The moonlight spills onto the beach as I make my way out, turning the sand into swirls of silver and shadow. I slip off my shoes and dig my toes in, reveling in the cool softness. With each step, I feel myself letting go of the weight I've been carrying.

In the distance, I see the flicker of a bonfire surrounded by familiar faces. Devon waves me over enthusiastically, her smile bright even in the darkness.

"Hey Angel! Come join us!" she calls out.

As I approach, the firelight paints the scene in warmth—friends laughing, drinks flowing, music playing softly. This is my family, my people. We've been through hell together, but here we are, still smiling, still celebrating life.

I find an open spot next to Devon and she wraps an arm around me in an easy, affectionate gesture.

No words are needed between us.

The fire crackles, the ocean whispers, and I know I'm exactly where I'm meant to be.

CHAPTER THIRTY-EIGHT

AIDAN

The monitors glow in the darkened control room, casting an eerie blue light across my face. I lean forward, my eyes darting from screen to screen, taking in every detail of the compound's exterior. The perimeter is secure. For now.

Motion at the front gate draws my gaze. Two of our guards approach a nondescript delivery van, hands hovering near their holstered weapons. They exchange terse words with the driver before stepping back and waving the vehicle through. It comes to a halt outside the main building.

My pulse kicks up a notch as I watch the scene unfold. What new threat is at our doorstep now? Tension coils through my muscles. I'm on high alert, ready to act. I know it's only a matter of time before Tane tries something. We did almost kill him, after all.

The driver emerges clutching a small parcel. No sudden moves or suspicious bulges to his clothing. Still, my gut twists. Nothing good ever comes wrapped so neatly.

I meet him at the entrance, my features schooled to reveal none of the apprehension roiling beneath the surface. With steady hands, I accept the envelope. Light. Just paper inside, maybe something small. But paper can do plenty of damage in the right hands. Or the wrong ones.

Back in the control room, I slide a finger under the sealed flap and remove the contents: high-quality stationery and a small USB drive. Cryptic and troubling. But we've handled worse before. I pocket the items to bring to Zeke. If answers exist, he'll uncover them.

I make my way through the compound, my footsteps echoing off the concrete floors. The décor here matches our own exterior, a sophistication that doesn't quite manage to hide the roughness inside—solid doors, bare walls, utilitarian furniture.

I rap my knuckles twice on the metal door, more out of courtesy than necessity. Zeke startles easily when deep in concentration. A muffled "Come in" reaches my ears.

Multiple computer screens cast an eerie blue glow over the room. Hunched in the center, Zeke types rapidly, his eyes glued to the monitors. For a makeshift office, he's quickly managed to turn this into some kind of brilliant tech oasis.

"Zeke, we got a mysterious note with a USB stick. It's encrypted. Think you can crack it?" I hold out the stationery and drive. Zeke's eyes light up, his mouth curving into a sly grin. He loves a challenge.

"Let's see what we've got."

He spins in his chair, cracking his knuckles before taking the items. I clasp my hands behind my back, watching as he examines them. Even handling such innocuous objects, his movements hold precision. Caution.

After a moment, he plugs the USB into a device designed to isolate and analyze files. I resist the urge to peer over his shoulder. Zeke requires space to work his peculiar brand of magic.

For now, we wait. But if answers exist, Zeke will uncover them. And if it's a threat, we'll be ready. Always vigilant. Always prepared.

Zeke's fingers fly across the keyboard, inputting commands that—despite a reasonable degree of tech savvy—I can't begin to comprehend. The rapid clicking fills the tense silence. His brows knit in concentration, his mind almost visibly racing to solve the encrypted puzzle.

I pace the room, too restless to sit. The computers hum monotonously, punctuated by beeps and whirs as Zeke runs program after program. He tries different cryptographic algorithms and reverse engineering techniques, searching for the right key to unlock the message.

Who sent this, and why such secrecy? My gut says whoever it is, they want to help us. But years in this life taught me to be wary of unknowns. For all I know, it's a warning from Tane, or a dissatisfied client trying to fuck with our IT systems. It really could be anything.

"Got it," Zeke says suddenly, breaking me from my thoughts.

I stop pacing and join him at the desk. Lines of code fill the screen—the decrypted message. He highlights it, preparing to translate it into readable text. I clench my fists, muscles taut with anticipation.

With a few more keystrokes, the message appears. Zeke's voice is solemn as he reads aloud the decrypted message:

I can't risk being there in person, and I wish I had something more tangible to help you destroy Tane. But you're doing the right thing. Never doubt that. I've seen how his business, and he as a person, are rotted from the inside. I've seen the destruction he causes, and the pain and suffering he happily doles out like some sick candy man. Hit him hard, hit him from multiple angles. And more than anything, play with his weak spots—his massive paranoia, his secret insecurities about his men's loyalty, his constant fear that one of them is scheming to take his place. And once you start the attack, keep going until he is finished. Don't back off until he's permanently destroyed, or he'll lash out like a caged animal, and that's when he's at his height of lunacy as well as at his strongest. You can do this. I believe in you.

-MB

The words hang heavy in the air. I meet Zeke's gaze, seeing my own shock reflected in his eyes. This message is from Minka Beckett—a former member of Tane's most inner circle. She turned against him back on the other island, essentially saving our lives in our last attempt to take him down. When she found the girls on their undercover operation deep within Tane's compound, she had the opportunity to capture them and turn them in where they almost certainly would have been killed. But instead, she helped them to escape.

It turns out that Tane's ruthless approach was beginning to grate on her, and it was her act of defiance before slipping out of his grasp. Another one of his top officers, gone.

Since then, I've only heard whispers about her living her life in some sort of exile, away from Tane's vengeful reach. You can't just put in a letter of resignation with a two week notice when it comes to a monster like Tane. With him, quitting is a personal affront and therefore a death sentence.

My mind reels, my thoughts crashing like waves. Minka has essentially confirmed what we thought we knew about Tane's weaknesses, and in some ways that's handed us the tools to exploit them. She knows him intimately, and has seen the rot festering beneath his polished veneer. And the information she's just shared with us could bring his empire crumbling down.

But it also puts her at great risk. If Tane discovers her further treachery, his wrath will be apocalyptic. I hope Minka finds a way to stay hidden before that happens. Because despite our differences, no one deserves Tane's brand of punishment.

"This doesn't necessarily change our overall approach," I say finally, my voice low. "But it sure does give us a clue that we need to amp things up and go for the jugular. Minka just gave us a roadmap to destroy him. We know his pressure points now, and they're more than just calculated guesses. It's time to start planning our attack."

Zeke nods, a hungry gleam in his eyes. "Let's call a meeting. We have work to do."

There's no time to waste. Tane's reign of terror ends now. Minka handed us the weapon—Tane's own mind—and now, we just need to strike the killing blow.

The war room hums with tense energy as we gather around the heavy oak table. Maps and diagrams cover the walls, remnants of past schemes and battles. But now, the only target in our sights is the man who started it all and now needs to be finished—Tane Brown.

I meet the eyes of each team member in turn. Loyal soldiers ready for war. "Minka confirmed Tane's weaknesses," I say without preamble. "Paranoia. Insecurity. Fear of betrayal. We knew we need to exploit these cracks in his armor, but it looks like we'll need to double down. Any plans we already have? Amplify them. Think something seems over the top? Make it bigger."

Suggestions come rapid-fire. Whisper campaigns to stoke distrust between Tane and his men. Anonymous threats to feed his paranoia. Carefully leaked information to spark suspicion. We dissect Tane's psychology, searching for further vulnerabilities to attack.

The hours fly by in a blur of strategy and planning. Our focus narrows to a single purpose—destroying the monster who has tormented this island chain for too long. I glance around at my inner circle, seeing iron determination etched on each face. Failure is not an option.

As midnight nears, we finalize our battle plans. The work ahead will be grueling, requiring patience and total commitment. The timeline has been condensed, and with it the pressure has increased exponentially.

But we have no choice. Tane's reign ends now. By any means necessary.

I nod in approval as we review the final plans. Psychological warfare designed to fracture Tane's organization from within. An onslaught of anonymous threats and misinformation to feed his paranoia. Strategically placed rumors to turn his most trusted men against each other. We'll chip away at the very foundation of his empire. But we have to do it quickly. There is no time to waste, and Tane amasses more power with each passing moment.

"This ends now," I say, steel in my voice. "We won't stop until Tane is destroyed, until he can never again terrorize our home and our people."

I meet each pair of eyes, seeing my own relentless determination reflected back. We've sacrificed too much already to fail now.

"Minka took a huge risk sending us that message," I continue. "It would have been far easier, far safer for her to stay silent. In the shadows. But she clearly believes in us. Let's make damn sure her courage wasn't in vain."

A ripple of agreement goes through the room. We all understand the stakes. If we falter, the consequences will be severe. But united by a common purpose, we are an unstoppable force.

"For too long, Tane has crushed our islands beneath his boot. Take more than he gives. Destroyed families, lives, hopes and dreams. But no more. The time has come to fight back, to reclaim our freedom." I pause, feeling the weight of this moment. "We end this. Now."

One by one, they nod. Jaws set, eyes blazing. Ready for war. We will not rest until Tane is dethroned, until his empire lies in ruins at our feet. Until his power becomes ours.

As the meeting concludes, there's a sense of destiny hanging thick in the air. The team disperses to begin executing our plans, each carrying the fate of the mission on their shoulders.

But despite the burden, we share a flicker of hope for a future free from Tane's tyranny.

The first rays of a new dawn can be glimpsed on the horizon.

CHAPTER THIRTY-NINE

ANGEL

The creaky wooden stairs groan under my feet as I descend into the dimly-lit basement. The cool, damp air prickles my skin and the earthy scent of soil fills my nose. I'm used to blood, screams, the occasional pool of vomit—but this is different. What is Brick up to down here?

My eyes adjust to the shadows and I spot him hunched over a makeshift table, intensely focused on the containers and tubes spread out before him.

"What are you doing?" I ask, sidling up behind him and placing my hand on his lower back.

He glances up, a devilish grin spreading across his rugged face. "Oh this? Just a little worm farm I'm experimenting with. Something Dom inspired me to do."

I peer closer at the writhing creatures in the soil. "Slade said you were up to something." I nudge him playfully. "But worms?" I quirk a brow.

"They really are remarkable creatures," he says, clearly enthused. "They can take shit, actual crap, and convert it into fuel to keep on living. Meanwhile, the rest of us can barely handle a little criticism."

I have to laugh. Only Brick could find beauty in a pile of worms. But that's what I love about him—he sees potential where others only see garbage.

"So what's the grand plan for these wriggly little guys then?" I ask, leaning in close to meet his glittering eyes.

"Who knows? But if worms can turn crap into something useful…" He pauses, tucking a strand of hair behind my ear. "Maybe we can take the shitty hand life's dealt us and turn it into something beautiful, too."

My heart swells, overflowing with admiration for this brilliant, unpredictable man. No matter how dark things seem, Brick always finds the light.

I'm lost in thought as Brick gazes at me, his eyes full of warmth despite the cool basement air. There's always more swirling beneath that rugged exterior than anyone realizes.

"You really think we can turn all this around?" I ask softly.

He brushes his thumb across my cheek. "With you by my side? We can do anything, my Valkyrie. I know things have been difficult lately, and we're about to take some huge risks. But I really believe we've got this."

I raise my eyebrows. "Oh yeah? How so?"

Brick grins. "I say we take all the bullshit Tane's put us through and turn it into power. Use it as fuel to destroy that handsome gargoyle once and for all. If worms can thrive on shit, we can take whatever Tane dishes out and come back stronger."

A smile spreads across my face. Trust Brick to find inspiration in the unlikeliest place. But he's right. We've turned garbage into gold before. We can do it again, no matter how deep of a hole Tane's dug for us.

Brick pulls me close, his breath warm on my skin. "As long as we stick together, we can handle anything. Together, we're pretty fucking unstoppable."

I laugh, squeezing him tight. Leaning into his embrace, I'm comforted by his solid strength. This man has been my rock through countless storms. No matter how chaotic life gets, I can always count on him to be my anchor. My insane, ruggedly handsome anchor.

"I don't know what I'd do without you," I murmur into his massive chest.

He strokes my hair gently. "You'll never have to find out. I'm not going anywhere, my Valkyrie. Whatever that snake throws our way, we'll power through it together." He pauses. "Don't tell Skyler and the guys I called him that. Oops."

I look up at him, my eyes tracing the rugged lines of his face. Even in the dim light of the basement, he takes my breath away.

"Promise me it'll always be like this," I whisper. "Just you and me and Aidan and Slade and Roman against the world."

Brick tilts my chin up, his piercing gaze meeting mine. "I promise. No matter what happens, we've got your back. Partners in crime, now and always."

His lips find mine in a searing kiss that steals the air from my lungs.

My hands grip his muscular shoulders, pulling him closer until no space remains between us.

The rest of the world fades away. In this moment, it's only me and my rock, my anchor, my everything.

When we finally break apart, both gasping for air, Brick rests his forehead against mine.

"We should get back upstairs before the others send out a search party," he says with a roguish grin.

I roll my eyes playfully. "Alright, but we're continuing this later."

Brick smacks my ass as I turn to leave. "Yes ma'am. I'll be ready and waiting."

I throw a flirty glance over my shoulder as I climb the basement stairs. No matter what happens, I know these guys will be by my side.

Worm farm and all.

CHAPTER FORTY

ROMAN

I walk the perimeter of the courtyard again, my boots crunching on the gravel with every step. This is where I like to come when my mind is troubled and I don't want to go all the way to the beach.

My thoughts keep looping back to the image of those rotting corpses, flesh sloughing off bone in a grotesque parody of humanity.

Mass graves. A shiver runs down my spine.

Brick approaches, brows furrowed. "You've been pacing for hours. Talk to me."

Taking a leaf from Aidan's book, I rake a hand through my hair and sigh. "Those fucking mass graves on the other island. I can't stop thinking about them."

"You've seen worse." His tone is gentle but matter-of-fact.

"Not like that." My fists clench at my sides. "Tane's always kept the real ugliness at a distance. But the graves?" I gesture vaguely, even though they're many miles away. "They're a reminder that he sees the people of these islands as nothing more than obstacles to exploit or remove. And if he can do that to them..." I trail off, unwilling to voice the fears churning in my gut.

Brick's hand lands on my shoulder, warm and solid. "You're wondering where it will end?"

"Yeah..." My voice comes out rough. "You've seen what he's capable of. What if—?"

"Stop." Brick gives me a little shake. "We're ready for him. Always have been. He'll get what's coming to him, but not before we're good and ready. You know

I'd attack him today if I thought it would be beneficial, but we have to plan this just right."

His confidence is reassuring, but it does little to quiet the unease whispering at the back of my mind. I know Tane won't stop until he's eliminated any threat to his control.

And we're the biggest threat of all.

Brick squeezes my shoulder. "Come on. Let's get something to eat."

My stomach rumbles in response and I realize I haven't eaten all day. Still, I hesitate. "I'm not really hungry."

"Wasn't a suggestion." He steers me toward the kitchen. "When's the last time you took a break? You'll run yourself into the ground at this rate."

I open my mouth to argue but decide against it. Maybe a distraction is exactly what I need right now. And if anyone can take my mind off things, it's Brick.

"Fine," I concede. "But if I'm eating, you are too."

Brick grins. "Wouldn't dream of letting you suffer through a meal alone."

As we walk, some of the tension eases from my shoulders. Our enemies may be gathering at the gates, but my family is here. Ready to face whatever comes.

Together.

The kitchen is empty when we arrive, the counter bare except for a few stray crumbs. Brick rummages through the cabinets, emerging with a triumphant "aha!" as he produces a loaf of bread, a wedge of cheese, and a jar of olives.

"It's no five-course meal, but it'll do." He slices the bread and cheese, arranging them on two plates along with a handful of olives. "Just don't tell Slade we're messing with his stuff."

I smirk. Slade is rather particular about people touching his things, and the kitchen is his official domain. Although I've noticed he's finally started letting Angel make herself at home in there.

We take a seat across from each other, the empty room echoing with each bite.

I study Brick as he eats, noticing the shadows beneath his eyes and the tense set of his jaw. He's just as on edge as the rest of us, though he does his best to hide it.

"You don't have to put on an act for me, you know." I meet his gaze. "It's okay if you're worried too."

He sighs, scrubbing a hand over his face. "Is it that obvious?"

I nod. "We've known each other too long for you to hide it."

"I just—" He hesitates, frowning at his plate. "What if it's not enough? What if we can't beat him? I feel like I'm reassuring everyone else, but I'm human. I have my own doubts, too."

"We will beat him." I speak with a conviction I don't entirely feel, hoping to reassure him as much as myself. "Tane has no idea what he's up against. We're smarter, we're faster, and we've got way more to fight for. And we're just as strong as he is."

Brick looks up at me, a smile tugging at the corners of his mouth. "And you always know just what to say."

"It's a gift." I lift my glass in a mocking toast. "And don't you forget it."

The tension in the room breaks as Brick laughs, the sound ringing out through the empty hall. I join in, the two of us chuckling like idiots over our makeshift dinner.

In this moment, Tane feels far away.

I wake with a start, my heart pounding as wisps of a nightmare fade from memory. Beside me, Angel stirs but doesn't wake.

The room is dim, shadows flickering in the corners. Moonlight streams through the window, pale and milky. I turn onto my side, studying Angel's profile in the darkness. Her chest rises and falls with the steady rhythm of sleep, her lips slightly parted. God, she's gorgeous.

My pulse slows as I watch her. There's something calming about her presence, as if the chaos and violence that surrounds her in waking hours can't touch her here. I reach out, brushing a stray lock of hair off her forehead. She leans into my touch with a soft sigh.

The mass graves flash behind my eyes, and I squeeze them shut against the memory. I can't escape the knowledge of what's waiting outside these walls. The war isn't over, and more bodies will pile up before the end.

"Hey." Angel's voice is thick with sleep. "You okay?"

I open my eyes to find her gazing at me, concern etched into her features. There's no hiding from my Angel.

"Just thinking about the graves again." I lace my fingers through hers, holding on like she's the only thing tethering me to shore. "I can't get the images out of my head."

"I know." Her thumb rubs slow circles over my knuckles. "But we'll make him pay for every single one. For now, try not to dwell on it."

"Easier said than done." I stare up at the ceiling, watching shadows dance in the dark. "I keep seeing their faces. Wondering who they were, how they ended up there. What kind of lives they might've lived if—"

"Shh." Angel pulls me against her, wrapping her arms around me. She's warm and cozy. "You'll drive yourself crazy thinking like that. What's done is done. But we can still avenge them, bring their killers to justice. Focus on that."

I exhale, relaxing into her embrace. The steady beat of her heart drowns out the whispers in my mind, at least for now.

"You're right." I tilt my head up, finding her mouth in the dark.

The kiss is slow and deep, a tangle of lips and tongues that leaves me breathless.

When we break apart, her eyes gleam down at me. "Feeling better?"

"Getting there." I smile, the shadows in my mind receding to make way for her. "Keep going."

Angel chuckles, rolling me onto my back to hover over me. "With pleasure."

The nightmare slips further away with each kiss, each caress. In the shelter of Angel's arms, the darkness holds no power.

The mass graves can't get me. Here, I'm safe.

Here, I'm home.

CHAPTER FORTY-ONE

ROMAN

The next morning

We're gathered in the courtyard to discuss our next moves. "We need to put him on the back foot now," Slade says, cracking his knuckles. "Then we can sit back and watch as he begins to unravel."

"I agree." Angel nods, her eyes hard as flint. "Messing with his meat supply on the other island really got to him. It made him vulnerable. We can do it again. We need to fuck with his business, for sure."

"And his people." A grim smile tugs at Brick's lips. "An eye for an eye. We take out whoever's responsible for those graves, and then some."

Brick's suggestion makes my stomach churn, because that type of vengeful plan usually involves collateral damage. There's a chance more innocent lives could be lost while we carry out this plot. But I know he's right. Tane understands violence, and violence is the only language he speaks.

"Do it," I say quietly. "Take out whoever was involved, and send them back in pieces. We'll dump them on Tane's doorstep."

A savage grin spreads across Brick's face. "With pleasure."

Angel smirks at his side. "This is going to be fun."

Slade cracks his knuckles again, anticipation etched into the sharp lines of his face. "We'll make sure Tane never forgets us."

I nod, steeling myself against the nausea rising in my gut. This is war, and war means sacrifice.

We surge into action, preparing for the bloodbath to come. But when I close my eyes, all I see are piles of rotting corpses stretching out into the distance.

And I wonder if we're any better than the monster we're trying to stop.

The raid of one of Tane's local outposts goes off without a hitch, our men descending on Tane's like a plague of locusts.

By the time the sun dips below the horizon, three of Tane's captains are dead —and in pieces, just as we ordered. Our guys made it look like a botched drug interception. Something that wouldn't link directly back to us, just enough to thoroughly unsettle Tane and set him on a wild goose chase.

Brick and Angel return with blood on their hands and victory in their eyes, Slade on their heels with a shark's grin on his face.

"Message sent," Brick grins, pulling Angel in for a deep, hungry kiss. I can only imagine she tastes blood and death on his lips, and my stomach churns.

But she kisses him back, and I understand the need to cling to the familiarity of his embrace. This is our world, our life, and we can't afford to flinch from the violence that sustains it.

"Well done," she murmurs against his mouth. Brick hums, nipping at her lower lip.

I close my eyes, trying to clear my mind. But the ghosts of rotting corpses still linger at the edges, silent witnesses to the bloodshed we've wrought.

And I wonder if there will ever come a day when I can no longer ignore their accusing stares.

I scan the courtyard where everyone has gathered to discuss today's events. Angel and Slade are now tangled up in each other, a mess of hungry lips and roving hands, while the others laugh and trade stories of the raid.

They're alive. They're whole. And for now, that's enough.

"You did good today," I tell Brick, patting him on his massive shoulder. He grins, pulling a cigarette from his pocket and lighting it with a flick of his lighter.

"All in a day's work."

I pluck the cigarette from his lips, taking a deep drag and blowing smoke up at the darkening sky. The nicotine buzzes in my veins, calming my frayed nerves.

Angel notices us, and narrows her eyes from across the courtyard. She's not fond of our habit, but knows right now isn't the time to ride us. The last thing we need is nicotine withdrawal while trying to take down Tane. Besides, I hardly pick up a cigarette when I'm not under extreme stress.

"I don't know how much longer we can keep this up," I admit. Across the courtyard, Slade now has Angel pressed up against the wall, her legs wrapped around his waist.

Brick's gaze follows mine, his brow furrowing. "What do you mean?" He quirks a brow at me. "Get a room!" he yells at Angel and Slade, and they both laugh, but don't stop their canoodling.

"Tane's not going to back down. He's going to keep coming at us, and if we don't put him down for good..." I trail off, passing the cigarette back to Brick. "Sooner or later, one of us isn't going to make it back home."

Brick is silent for a long moment. "Then we end him," he says flatly. "However we have to. Before he has the chance to hurt anyone else."

His words should fill me with relief. But all I can see are the piles of rotting corpses, innocents sacrificed in a war that will never truly end. And I know it's way too late to walk away from this life of violence.

"Roman." Brick's voice cuts through my brooding thoughts. I look up to find him watching me, eyes gleaming gold in the fading light.

"We're together until the end. Whatever happens." He places his huge hand on my shoulder, squeezing tight. "You don't have to face this alone."

I nod and let him keep his hand there, holding on through the tumult of emotions crashing inside me. And for the first time since hearing about those graves, they're not front and center images in my mind.

My family is my light in the darkness.

Maybe together, we really can find our way out of this.

CHAPTER FORTY-TWO

ANGEL

T he sun melts into the ocean, bleeding brilliant hues of orange and pink across the darkening sky. I find Aria outside, her silhouette backlit by the sunset's glow.

"I've been thinking about our conversation the other day," I say, joining her on the porch steps.

Aria turns to me, curiosity in her eyes. "Oh yeah? What about it?"

I take a deep breath, choosing my words carefully. "I think in a lot of ways, your experience mirrors my own. There are definitely parallels with what we've both been through."

She nods, understanding dawning on her face. "I'm not surprised. But how so? Like, anything in particular?"

I stare out at the sunset, memories of my past swirling through my mind. "For a long time, I didn't think I was capable of love. Not for myself, or for anyone else. I was broken, you know?"

Aria places her hand on mine, grounding me. "Having a deranged stalker will do that to you." Her voice is warm and full of understanding.

"Right?" I nod. "But once I started to heal and learn to love myself, everything changed. I finally opened myself up to love, and found it in the most unexpected places." I turn to Aria, emotion thick in my voice. "With them—with all of you—I feel whole for the first time in my life."

Aria squeezes my hand, smiling softly. In this moment, no words are needed. The silence wraps around us like a warm embrace as the last sliver of sun dips below the horizon.

I take a deep breath, letting the salty ocean air fill my lungs.

"It wasn't easy, learning to love myself," I say quietly. "For a long time, I didn't think I deserved it. I was my own worst critic, you know? But eventually I realized—I had to stop beating myself up over things that weren't my fault."

Aria nods, her eyes filled with understanding. She knows this struggle all too well.

"I had to re-learn how to be gentle with myself. How to quiet those critical voices in my head." I pause, searching for the right words. "And little by little, the more compassion I showed myself, the more I could open up and love others. The more that little voice faded away. I called it 'Veronica', and told her to go back where she came from." I smirk, and Aria smiles.

I turn to her, conviction in my voice. "So when Aidan and the guys came into my life, I was finally ready. Ready to give myself to them fully, without holding back. And it's been incredible, experiencing the depth of love between us all."

A soft smile plays on Aria's lips. "It's amazing what we're capable of, once we heal our own wounds," she says.

"You got that right." I let out a small laugh. "Who would've thought I could love not just one man, but four? And that they could all love each other, and me, with such passion and devotion?" I shake my head in wonder. "We're rewriting all the rules out here."

Aria grins. "We sure are. And I wouldn't have it any other way."

Silence settles between us once more as we watch the moon rise over the sea. A new understanding flows between us, two women traversing an unconventional path side by side.

"Makes you realize how universal some things are," I say. "Like the journey to self-love, and opening yourself up to new kinds of relationships."

"Yeah," Aria agrees. She pauses, seeming to gather her thoughts. "You know, I was skeptical at first too, when the guys proposed the reverse harem thing. I mean, three alpha males agreeing to share one woman? Sounded crazy."

I chuckle under my breath. "Right? Not exactly the conventional romance."

A small smile plays on Aria's lips. "But they wooed me, slowly and persistently. And once we established some clear boundaries and expectations, I realized it could work. There were definitely some messy moments at first, of course."

"Oh I bet," I say. "My guys had some jealous moments early on too, before everyone got more comfortable with the arrangement."

Aria nods in understanding. "Now though, it's like...we're a family. A highly dysfunctional, passionate, messy family." She lets out a throaty laugh. "But that's part of what makes it so beautiful. We embrace each other fully, flaws and all."

I take in her words, a warmth blossoming in my chest. "That's exactly it," I say softly. "The ups and downs just bring us closer together."

We share a look of knowing, two women who have found love and fulfillment in the most unexpected places and unanticipated manner. The setting sun bathes us in a golden glow, and I feel at peace.

As the last sliver of sun disappears below the horizon, I think about how much we've grown together. Once lost souls, now intertwined in a complex web of passion, trust, and understanding. We started out as individuals, but now we're all part of something so much greater.

A gentle breeze rustles through the trees, carrying the scent of the sea. I close my eyes, breathing it in. No matter how chaotic things get, this place centers me.

Beside me, Aria sighs contentedly. We don't need to speak—our shared experience connects us on a deeper level. In this moment, I feel profoundly grateful to have her wisdom and empathy to guide me.

Stars begin to peek through the dark blanket of night. Each one a pinprick of light, even against the blackness. Just like the hope we give each other, illuminating our lives when things seem darkest.

I reach for Aria's hand, squeezing gently. She looks at me, her eyes glistening, and smiles.

I've found a new sister in her, a close friend. And together we'll embrace our darkness and find our inner light.

CHAPTER FORTY-THREE

DEVON

The Next Day

My mind has been racing with thoughts of taking Tane down. It's bubbling up unpleasant memories—my father's debt, my kidnapping, his ultimate demise. But those things had their upsides, too. Like meeting my guys. And, as it turns out, in the midst of this chaos we have a little time to spend together. So I've planned a special surprise for them, something I've been wanting to do for a while.

All I told them was to bring decent walking shoes, and the rest will take care of itself.

"Please tell us where we're going," Zeke had said, frowning. "You know how I feel about surprises."

"I promise this is a risk-free adventure," I laugh. "Be a bit spontaneous, please. The worst you're going to do is get a mosquito bite, or maybe trip over something if you're not careful where you're going."

"If you say so," he sighs. "Good thing I trust you."

Rake, on the other hand, is a bundle of excitement, jumping from one foot to another. Grinning at me. He's childlike in his enthusiasm, but it somehow translates into sexiness in this handsome, tattooed giant of a man.

Dom and Skyler are more go with the flow with the plan, and they hop into the vehicle, both wearing sneakers as instructed. We drive for a while, curving our way along winding roads lined with lush palm trees and other vegetation.

There's not a ton of traffic, but I really don't mind being stuck in a row of cars in a place like this. As long as I'm with these incredible men.

We make our way down the winding path, the thick canopy of leaves overhead filtering the golden sunlight into dappled patterns. The distant roar of water grows louder with each step, anticipation building within me.

The leaf canopy parts before us, revealing a hidden paradise tucked away in the heart of the forest. My breath catches in my throat at the sight that unfolds before our eyes. I'd seen it in Instagram pictures before, but nothing could have prepared me quite for what this looks like in person.

We emerge into a sun-drenched clearing where a towering waterfall cascades into a crystal-clear pool, rainbow-hued mist swirling at its base. Mist rises from the base of the falls, rainbows dancing across its surface.

The air is alive with the roar of rushing water and the sweet scent of tropical flowers: plumeria, lobster-claws, birds of paradise, Kahili ginger, each scent more enticing than the next. Sunlight filters through the treetops above in dappled patterns, dancing across the surface of the rippling waters.

I glance over my shoulder to find four pairs of eyes gazing at me in wonder, their expressions a mixture of astonishment and delight. I've never seen the four of them speechless at the sight of something new. A surge of pride washes over me at the joy I've brought to my men.

"Surprise!" I announce with a mischievous grin.

"Holy shit, Dev. This place is incredible!" Zeke breathes, his analytical mind momentarily silenced by the magnificence of the natural world.

"It's like something out of a dream," Dom adds, his voice tinged with awe.

Rake lets out his trademark low whistle, his gaze lingering on me with unveiled admiration. "You never cease to amaze us, Dev."

Warmth floods my cheeks at his praise. I may have led them to this hidden paradise, but they're the ones who bring color to my world.

My lips curve into a smile as I meet Skyler's gaze, his eyes glinting with wonder as he takes in the spectacle before us. I knew that he, out of all four of them, would likely appreciate this the most.

"Wow, Dev. This place is amazing." Genuine admiration fills his voice, igniting a surge of warmth in my chest.

"The water's perfect too," I say, kicking off my sneakers and socks.

I dash forward with a laugh, plunging into the crystal clear pool. The guys' surprised shouts and curses echo behind me as they scramble to catch up, their playful threats of punishment bringing a grin to my lips.

The cool water envelops me, its refreshing embrace chasing away the lingering heat. I surface with a gasp, pushing back my tangled hair as I find myself gazing up at four grinning faces.

I glide effortlessly through the glittering blue pool, my arms and legs slicing through the water with ease. I reach the deepest part and glance back at the guys.

A mischievous grin spreads across my face as I slowly peel off my bikini top, revealing my breasts. I twirl around as I remove my bikini bottoms and toss them, and they land on a nearby rock with a satisfying thud. The water ripples around me as I wink playfully at the guys, all who are mesmerized by my little striptease.

"Well?" I call out, arching a brow. "Are you coming in or not?"

That's all the invitation they need. The guys strip all of their clothes off, their eyes dancing with laughter and desire as they join me in the pool.

Within moments, four pairs of hands grasp at my ankles and waist, dragging me under the churning waters.

I break free with a splash, my hair clinging to my face in wet strands as I surface.

"Thought you'd get away that easily, did you?" Rake teases, his hands closing around my waist to pull me against his chest. I laugh, the sound echoing over the rushing waters.

"There's no way I would try to run."

Skyler pulls me close, claiming my lips in a searing kiss that leaves me breathless. I melt against him, my hands roaming over the hard planes of his chest.

We're interrupted by a splash of water, courtesy of Zeke and Rake. I laugh, grabbing Skyler's hand as we launch a counterattack. Soon we're engaged in an all out war, the air filled with laughter and playful shouts.

At last we call a truce, collapsing against each other in a tangle of limbs as we catch our breath. My heart swells with joy, overcome by the simple pleasure of being together.

Laughter mingles with the roar of the waterfall, the guys' eyes dancing with mirth.

In this place, there are no Snakes or jobs or threats of danger looming on the horizon. Here, we are simply me and my men, embracing the joy of living in the moment. A contented sigh escapes my lips as I float into Skyler's arms, the stresses of the outside world melting away.

We have found our paradise. At least for this snapshot in time.

Skyler shakes his head, droplets of water flying from his hair. "We're not done with you yet, Dev." His eyes gleam with mischief as he closes the distance between us, his hands roaming over my hips beneath the water. "The party's just getting started."

Heat coils in my belly at his words, anticipation building inside me. We're alone out here, free from prying eyes and listening ears. A thrill courses through my veins, my heart racing with excitement at the promise of what's to come.

It's not why I picked this place, but I'd be lying if I said the thought of the five of us enjoying each other out here hadn't crossed my mind

I reach out to curl my fingers over Skyler's shoulder, pulling him closer until our lips meet. The kiss is hungry and demanding, full of heat and promise. My body comes alive under his touch, desire igniting my nerves like wildfire.

We break apart, breathless, our chests heaving. Skyler's eyes darken with lust as he takes in my disheveled appearance.

"Well, guys," he says, his voice a low rumble. "Shall we give our girl something extra special to remember about this amazing place?"

Groans of anticipation escape my lovers' lips. Four pairs of hands close around my body, lifting me from the churning waters. Joy and desire mingle inside me as I'm carried towards a large, flat rock that pokes its way out of the shimmering pool, the guys' hungry gazes devouring every inch of my skin.

Today, I'm going to let pleasure take over. And by the time the sun dips below the horizon, I'll be a quivering, sated mess in the arms of the men who own my heart, body and soul.

They aren't the only ones who I intend to benefit from this surprise.

Skyler's lips crash against mine, hungry and demanding. I moan into his kiss, desire igniting my veins like wildfire. His hands roam over my naked body as he lays me out on the sun-warmed rock, my skin tingling under his rough, calloused touch.

"So beautiful," he breathes, gazing down at me with lust-darkened eyes. "All ours."

A thrill courses through me at his possessive words. "Yours," I whisper, arching into his touch.

Skyler growls low in his throat, the sound sending shivers down my spine. His mouth descends to my neck, lips and teeth marking a trail of fire across my sensitive skin. I gasp as he closes his mouth over my nipple, fingers twisting and pinching the other.

"Look at her," Zeke rasps, his eyes drinking in the sight of me writhing under Skyler's ministrations. "So eager to please."

"Our little slut can never get enough," Rake adds with a throaty chuckle. He grabs hold of the rock, his free hand sliding between my legs to stroke my aching core. I cry out at the sensation, trembling under the dual assault of their hands and mouths on my body.

"Please," I whimper, desire coiling tight inside me. I'm desperate for more—to feel them moving inside me, claiming me as theirs.

"Patience, mermaid," Dom croons, trailing a finger down my cheek. His eyes gleam with hunger and affection as he gazes down at me. "We're going to take our time with you."

The anticipation is almost too much to bear. I lick my lips, gazing up at my lovers with unabashed desire. "I'm all yours."

Skyler smiles, slow and predatory, his eyes gleaming with lust. "That's right, sweetheart," he purrs. "Ours to do with as we please."

His words ignite the fire in my veins, sending heat pooling between my legs. I'm clay in their hands, ready to be molded and shaped into whatever they desire.

Today I surrender myself completely to pleasure from the men who I love with all my heart.

Skyler lowers his head between my thighs, his hot breath fanning over my sensitive flesh. I gasp as his tongue slides through my slick lips, teasing and tasting.

Rake captures my mouth in a searing kiss, muffling my moans of pleasure. His clever fingers pluck and roll my nipples, sending jolts of electricity shooting through me.

I'm drowning in sensation, surrounded by the men I love.

Skyler's talented tongue works magic against my aching core, pushing me ever closer to the edge.

Rake swallows my cries, his kiss deepening as desire burns in my veins like wildfire.

Dom and Zeke press closer, their mouths finding my breasts, teasing my nipples with lips and teeth.

Their hands roam over my body, stroking and caressing my heated skin.

I'm surrounded, engulfed, claimed in every way possible.

Pressure builds inside me, threatening to shatter my control. I'm balancing on a knife's edge, ready to fall into sweet oblivion.

Skyler slides two fingers into my dripping entrance, curling them against my inner wall. The sensation rockets through me, shattering my restraint.

I come with a muffled cry, pleasure rippling through my body in intense waves.

My lovers ease me through the aftershocks, their hands and mouths gentle yet possessive. I float in a sea of bliss, sated yet craving more.

I come down from my high to find Skyler gazing up at me from the base of the rock, his lips curled in a smug grin. "Enjoy the ride, darling?"

I laugh breathlessly, running my fingers through his hair. "You know I always do."

Rake releases my lips, trailing kisses along my jaw. "She tastes even sweeter than usual today." His voice is rough with desire, igniting sparks deep within me.

"Our little vixen was extra naughty this morning," Zeke remarks, giving my nipple a gentle pinch. I gasp, heat flooding my cheeks at the memory. "She deserves to be rewarded."

"And we have so many rewards in store for you," Dom purrs, locking gazes with me. His eyes are dark, filled with promise and passion. "The day is still young, darling."

My heart pounds with anticipation. Today is going to be deliciously exhausting.

Skyler pulls away, wiping his mouth with the back of his hand. His gaze burns into me, pupils blown wide with lust. "On your hands and knees against this rock, pet. It's time for your next reward."

Shivers of delight race down my spine at his commanding tone. I eagerly assume the position, presenting myself for their pleasure. What will they do to me next? My mind spins with possibilities, craving their intimate touch.

Warm hands grip my hips, steadying me. Hot breath ghosts over my entrance, then a slick tongue delves inside. I gasp at the sensation, heat and moisture pooling between my thighs.

Zeke. Only he can work me so thoroughly, reducing me to a quivering mess with only his mouth. He has a gift, and he uses it well.

Rake claims my lips in another searing kiss, muffling my moans. His clever fingers pluck and roll my nipples, sending jolts of electricity shooting through me. I'm drowning in sensation, surrounded by the men I love.

Today is turning out even better than I imagined.

Dom kneels before me, his eyes burning with lust as, over my shoulder, he watches Zeke pleasure me.

I reach for him, tugging his mouth to mine. Our kiss is hungry and desperate, filled with longing.

I break away with a gasp as Zeke's tongue flicks over my clit, sending sparks of ecstasy ricocheting through me. "Please," I whimper, writhing against his mouth. I'm so close already, teetering on the edge of bliss.

With a smug grin, Zeke pulls away.

I cry out in protest, trying to chase his retreating mouth. He only chuckles, clearly enjoying tormenting me.

Rake takes my chin in his hand and turns me to face him, desire darkening his eyes. "Patience, Dev. We're not done with you yet."

Before I can respond, Skyler swims away and returns with ropes from his backpack. He uses them to encircle my wrists, binding them behind my back.

I glance over my shoulder as Skyler secures the knots, an impish grin playing over his lips.

"Trust us," he whispers, lips brushing the shell of my ear. A delicious shiver races down my spine as his hands glide over my hips, settling into a possessive grip.

And I really do have to trust them. Out here, in the middle of nowhere. In a pool of deep water, no longer with the use of my hands. In any other situation, this would be terrifying. But with these four? Exhilarating.

I kneel back, sitting on my calves, still atop the large, flat rock.

Dom steps forward, trailing a single finger down the valley between my breasts. "So beautiful like this, completely at our mercy." His voice is rough with longing, pupils blown wide with lust. "The only question is, what should we do with you now?"

A slow, Cheshire grin spreads across Rake's face. He leans in, nipping at my earlobe before whispering, "I have an idea."

My heart pounds in anticipation. What do they have in store for me that they haven't already done?

Rake grips my bound wrists and gently leads me off the rock, guiding me towards the cascading waterfall. The spray mists over my skin, droplets clinging to my eyelashes and trickling between my breasts. I gasp at the sensations, desire coiling hot and insistent within me.

They maneuver me until I'm positioned directly in front of the thundering cascade, the full force of the waterfall pounding against my flesh. I cry out at the exquisite pleasure-pain, desire burning white-hot in my veins.

Trapped in their embrace, surrounded by the raw power of nature, I've never felt more alive.

Skyler presses against me, his hardness nudging between my thighs. I gasp as he slides inside, stretching me open around his cock.

"So tight," he groans, grasping my hips. He pulls back slowly before thrusting deep, wrenching a strangled cry from my lips.

Pleasure spikes through my veins, heightened by the pounding spray of the waterfall against my flushed skin. I'm drowning in sensation, surrounded by the roar of the falls and the growls of pleasure from the men holding me captive.

Skyler sets a brutal pace, his hips slamming into me as I cry out with each thrust. The coil of desire within me winds tighter and tighter, threatening to snap.

A large hand closes around my throat, forcing my head under the ferocious downpour of the waterfall. I gasp, choking on mouthfuls of falling water as Skyler continues to pound into me mercilessly. I can only hear the rush of the water, and feel Skyler's rock hard cock slamming into me.

Panic rises in my chest, my lungs burning for oxygen. Just as darkness threatens to overtake me, Skyler pulls my head away from the waterfall. I cough and sputter, gulping in deep breaths of air.

"Still with me?" Skyler rasps, his thrusts slowing.

I nod, eyes locking with his. "Don't stop," I plead, desire eclipsing any trace of fear.

A devilish grin curves his lips. "As you wish."

He pushes my head under the waterfall once more, fucking me with abandon as I struggle for air.

The coil of pleasure within me snaps, ecstasy flooding my senses. I come undone around him, writhing helplessly in his grasp.

Skyler groans, burying himself to the hilt as he finds his own release. We emerge from the water, chests heaving as we cling to each other.

"You're incredible," he whispers, lips brushing over my throat.

I smile up at him, sated and breathless. "So are you."

Exhaustion washes over me, limbs heavy from our passionate encounter. Skyler scoops me into his arms, carrying me from the pool. The others are quick to assist, bundling me in towels and tending to my every need.

I nestle into Skyler's embrace, warmth flooding my chest at the affection and care shown by my men. They lay out a picnic blanket and settle in around me, pulling me close as we bask in the afterglow of our shared experience.

"How was it?" Rake asks, a teasing glint in his eyes. "Everything you hoped for and more?"

A blissful sigh escapes my lips as I nod. "It was incredible. All of it."

"Good," Dom says, brushing a kiss over my forehead. "You deserve to have your every fantasy fulfilled."

"And we aim to please," Zeke adds with a roguish wink.

I laugh, giving his arm a playful swat. "Oh, I'm well aware. You lot spoil me rotten."

"Only because you deserve to be spoiled," Skyler says, tightening his arms around me.

Warmth floods my chest at his words, touched by the depth of affection and care shown by the men who have captured my heart. To think our relationship began as a power struggle—captors and captive—each vying for control until we realized the true strength to be found in surrender.

The bonds we have forged are unbreakable, built on trust, desire and a love that knows no bounds. And it all began with a kidnapping, a fleeting moment in time that could have resulted in fear and violence and even death, but instead which set our souls alight and destined us to be together.

Fate brought us together, but it's choice that has bound us so tightly. The choice to love each other wholly, to embrace both the light and the dark, to share in life's adventures together.

And as I gaze into the eyes of the men who have claimed my heart, I cherish having found my home. My family.

"Thank you for this," Skyler says softly, his lips brushing against my temple. "You always know how to brighten our days."

"You're most welcome," I reply, nestling closer against him. "But the pleasure is mine, I assure you."

A comfortable silence falls over us as we bask in the beauty of our surroundings and the intimacy of the moment. The only sounds that break the stillness are the gentle lapping of water against stone and the distant calls of birds echoing through the forest.

Peace and contentment wash over me in waves as I surrender myself fully to the embrace of the men who hold my heart. This is bliss, a slice of heaven on earth that I never wish to leave. I close my eyes and inhale the sweet scent of tropical flowers, enjoying the sun's gentle warmth on my face.

Dom lifts my chin, his eyes searching my face. "You good, angel?"

I smile, reaching up to caress his cheek. "I'm wonderful."

He grins, pulling me in for a searing kiss. I moan into his mouth, desire igniting in my core once again as his hands roam over my naked skin.

When we break apart, I find myself gazing into Rake's smoldering eyes. A slow, wicked smile spreads across his lips as his gaze travels the length of my body.

"Well, don't you look delicious," he growls, trailing a finger down my throat. I shiver, heat pooling between my thighs in response to his touch. "All wet and ready for us."

"All this for you," I reply breathlessly.

Rake's eyes darken, his smile turning predatory. "Is that so?" He growls, pulling me flush against him. I gasp as his hard length presses against my stomach, desire burning bright within me.

"Please," I whimper, grinding shamelessly against him.

Rake lets out a low chuckle, pinning my wrists above my head. "Patience, little one."

I cry out in frustration, struggling fruitlessly against his grip. He only tightens his hold, a smug grin tugging at his lips.

"Relax," he purrs, trailing kisses along the column of my throat. "We have all day to play. No need to rush."

I whimper in protest, desperate for more, but relent against his firm grip. When I stop struggling, Rake rewards me with a searing kiss that leaves me breathless and trembling with need.

"Good girl," he murmurs, his eyes glowing with approval. I preen under his praise, my heart swelling at the knowledge of pleasing him.

Dom steps forward, his eyes dark with desire as he takes in the sight before him. "My turn."

Dom pulls me into his arms, his lips claiming mine in a possessive kiss. I moan against his mouth, desire igniting my veins as his hands roam greedily over my body.

When we break apart, I'm breathless and trembling. Dom grins down at me, his eyes glowing with lust. "On your knees," he commands, his tone leaving no room for argument.

I drop to my knees without hesitation, gazing up at him through lowered lashes. Dom strokes my hair in approval, guiding my mouth to his throbbing cock. I take him in eagerly, relishing his strangled groan of pleasure.

As I pleasure Dom, I feel a pair of hands grip my hips from behind. I gasp around Dom's length as Zeke enters me in one smooth thrust, filling me to the brim.

I cry out in ecstasy, writhing between them as they establish a punishing rhythm. Dom's hands tighten in my hair, forcing me to take him deeper. I moan wantonly, arousal burning through my veins as I surrender to their primal rhythm.

Rake crouches before me, guiding my hand to his aching cock. I stroke him eagerly, desperate to give him pleasure as my lovers plunge into me from both ends.

When Dom spills down my throat with a guttural groan, I swallow greedily, craving every last drop of his release. Zeke quickens his pace, his fingers digging into my hips as he hurtles towards his climax.

With a strangled cry, Zeke erupts inside me, his warmth flooding my core. The feeling sends me tumbling over the edge, my vision going white as pleasure overwhelms my senses.

I collapse against Zeke, spent and trembling in the aftermath of my climax. Strong arms lift me against a firm chest, cradling me close. I nuzzle into the comfort offered, a contented sigh escaping my lips as the cool mist caresses my heated skin.

My lovers join us, their arms encircling me in a cocoon of warmth and affection. I smile, basking in the intimacy of our embrace and the profound joy that fills my heart.

Here, surrounded by the men who have captured my heart and given me reason, I have found my place in this world.

Here, in their loving arms—and regardless of the danger we're about to face—I am home.

CHAPTER FORTY-FOUR

SLADE

The smell of sizzling bacon fills my nostrils as I flip the pancakes on the stove. Brick and Angel are parked on the barstools behind me, and Angel has had an extra coffee and is chattering away like a fucking magpie. Brick is glued to his computer, half-listening to Angel while tapping at his keyboard.

"What are you doing, Brick?" Angel asks. Her voice is like a melody, even this early in the damn morning.

"Reading about polycules," he replies, not even looking up from his laptop screen. Fucking weirdo's always got his nose buried in some new research obsession.

I glance over my shoulder, eyebrow raised. "What the hell is a polycule?"

Brick's face lights up like he's just discovered plutonium. "It stands for polyamorous molecule!" He's grinning from ear to ear. Jesus, he looks deranged when he's this excited. Of course he would find the most ridiculous-sounding term in the English dictionary and apply it to us.

I shake my head and turn back to the sizzling pans. Fucking polycules. Just another one of Brick's harebrained schemes to organize our twisted little family unit. That psycho probably already has the tattoo sketches done for each of us. Like one of those stickers people get for their cars where it shows the parents and each of the children. Sometimes the dog. Except in our case it'd be four tattooed rectangles and one hot female with bright purple hair and nipple piercings.

The pancakes are a perfect golden brown. I slide them onto a platter just as the coffee maker beeps. The rich aroma mingles with the bacon.

Brick is still rambling about relationship diagrams or some shit. I tune him out and focus on the food. This is my love language, and I think everyone in the house knows that.

I plate the pancakes, eggs, and bacon, then set them down on the counter with a satisfying thunk. Brick and Angel dig in eagerly, Brick of course opting out of the bacon and the eggs. Nothing more satisfying than watching people enjoy my cooking, even if they're vegan.

Except maybe listening to the screams coming from Brick's basement. But that's a different kind of satisfaction.

Brick shovels a forkful of pancakes into his mouth, talking around the food in his usual charming way.

"But you know what this means?" He's practically vibrating with excitement. "We get to make one of those relationship map things, with all the lines connecting us!"

I roll my eyes so hard it's a wonder they don't detach. "Yeah, I don't think so. The only lines I want connecting us are handcuffs and whips."

Angel giggles at that, the sound light and musical. God, I love this woman. She appreciates my special brand of humor.

Brick is undeterred, already sketching something on a napkin. "It'll be so cool, though! I can draw Angel's nipple rings and everything."

Of course. Any excuse for him to draw Angel's pierced nipples. Called it. The things that turn this guy on never cease to disturb me... I mean, her nipple piercings turn me on as well, but I don't feel the need to draw them. Although, maybe if I arrange the pancakes just so...

"Eat your breakfast," I growl. "No relationship diagrams at the table. We'll make sure the nipple piercings are still there later."

Brick pouts, but shovels another bite of pancakes into his mouth. At least I can distract him with food.

We eat in comfortable silence for a few minutes. But I can see the wheels turning in Brick's twisted brain. No doubt he's imagining all kinds of deranged illustrations for his imaginary polycule.

Some things never change. Brick and his freaky obsessions. Me cooking breakfast. Angel lighting up the room with her smile.

I guess we make it work, in our own dysfunctional way. Just another day with my polycute little family. UGH. Gross. I can't believe I even thought that.

I glance over at Angel as we eat, taking in her delicate features. Her eyes shine in the morning light, and her full lips curl into a soft smile when she catches me looking.

There are words I want to say, but I couldn't possibly. How having her here makes everything better.... my cooking, this house, my whole damn life. How she's the sunshine that makes the rain and the murky clouds go away.

I think she knows, without me needing to speak the words. At least, I hope she does. I try to show her through my actions whenever I can.

"You know what, Slade?" Brick booms. "You've always been a good cook, but you were a miserable bastard before Angel came along." He shakes his head and grimaces, as if recalling me at my most curmudgeonly. "But now? Waking up next to Angel, seeing that beautiful face across the table from you? It's changed everything. You're a whole new man."

I sigh, my cheeks reddening. "Yep, you're it for me, baby," I glance at Angel and she meets my gaze with a smile. "The only one I'll ever need."

Weight lifts from my shoulders the moment the words come out. As if by admitting the truth I've released some of the pressure I've been holding in for goodness knows how long. It's not the emotions behind the words that scare me. It's saying them out loud... as if by revealing my true feelings I'm going to be judged, or the universe is going to say 'haha! Got you!', and everything I've wished for is going to be ripped away.

Brick makes a retching sound. "Oh my god, you two are disgusting. Please get a room before I vomit up this delicious breakfast."

I flip him off, but can't keep a grin from spreading across my face. "Shut it, pretty boy. I'm trying to have a moment here..." I pause and narrow my eyes at him. "Which you very obviously orchestrated."

Angel laughs, her nose scrunching up adorably as her eyes meet mine. "It's okay, Slade. I feel the same way about you. About all of you. I finally found where I belong." She pauses, reaching over the counter to squeeze my forearm. "And I know words like that don't come easily to you. I know you mean them very much."

Brick pretends to retch again, but I can tell he's pleased. He got me to verbally demonstrate my feelings to the woman we both love.

We've got our issues, but together we make one hell of a team. A family. Or I guess you could call us a polycule, according to Brick's relationship vocabulary lesson.

I shake my head, chuckling to myself. However we label it, Angel's right. This right here is home.

"Alright, enough with the feelings circle, Slade," Brick says, basically accusing me of starting the sappiness. "We've got business to discuss."

The urge to dive across the counter and throttle him is real, but I take a few deep breaths instead, just the way Angel taught me, and the urge diffuses.

Angel nods, her playful demeanor shifting to something harder and more calculating. My fierce little Valkyrie, always ready for a fight.

I reach across the counter to take Angel's hand, pressing a kiss to her knuckles. She smiles, softening for a moment, then meets my eyes.

Brick chuckles darkly. "I've got some new toys I've been wanting to try out. There's another sleazeball fucking with Roman's girls at the club. This seems like the perfect opportunity for a test run."

Only Brick would see an impending torture session as a chance to play with new gadgets. But I know once he gets going, the Snakes will be begging for mercy.

Angel grins, a wicked glint in her eyes. "I'll make sure to pack my favorite knives. It's been a while since I got my hands dirty."

A flare of desire courses through me at hearing the anticipation in her voice. My fierce little warrior. So beautiful on the outside, and so very depraved on the inside.

"Okay, I know we can go and find trouble if we want to. But I really think we should stick to the plan and focus on Tane."

"You're right, Slade," says Angel. "We can practice with the new tools later. At least, the new tools not intended for our operation."

Brick claps his hands together. "It's settled then. " His smile widens, edging toward unhinged. "This is going to be fun."

I take a long sip of coffee, savoring the calm before the storm.

We've got a big few days ahead of us, but I know one thing's for certain—Tane and his men will not be fucking with our business again.

Not after we're through with them.

CHAPTER FORTY-FIVE

SLADE

*T**he Following Day*

The room grows silent as he enters. Previously filled with excited chatter and casual banter, and the clinking of glasses and cutlery against plates, the space is now eerily still as people turn to look. Ever the sophisticate, Tane wears another of his immaculately tailored suits, a navy blue that brings out the untold depths of his eyes.

I have to give it to him, Tane is one handsome dude.

Angel and I are watching him on camera, from the surveillance room on the other side of the building. The camera setup bears the standard offerings you'd expect from a restaurant—eyes on the cash register, the kitchen, the host stand and a general view of the dining room. But ours also offers a more detailed view, and one that gets us close to exactly where we need to be.

Aria flits to his side. "Welcome, Mr. Brown. We're honored you could be here today. We do hope you enjoy our soft opening."

What Tane doesn't realize is that this isn't Aria's official soft opening. This is a very special one, just for him. The other guests are just for show, a curated list of well-behaved influencers who will stick to themselves. And, just to keep them safe from any collateral damage, they all happen to be vegan. We're saving the meat for Tane and his men.

Of course, when Tane received a VIP invite, he didn't question it. As notorious as he is, and with his own network of restaurants around the islands, he's always attending these types of events. Even if his men vetted everything beforehand, all roads from this restaurant lead back to shell corporations. If they got to the bottom of things, everything is in Aria's name and she's still not well known to them.

Aria winks at the camera as she walks past, on her way to the kitchen where she and I spent close to forty-eight hours over hot grills. At times, the aromas coming out of the kitchen sickened me, but only because I knew what was really at play.

As I realize that this is actually happening, I watch with glee as Tane and his men make their way further inside the colorful space. They each take a champagne flute from a passing server, and take a seat at the communal table which has been reserved just for them.

Tane is positioned next to his current top man, Lawrence, a very large man with a scar running down the side of his face. His head is shaved, the elegant lighting bouncing off his bald pate as he cranes his neck to take everything in. "Wow boss, this place is alright." He nods as he surveys the crowd. "Some really elegant stuff here."

Tane murmurs his assent, preferring to keep to himself.

A server approaches, tray in hand topped with matching small plates. Each is covered with a sticky red sauce, two riblets on each, dotted with a sprig of microcilantro. "This is the smoky glazed ribs. You can expect them to be sticky, unctuous morsels. You will need to use your hands, and these can get messy, but we've provided each seat with its own finger bowl so you can rinse off."

She carefully places a small plate in front of each of the giant men. It's almost comical, her tiny frame dwarfed by these large henchmen that look like... well, henchmen. They all stare at the plates before them, and then at Tane, as if awaiting his permission to eat.

"Oh wow, these are some sticky ribs," the bald guy says, shoving his meaty thumb into his mouth, first to eat out of the group. I try to hide my grimace as a glob of sauce starts to dribble its way languidly down his stubbled chin. "This sauce is to fucking die for."

And some people did.

"Boss, trust me. You gotta check this out," he continues, a testament that the dish at least hasn't been poisoned.

Tane glances over. "I'm cutting down on my red meat at the moment."

"Oh trust me, boss," he insists. "Everyone needs to color outside the lines a little every now and then. It's just a teeny tiny piece of beef, right? One little sliver of red meat isn't going to hurt anyone. And none of us are going to tell your nutritionist team, are we now?"

He glances around the rest of the group exaggeratedly, accompanied by a stage wink.

What an absolute pillock! But I guess not even Tane can be picky with his help when his best men are disappearing all over the islands.

Before I have a chance to get frustrated, Angel catches my eye. She reaches down and squeezes my hand and together we continue to view the live video stream.

Aria's voice is confident, airy, as if she's taking a group of investors through her restaurant. "One of the biggest issues I find these days is that we really don't know what goes into our food. But I can tell you about where each and every item in the plate before you was carefully sourced. 'Intentional cooking', we like to call it."

I hold back a smirk. Oh my god, she isn't. But she is. The words roll off her tongue in an exquisite display of double entendre.

"We grow our protein to be tough, but in the end we find the meat is all the same. We take great care in preparing it. Every life should mean something, right?"

"I, uh—I guess. All I know is I like ribs." Lawrence sucks the sauce off each finger, and my stomach roils seeing his meaty fingers stuffed into his loud, greasy mouth.

Suddenly, Tane speaks up. "You know, this is where you and I appear to differ," Tane smirks at Aria. "Because I'm a firm believer in the circle of life. There's a hierarchy of power and control in the animal kingdom, and at our very core aren't humans just animals, too? Only the strongest survive. Only the ones prepared to do whatever it takes to get what you want. What you *deserve*.

That's what gets rewarded. Tenacity. Self-belief. None of that generosity and gratitude mumbo jumbo I see spouted all over the place these days. It's about grit. Chutzpah. Something that's severely lacking in most people these days."

"Oh, well I still trust you'll enjoy the dish," says Aria, politely.

We all hold our breaths as Tane picks up a rib with his elegant fingers and glances at it more closely. "It is quite beautifully prepared," he says. "Just the way I like my meat."

"Human and dead?" Angel whispers, and I fight the urge to laugh out loud. She's warped, and it's one of the things I love most about her.

With that, Tane takes a bite, closing his eyes as he savors the rich taste. I never thought I'd say this, but I'm getting really good at cooking people. I've come a long way since sautéeing pieces of Angel's stalker and his cousin's dick.

"This is quite nice," says Tane, taking another bite. Before long, he's devoured both ribs, oblivious to having just consumed actual pieces of two of his formerly esteemed men.

The rest of the meal goes off without a hitch, and we watch with glee as Tane continues to unknowingly eat some of the men who delivered so much agony, so much heartbreak, on his behalf. Lardons, rissoles, even a dessert using gelatin made by melting down their fingernails and eyeballs, and Tane—none the wiser.

"Is this really going to make him paranoid, if he doesn't know what he's eating?" Angel whispers, a brow quirked.

"Oh, that's part of the mindfuck," I explain. "We let him enjoy this, savor every last bite, truly enjoy it. And then when we break the news, it will be all the sweeter. It'll unseat him from his foundation, knowing he ate his men and had no idea. Complete loss of control."

"Genius," Angel exhales, shaking her head as Tane takes a final bite of his dessert. "Absolute genius."

CHAPTER FORTY-SIX

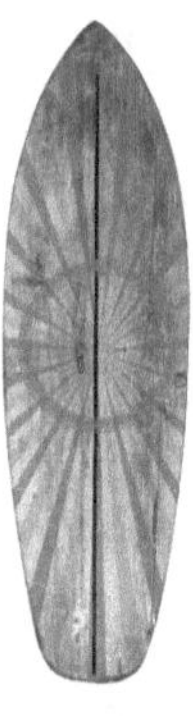

RAKE

Two Days Later

We watch through the cameras as one by one, Tane's men file in through the door in the corner of the room and take their seats around a large meeting table.

I recognize nearly all the faces in the room from their visit to the spiritual store and our special room in the back. As well as from the profile sheets Zeke and Aidan pulled together on each of Tane's top men.

This is definitely a starting team, each of Tane's star quarterbacks are basically seated around the table. Well, the ones that are left, anyway.

I've never really taken the time to appreciate just how good Tane has been at assembling his men. They're all so similar, devoid of individual personalities for the most part. They wear signature dark suits, and bear impenetrable expressions on their faces, the only sign of personalities buried deep inside coming from the variations in the timbre of their voices, and the occasional twitch of the corner of their mouth or eye when something is said involving danger or a change of plans.

He's deliberately molded them like this, into mini versions of himself. But there's one distinct difference. Where Tane himself is a master of strategy, treating his men and everyone else like chess pieces—pawns specifically—in his sick games, these men don't have the same desire to control things.

They're perfectly content to take instructions from the man, just eager to be affiliated with him in some capacity. And don't get me wrong, they are ambitious—but not in the way that they want to overthrow Tane and take over his share of power. Just the opposite, in fact. They're motivated by working their way up his ranks, of proving their fierce loyalty to him.

Tane has carefully cultivated urban legends about how well he treats his men at the top, the power and untold wealth they'll accumulate for themselves and their families. How they'll be set up for life by the time they retire.

So what better strategy than to use that to our advantage? Tane is obsessed with loyalty, and he's constantly wanting to test it with his guys. We know that, which means they definitely know that.

The second he gives them a task, they morph into a team of pick-mes. I get the image of a group of kids in class really wanting the teachers attention, raising their hands and grunting 'mm mm' in an effort to be selected. 'I did the homework, miss. I'm your best student ever! You must see me!' Just like that.

But, as it turns out, Tane is just as susceptible to a struggling labor market as the rest of us. While it might sound glamorous, living on the islands is a whole new beast from vacationing here. People perceive greater opportunities in bigger cities on the mainland. And, of course, it doesn't help when we've been picking off his best men one by one. It tends to serve as a deterrent to people with other options.

I still have no idea what Brick hoped to achieve with this little stunt of his. There's always some genius end-game, and this appears to be no exception. He usually brings me into the details early on, but it's almost like he wants me to experience this one as a spectator... which makes me think this is going to be really fucking good. And really fucking bad for Tane and his men.

The room goes silent as Tane enters, flanked by two more giant men, and takes his place at the head of the table. "Right, men. We've achieved a critical state of alert. People will relentlessly try to take what's ours. Your one and only goal is to protect our bottom line and any threats to our power by any means necessary."

"What does that mean, boss?" asks one of the men sitting near the head of the table.

"Well, for starters, we won't be attending any further events. That restaurant thing was fine, although it was a pitiful attempt to compete with the standards set by my restaurants..." He smirks, and I want to punch the arrogant fucker in the fact on Aria's behalf. The audacity...

"Okay, get ready." Brick nods at the rows of tiny remote controls in front of us.

I have six, he has six.

"On my count, activate them one by one. Wait five or so seconds between each."

"Wha–what are these for, anyway?" I ask, still confused. All I know is I trust him, and I'm going to go along with his request for help, no matter how weird it might seem.

Brick presses the big button on the first of the remotes.

"Go!" Brick urges me, and I do the same.

Right on cue, one of the men stops short. His brows knit together, confusion clouding his features. He shifts his weight, hand drifting to his arm and he pats at himself near the incision site. Discomfort flickers across his face. "What the hell...?"

A second man looks down and I see him adjust in his chair. It's as if he's trying and failing to maintain a neutral expression, fighting the urge to fidget.

One by one, we press the rest of the activation buttons and each man around the table begins to act in a similar way.

A fierce joy ignites within me. "Here we go. It's starting."

The man's discomfort slowly morphs into panic. He tugs at his shirt, his breathing accelerating. The toy buzzes relentlessly, driving him mad from the inside out.

Across the room, his compatriots exhibit the same dismay. They clutch at themselves, faces contorting. One by one, Brick's genius plan unfolds.

I glance at Brick, my lips curving. His eyes glitter with that sadistic gleam I've come to adore. Tane's men have no idea what's about to hit them. But we do. And we're ready.

The men's confusion shifts to alarm as the vibrations intensify. Their muted discomfort transforms into outright panic under the harsh fluorescent lights.

"Something's wrong!" one exclaims, beads of sweat dotting his brow. "I'm...I'm vibrating!"

I lean forward, pulse racing. "They're realizing it's not just in their heads."

"Okay, now increase the intensity."

I observe as he taps on the second button on one of the remotes, until it reaches its maximum. The corresponding henchman starts to writhe around in his chair, horror written on his face.

Tane looks on as we crank the remaining remotes and his top-ranking men all start dancing around.

"Wha-what in the world?" I ask.

"Good vibes only!" Brick yells, cackling with glee as the remaining men jump from their seats.

They're clawing at themselves now.

"What's that buzzing noise?" Tane yells. "Control yourselves, men!"

"These GPS chips you had us install, they're buzzing! Mine's buzzing inside me!"

Some of the men start clawing at their arms.

"GPS chips?" Tane asks, confusion painted on his face which is turning an infuriated shade of red. "What the hell are you talking about?"

"The ones you had us go get at the woo-woo shop," the spokesperson pants as he grates his fingers over himself in a desperate attempt to remove the buzzing situation.

"Huh?" Tane doubles down on his confusion. "The 'woo-woo shop'? You're not making any sense."

"Oh my god, did we really just... ". I stare at Brick.

"Abso-fucking-lutely that's what we just did," he grins. "I guess you could call this a bzzzzzz-ness meeting."

My eyes grow wide. "Oh my fucking god. This is insane..." I pause and glance at Brick. "Even for you!"

"Get mine out!" another man yells. One of them runs over to the table at the side of the room and grabs a knife intended to cut through an eye of beef after the meeting.

But instead, he digs it deep into his arm and then drops the knife as he uses his free hand to desperately dig around in his arm. He screams in pain and terror as he retrieves the small black item from deep inside his arm.

"This looks like something... familiar, but i can't place it. It's just not like any GPS chip I've ever seen before."

"That's because it's not a GPS chip, you idiot!" Tane screams. "It's one of those remote control vibrators you can get at the adult store. My wife has one just like it! Have you ever seen a GPS chip that huge, you fucking moron?!""

"What the hell? A vibrator?! What's it doing in my arm?"

The revelation just makes the other men work themselves into even more of a frenzy, and two of them clash heads in their simultaneous effort to dive for the knife that clattered to the floor earlier.

The glow of the monitors lights up Brick's face, casting harsh shadows across his chiseled features. I study his expression, searching for any cracks in that impenetrable façade. As always, I find none.

"This is wild," I exclaim as one of them starts digging in his arm in an effort to extract the vibrator and stop the buzzing. He seems oblivious to the blood that pours from his arm, a tangle of flesh and bone getting in the way as he attempts to remove the device.

My pulse kicks as the live feed plays. My thoughts drift to everything these men have done, everyone they've hurt. Including me. Heat blooms in my core, primal and aching. I want them to suffer. To feel even a fraction of my pain.

Another vaguely familiar face twists in confusion, then panic. His hand gropes at his arm. Right where the toy sits, buzzing away. "What the hell...?"

Excitement spears through me. My lips curve as I imagine the vibrations working deeper, driving them mad.

Brick's eyes gleam, feral and pleased. He knows what this will do to them. And he can't wait.

Neither can I.

The scene descends into chaos. Men stumble about, shouting and grappling at themselves in a futile effort to stop the relentless buzzing. Their lieutenant tries to restore order, arms raised placatingly.

"Everyone, calm down! We need to—"

"Calm down?" another interrupts, face twisted in disbelief. "Are you feeling this? We've been sabotaged! Operated on. *Someone has been inside our bodies*!"

Their panic is palpable through the screen. A heady rush courses through me as I take it all in. Brick outdid himself this time. Tane's men are coming undone at the seams, all thanks to us.

I meet Brick's eyes, lips curving wickedly. "They're falling apart," I purr. "This is our chance."

His answering smile is nothing short of feral. We've set the perfect trap, and now it's time to spring it. Tane won't know what hit him.

Tane's eyes flash dangerously. He grabs the nearest afflicted man by the shirt, giving him a rough shake.

"Tell me!" he roars. "How did this happen? Who did this to you?"

The man can only shake his head helplessly, teeth chattering from the relentless vibrations wracking his body. Tane shoves him away in disgust before rounding on the others.

"I want answers, now!" He slams a fist on the table, making them all jump. "Find out who sabotaged us. I'll flay them alive for this."

His men scramble to obey, fleeing the room. But it's no use. There's no stopping what Brick has unleashed in them. No countermeasure or antidote that can save them now.

Tane just doesn't know it yet. But he will.

And when he does, we'll be there to finish him off for good. I lick my lips in anticipation, adrenaline singing through my veins. The game is on.

The monitors go dark as we turn them off, the glow fading from our faces. Brick's vibrations have thrown Tane's men into chaos, just as planned.

Now it's time to act.

We gather around the table with the others, urgency charging the air. Aidan leans forward, his eyes blazing.

"This is our window," he says. "We need to hit them while they're disoriented."

"Agreed." I nod. "Let's let the others know we need to mobilize and take advantage of the chaos."

My pulse thrums with excitement. After waiting so long for this moment, it's finally here.

Brick grins, cracking his knuckles. "I've been looking forward to this. I knew it would create a real buzz."

I shake my head and laugh. This guy.

We head back to the compound, adrenaline surging through our veins.

Outside, the ocean crashes serenely against the shoreline. Inside, we gear up for war.

We've destabilized Tane's empire. Now it's time to tear it down for good.

As the others assemble so we can share what happened, Brick claps my shoulder. "Remember, this is just the beginning," he says, eyes glinting. "Stay sharp."

I meet his gaze and nod. We're ready.

CHAPTER FORTY-SEVEN

AIDAN

*T**he Following Day*

We're sitting at the large table in the kitchen, scanning websites for additional intel, when Dom's phone lights up. He glances at the caller ID and his shoulders tense.

"Yeah," he answers gruffly. There's a pause as he listens, his jaw clenching. "How bad?"

Another pause. Dom's eyes meet mine, his expression grim.

"Shit. Alright. Keep me updated." He ends the call and slams his phone down, his eyes wide.

"Tane's lost it. Fired his whole inner circle today, replaced them already with some secret team he's been training."

"Shit," I echo. My mind races, thoughts of Tane's ruthlessness swirling. This is bad news. Real bad. Or is it? It might be helpful to have him off-kilter from his usual poised self.

Dom runs a hand over his face. "He's getting paranoid. Desperate. That kind of move never ends well."

I nod, dread pooling in my gut. If Tane unravels, the whole island could erupt into chaos. We've seen what he's capable of when he feels threatened. How far will he go to maintain control?

"We need to keep our ears to the ground," I say. "A storm is coming, but we need to make sure we follow our plan, even if Tane is losing it."

Dom's eyes meet mine again, steely with determination. "We'll ride it out. We always do."

His words steady me. Together, we've weathered worse.

I take a long sip of my water, letting the icy cool liquid ground me. There's a tension in the air now, a shift. Word of Tane's power play will spread quickly through the island's underbelly.

"He's not just replacing people, though," Dom says after a moment. "I'm hearing he's using their families as leverage. Threatening them to keep the new guys in line."

My blood turns to ice in my veins. Going after innocent family members isn't a new thing for Tane, but as far as I know he hasn't targeted the families of his own men before.

"Fuck," I spit out. "That's not going to go over well."

Dom shakes his head, his expression thunderous. "No. Morale is tanking. People are questioning their loyalty. It's a mess."

I rake a hand through my hair, adrenaline spiking through me. "If his crew abandons him, Tane won't hesitate to burn everything down on his way out."

The thought makes my pulse pound in my ears. What will that mean for the rest of us, caught in the crossfire of Tane's breakdown? How do we protect ourselves and the people we care about from the wrath of a madman?

Dom's hand clasps my shoulder, steadying me. "We've got this, brother. One day at a time. We look out for our own."

I meet his resolute gaze and nod. Together, we've got this.

I grimace. "Let me make a few calls. Maybe we can use this to our advantage. I'm guessing the old crew didn't take kindly to being replaced."

"That's putting it mildly. Word is, anyone who walks gets a bullet in the back of the head." Dom's jaw clenches. "Lawrence tried to resign this morning... you know, the one who was raving about Slade and Aria's sticky man ribs. Tane had him executed on the spot. Shot him right in the head as he went to leave through the front door."

"Fuck," I curse, shock rippling through me. Lawrence was one of Tane's most trusted men. Ruthless, but we'd broken bread together over the years before he worked his way up. And he really did like those sticky ribs at Aria's soft opening. I guess he'll never get to know what was in them. Sometimes it's better not to read the nutritional label.

Dom nods, his eyes hard. "The ranks are turning on Tane. Nobody wants to work for a psycho who kills you for handing in your notice."

My mind races, thoughts of Aria and her safety overtaking everything else. "This could destabilize the entire island's underworld. We need to get in there first, before anyone else takes advantage of his doom spiral."

"We need to be ready for anything," Dom says grimly.

I grip my water bottle hard, fear and determination steeling my spine.

No matter what Tane does, I'll keep Angel and the rest of the Brixtons safe. Whatever it takes.

CHAPTER FORTY-EIGHT

ZEKE

The shadows dance across the dimly lit walls as I take my seat at the table with the others. Just when I think Aidan couldn't look more intense, he manages to, as he prepares to give us a rundown of what he was able to find out after Dom shared his news. His dark eyes meet mine, filled with that familiar sense of purpose and caution.

"So what's the plan, boss?" Brick asks, leaning forward eagerly. His rugged features are taut with anticipation.

Aidan runs both hands through his hair. "Tane's losing his grip even more now. It's time we make our move." His gravelly voice fills the room as the rest of us listen intently. "We have to act fast, because everyone else is likely hearing exactly the same information. We could set ourselves up for a bloodbath if we don't get in and get it done. We have one shot here."

A flicker of unease twists my gut. Tane won't go down easy. But the thought of finally taking him out, of watching his empire crumble...it makes my blood burn.

"Tonight's the night," Skyler says, his piercing gaze sweeping over each of us. "We've done the groundwork, and now we strike hard and fast before he has a chance to slither away."

Adrenaline surges through me as I picture wrapping my hands around Tane's throat. I want to be the one to squeeze the life out of him.

Dom grins, cracking his knuckles. "Let's do this."

I nod, resolve steeling my nerves. Tonight, Tane's reign of terror ends. By our hands.

I take a deep breath as I stare up at the looming silhouette of Tane's compound. Floodlights bathe the perimeter in harsh white, guarded by men with guns and snarling dogs straining against their leashes. Dom and the others fan out, melting into the shadows. My heart hammers against my ribs.

It's time.

I raise my hand in signal and the Snakes and Brixtons slither forward, dispatching the guards with quick efficiency. Screams and gunshots pierce the night but we move fast, swarming the grounds like a tide of vengeance.

Out of the corner of my eye I see Dimitri, his chiseled features set in a mask of cold determination. Our gazes connect for a brief moment before he disappears inside.

I follow close behind, my senses heightened. The interior is eerily quiet, like a held breath before a plunge. We clear room after room but find no sign of Tane.

A door creaks open at the end of a long hallway and I freeze. The barrel of a gun glints in the darkness.

Before the guard can fire, I lunge forward, knocking the weapon away.

We crash to the floor in a tangle of limbs.

I wrap my hands around his throat, squeezing until his struggles cease.

Panting, I get to my feet. A muffled shout echoes from behind the door and I feel a spark of savage delight.

I've found him. Tane's fate awaits.

For all of his power and self-belief, it doesn't take us long to subdue Tane. It makes me realize that he's not the giant monster character he'd become in my head. His power was bolstered by ruling a bunch of strong and loyal men. But loyalty only lasts so long when there's little payoff. And that's about to be Tane's fatal lesson.

"Oh, we're back here again? You idiots trying to get me?" He tries to play it cool as he glances around, no doubt willing his men to enter the room and save him in a hail of gunfire. "It didn't work last time, and it most certainly isn't going to now."

I smirk. "Dude, you're hardly in a position to negotiate." I gesture at his situation—tied to a chair in the middle of one of his ops rooms. Whiteboards line the walls, dotted with diagrams and dollar figures. But whatever dark deeds they're in reference to doesn't really matter. Not any more.

"Oh Tane, you think we came across you by accident tonight? That we haven't been planning this for a while?" Brick smirks.

"Well, your little plans didn't work last time and very nearly got the lot of you killed," Tane snarks back. What's the difference now?"

"You're hardly in a position to negotiate, bro," growls Brick. "Look at you in your tiny little chair."

Tane scowls and wriggles in his restraints, but there's no give and he quickly stops.

"Whatever. You guys are nothing. You run a tiny part of my operation. There are many men stronger than you, in mind and body. And I can't wait to watch you be crushed like the tiny little ants you are." He spits, and a glob of his saliva sails a few feet and lands on the tip of Brick's shoe.

Brick snarls and starts toward the elegant, suited man, but Aidan puts out a hand to stop him. Brick sighs and backs off, muttering about his shoe.

Tane glances around at each of us, his gaze settling on Dimitri and his group. "Jesus, every time I look there are more of you. You're multiplying like bacteria." He smirks. "Although this would be a case study to disprove survival of the fittest."

Brick snarls again.

"You look familiar," Tane says, glancing at Aria. "I know you from somewhere."

"Oh yes," Aria beams. "You were one of the first customers at my new restaurant. It was an honor having you under my roof, and being able to prepare a special meal just for you."

Recognition dawns in Tane's eyes. "Aha that's it," he nods. "I never forget a face..." he pauses. "Especially not one like yours."

Aria's facial expression remains neutral, but I notice the almost imperceptible shudder. But then she puffs herself up and smiles. "The ribs you ate? The one that your bald friend liked so much? They were human ribs. Ricky's in fact," says Aria.

Tane's face turns white as her words sink in.

"And in case that isn't enough for you, the paté was also made from several of your men. Those three guards of yours who disappeared. Oh, and the dessert, too. Fingernails, eyeballs, the whole shebang. A locally-sourced, farm-to-table approach where nothing goes to waste, you know?"

"Stanley, Boss and Takowsky?" His eyes narrow and his face grows mottled with rage. He's just about foaming at the mouth. "You're fucking with me."

"Nope," Aria shrugs. "Sorry, but you're a full-blown cannibal. And you really seemed to enjoy it, too."

Tane struggles in his restraints, just about turning green. Of course, he can't move, so he pukes his guts out on the floor beside him, for once his poised charm ruffled to pieces. A splash of his vomit lands on his no doubt very expensive shoes.

Brick snickers. "Well well well, karma is a bitch, and sometimes she's quick."

Dimitri clears his throat, and Tane's eyes fly to him. "You're an evil man, Tane Brown. And so it seems fitting to add cannibalism of your most loyal men to your list of atrocities. You do know, however, that eating the brains of another human is reported to make you crazy, right? Although clearly you've been able to check off that box for a while."

"You—you—" The normally very articulate Tane Brown cannot find words. Finally, he's able to spit it out. "Who the fuck are you? You look familiar, too?"

Dimitri's eyes darken. "So fitting for you. You annihilated my whole fucking family, killing my wife and daughter, and you don't even have the common decency to remember my face. We're really all nothings to you, aren't we?"

Tane's eyes narrow in confusion. "Oh, wait... was this several years ago?"

Fucking hell. For him not to remember, I can't even imagine how many people this man has killed... how many innocent women and children that he can't even have the decency to remember.

I snarl. "Enough!" I growl, and all eyes turn to look at me. "The truth, Tane, is that your men are a bunch of lemmings, idiots blindly loyal to you because of the chance at a sliver of your power. They don't care about you as a person, and many of them are clearly incapable of much except for following your instructions. And following instructions they think are from you."

Just when it seems like Tane's face couldn't get any paler, it somehow does.

"Even if today hadn't happened, we'd be coming after you again and again. Disrupting your business when you least expect it. You'd never be able to trust the ingredients in another meal. You'd never be able to trust any of your men to carry out the most basic of instructions without peering over their shoulder the entire time. You wouldn't be able to host a meeting without worrying your blathering idiot henchman have allowed us to insert personal pleasure devices *under their skin* like absolute morons! Is that the kind of life you want to lead, Tane? Is that really the quality of empire you're able to create?"

"Jesus. When you put it that way, I could probably go on Temu and find a better option," growls Brick as he sharpens a wicked blade. Tane's eyes flick to the shiny blade of the knife, and he visibly pales.

"I am a *businessman*!" Tane explodes. "I have done so much for these islands! Provided jobs, created charities."

"Everyone knows you've come here to exploit vulnerable people and make them do bad things, Tane. Nobody's falling for your philanthropy act."

"And you know what seems fitting? For someone like you to go out with a bang. And you know what this island is really good at? Fireworks. They're like the island's favorite pastime."

His eyes grow wide. "Please, no."

"But you love fireworks, Tane. Didn't you spend over a million dollars at your company's fourth of July bash? And didn't you ignore that the fireworks factory you commissioned them from went up in a blaze and killed all the workers?"

"Well, yes... but that didn't mean I want to be a firework myself. And as for the workers, that's just part of doing business."

"Come on, don't be so selfish," says Brick. "Appease the masses. After all you've put them through, the only fitting thing is for you to go out this way. In a way that nobody will ever forget. Isn't that what you've always wanted, anyway, Tane? To leave a legacy?"

"Yes," he splutters, "but not like this."

"Beggars can't be choosers, I'm afraid," Brick shrugs, his expression calm as if he's giving advice to an old friend. "You're going to have to take your lumps. Blood in, blood out and all that. All the things you drummed into your men over the years. And what did you say it was? Just business?"

For the first time, I see true fear in Tane's eyes. I didn't know if he was capable, but it turns out that inside, he's just a man. A scared man with a nice suit. "Listen, you've proven your point," he whimpers. "You want in on running the island business? I'll hand it over to you, no questions asked. I'll move to the mainland, you'll never hear from me again. I swear. Whatever you want... just not this."

I smirk at his attempt to negotiate with us, to offer us an attractive slice of his business pie after resisting us, keeping us small, for so long. I shake my head. "We're not idiots, Tane. Despite your more atrocious qualities, I'll give it to you that you're a shrewd businessman. Even if you did set up a satellite business on the mainland, these islands will forever be home to you."

"Right?" says Skyler, glaring at Tane. "You'll find a way back, and it'll be a constant game of wack-a-mole, finding out where you pop up next and having to smack you and your men down over and over again. It sounds exhausting, frankly, and while I'm confident we'll always find a way to beat you, it's going to drain our precious resources. We can't have you as a distraction any more, Tane."

"Yep, what did you call it?" Brick growls. "Just business? Collateral damage?" And with that, Brick puts a gun to Tane's head and pulls the trigger.

Tane's eyes go wide as the gun clicks and he braces for impact.

But nothing happens.

"Haha, just kidding," grins Brick. "Wanted to keep you guessing right until the end."

Relief is written all over Tane's face as he tries to catch his breath.

Without warning, Brick pulls another gun out of his waistband and shoots Tane right between the eyes.

Blood splatters on the opposite wall, along with pieces of Tane's skull and brain matter.

"That felt... anticlimactic?" Angel says. "He's really gone?" She walks over to make sure, as if him having his skull blown out at point-blank range left any room for error.

"He's had enough of a platform for far too long, and he just would have kept going on and on about how powerful he is, even when he's a husk of his former self. I was finding it depressing," Brick shrugs. "Him dead, that's all we needed. The show is yet to come. One that he, for once, doesn't get to enjoy. He'll be a posthumous star in the sky, just not the way he intended. Just you wait and see."

CHAPTER FORTY-NINE

DEVON

*L*ater that day

"Well, it's time for the finale," says Brick. "We couldn't just, like... bury him or cremate him in a traditional way. He was a special man, and he deserves a fitting sendoff."

"What are you going to do? Throw him a parade?" Slade looks at Brick like he's gone mad... even madder than usual. "Dedicate a public holiday in his honor?"

Brick shakes his head. "Don't be ridiculous. Just you wait for it. Look at the sky in about an hour."

"Okay...?" Slade replies, none the wiser, and he's not too happy about being kept in the dark.

"Trust.... trust and let go," says Brick, winking at Slade. "We're all on the same team, remember?"

"Oh okay, fine. I trust you, you psycho." Slade rolls his eyes, but I detect a smirk forming. He tries so hard to project a curmudgeonly persona, but we know that deep down Slade is as soft and fluffy as the delicious scones he bakes for us occasionally. Especially when it comes to Angel. "Wait, you were joking about the fireworks thing, I thought?"

Brick just laughs.

Exactly an hour later, we're standing outside and there's a huge bang and the sky suddenly lights up.

"What the hell?" I frown. My first thought is it's a bomb or someone storming our location, and I duck for cover, but then there's another bang and I realize this must be the sendoff Brick mentioned.

The fireworks burst into the air, shattering into what looks like a million pieces. Red, white and blue—to symbolize freedom. The freedom that's now possible for the people of these islands.

It's poetic, somehow. Watching someone so evil turn into something so beautiful.

I gasp as the finale begins, the remnants of Tane exploding into millions of tiny balls of light.

"It's fitting, in some ways," I say. "He did leave an impression on these islands, bad as though it may have been. And people are going to remember these fireworks forever." A thought strikes me. "Maybe it'll even serve as a warning to others not to challenge our new place here. If we can do this to someone like Tane Brown, who instilled terror for so long, maybe others will be hesitant to try."

"Yeah," Rake snickers. "I feel bad for anyone who puts on a display for Fourth of July or New Years after this. The baseline expectations for fireworks displays has increased exponentially."

I smirk. "If that's the worst part of getting rid of Tane—increased fireworks expectations—I think we're okay."

He laughs and wraps his long, tattooed arm around my shoulder, giving me an enthusiastic squeeze. "You're right. I think the positives far outweigh the negative here."

Together, with me leaning into his torso, we watch the rest of the show in silence, just taking it all in.

Just as the fireworks stop, the roar of a motorcycle gets louder and, soon, Brick comes into view. He's atop a brand new-looking machine, its chrome fixtures reflecting against the nightlights. And then I see the streamers. They're long, hanging off each of the handlebars. A fleshy tone, with an unmistakeable pattern. Tane's back tattoo, now in dangly tassel form.

As Brick makes his way past, he waves as if he's performing in some type of pageant, the streamers flying proudly as he goes. "I'll be right back!" he calls out. "Just need to take this through the main streets so everyone can see."

I shake my head and laugh, meeting Angel's gaze as she does the same.

There is no end to what this man will come up with, I swear.

And as he glances over at Angel, his eyes gleaming, I know that she wouldn't have it any other way.

CHAPTER FIFTY

SKYLER

I'm sitting with Zeke on the rooftop of the Brixtons' compound.

It's a calm evening with a cool breeze, the sky painted in hues of orange and purple as the sun sets. The sounds of the city are distant but present, providing a constant hum in the background.

We're seated on a bench, staring out at the horizon, both lost in our thoughts.

Zeke glances at me and clears his throat. "I'm proud of you, man. You finally got over yourself and now you get to be your real self. I've seen you grow so much since we first met, but this is different—you're a changed man. It's like you've finally broken free of the chains that were holding you back."

I turn to Zeke, a hint of a smile playing on my lips. "You see it?" Zeke's opinion means the world to me.

He nods. "Yes, I really do. Your dad had this invisible cage around you, but the actual guy would probably want nothing more than for you to succeed. But all the terrible things he did... it created a monster in your head."

I nod. "Well, I still think he was a monster. But there was good to him, too. He wasn't all evil. I don't think anyone is."

Zeke raises an eyebrow, contemplating my words. "Even Tane?"

I sigh, leaning back against the bench. "You know, I've thought about that a lot, and I think it applies to him, too. As much as I'd find it easier if we were certain he was this hundred percent evil guy, he still seemed to be a fairly decent family man. At least, he cared about his children from what I could tell." I shrug, thinking back to the family photos I saw taking pride of place across his various compounds. Maybe it was all for show, but maybe there was more to it. I guess we'll never know. "To them, I'm sure he wasn't the evil ogre and madman the rest of us knew him as. To them, he was probably dada or papi or something."

Zeke nods slowly and frowns. "Yeah, you're right. The world would be easier to understand if everything was binary. But we all live in the shades of gray when you think about it. Everyone's done something that goes against their own code. And everyone's code is vastly different."

We sit in comfortable silence for a moment, reflecting on our own experiences and the people we've encountered.

After a while, Zeke speaks up again. "If we saw the world in black and white, we'd miss the truth of what it means to be human. We all have our demons." He hesitates, but then continues. "You know, for a long time, I thought I was just as bad as the people we fight against. I've done things I'm not proud of, things that haunt me."

I look at Zeke and feel a surge of empathy. This man, so focused on making sure everyone else is safe and okay, rarely sharing the burdens he carries within himself. "We all have. But the fact that you reflect on it, that you strive to be better, it means you're not like them."

"Yeah, this whole thing has taught me that leadership isn't just about giving orders. It's about guiding others through the darkness and showing them the light. It's a heavy burden, leading this group. But it's moments like these that remind me why we do it. And there's nobody else I'd rather do it with."

I place a hand on Zeke's shoulder. "We're in this together, Zeke. And we'll keep pushing forward, for the sake of everyone who believes in us."

CHAPTER FIFTY-ONE

ANGEL

"Brick, why is there a parrot in our living room?" The brightly colored bird is sitting in a cage smack bang in the middle of the room, its claws wound tightly around a wooden rod as it shuffles from side to side. Occasionally, it cocks its head at me, and I have the overwhelming urge to do it back.

Brick beams and approaches the cage, sticking his finger out. "Look what a good girl you are. Yes you are," he says, in a voice typically reserved for puppies and kittens. He turns to me. "The parrot's name is Polly. Polly Cule.'

"Oh my god, Brick. Are you serious? You're too much."

"Actually, it was Rake's idea! We had a bird name-picking session!"

Slade walks into the room, a plate and dishcloth in hand and a frown on his face. "Are you fucking kidding me right now? You brought a bird and called it that annoying fucking word?"

"Polly Cule! Polly Cule!" the bird says, on queue.

"Oh jesus, there are two of you now." Slade shakes his head, rolls his eyes and stomps back into the kitchen, but I swear the corner of his mouth twitches as he goes by.

"Why am I not surprised?" I laugh. "Although I think you're making that up, the part about a name-picking session. Clearly, you brought the bird *after* you came up with the name. You didn't just go out and buy a bird and then name it."

Brick sighs. "Okay okay. That may be how it happened."

Devon comes rushing into the room. She gives the bird a weird look but clearly there's something more pressing than asking about Polly Cule.

"Well, it looks like we've officially made it!" she says, breathless.

"Why do you say that?" I quirk a brow.

"Good girl! Good girl!" Polly Cule suddenly shrieks.

Devon stops for a second, gives him side eye, then shrugs. She's just as used to Brick's shenanigans now as I am. "We got our first bad review on our clothing line..." her voice trails off.

"What kind of review?" I ask. "You seem disappointed."

"Well, there are a few of them. And we got a few one stars."

"Our collection hasn't even come out yet! How are people reviewing it? Nobody has even had a chance to see it, except for people who came to our little fashion show."

"I know! 'What the fuck did I just wear?' it says." Devon frowns.

"How bizarre! Who would write that?" Slade quirks a brow. "Me?"

"People will write anything for attention online these days," sighs Angel. "Aria said something similar happened to her with the restaurant. Said her salad had too much salad in it or something."

"Oh really?" Devon's eyes grow wide. "I want to check out her page."

"Jesus, it's full of one stars," she says.

"What do they say?" I ask, confused. "Her restaurant has only been officially open a few days."

"One star. Deducted four because there was a guest sitting near me that reminded me of the whole Scandoval situation."

"And that's her fault how exactly? What's she supposed to do... ban men with mustaches?" Slade stops. "Not that I know what that phrase means." He turns bright red.

Devon continues. "Another one star: 'Reminding myself to come back and eat here later.'"

"Huh?" I scrunch up my nose. "Make that make sense."

"Here's another: 'Loved it! Would recommend to everyone!'"

"And that's a one star??" I furrow my brow. Just when my life was starting to make more sense...

"Yeah, I guess that person has a reverse scale." Devon shrugs.

An idea strikes me. "Okay now do Skyler's surf school!"

"Are you sure you wanna do this?" Devon's eyes meet mine.

"Yes!" I pull out my phone. "Two stars. Expected to come out of 60 minute surfing lesson with the skills of Kelly Slater." I roll my eyes and continue. "One star. When I called about the lesson, he had the audacity to say I should be able to swim first. Can one not surf with water wings?"

Devon taps away at her phone. "Here's another one: I like my surfing instructors to say less and show off more. This was the most terrible surfing lesson I've ever had. I don't like the way he explained things in the lesson. I really wanted to like it but I just couldn't make it through, and ended the lesson early. I don't know.. someone else might like it, I suppose."

I laugh. "Wow. And the moral of the story is?"

"Never go online and read the reviews," Devon laughs too. "Some of them are brutal, and many are just unhinged and they're not helping anybody. They're not going to help us build a better clothing line—our actual customers who like our products will do that. Our teams and our focus groups. And the reviews will most certainly be there if and when you decide to read them. No need to force the issue now."

I nod as I absorb her words. She's right.

From now on, I'm going to focus on creating this incredible clothing line.

Haters can hate, but they never were the right people for me, anyway.

With Devon and my men, I have found my people.

There for the right reasons, and supporting me to achieve my dreams. Every step of the way.

CHAPTER FIFTY-TWO

ANGEL

"I know it probably sounds funny... hell, it sounds strange to me... but I'm going to miss Tane Brown in a way." As soon as the words leave my mouth, I flinch. What a cringe thing to say.

"You're going to miss Tane? What the fuck is wrong with you?" Devon narrows her eyes.

"I know, I know. Not the person... not the things he did or the people he hurt... but, you know. It feels like in a warped kind of a way he's the reason we're all here, together."

"I think I get what you mean but that's a weird way to say it. And yes, we're better for having known him. But I wouldn't say it's worth the cost... to us or anyone else." She gives me a pointed look. "In fact, if I had to call it, I'd say this feeling stems from your deep-seated daddy issues."

I laugh. Where her words would once have stung, I take them for what they are. A gentle poke at a truth. "I wholeheartedly agree. Maybe it's safer to say I'm grateful for the experiences that led us to this point rather than suggesting a Tane Brown Appreciation Day. And he, in fact, was quite insignificant to the whole thing once the ball got rolling."

"Yep, you're right. He just happened to be 'the guy'. The truth is, there are plenty more where he came from. Always will be. The next guys, bigger and better, readying themselves to take his place. We've just managed to eradicate the ones most interested in the island."

"We'll always have to be on the lookout. Remain vigilant. To some people, we're going to be seen as the new Tane Brown."

"Ugh. That's some terrible branding."

"Yep, won't be putting that on our sports bras, I can tell you that much," grins Devon.

"I can't help but think about how everything is coming to an end. How we've been through so much together," I say. "It feels a bit like when you finish high school and everyone writes, 'never change' in your yearbook, and promises to keep in touch. But in reality, we all know that's a lie. People drift away at the best of times. It's natural to grow in different directions. But the thought of being away from you guys now—it seems surreal and horrible to me. I don't want to go back to the 'before', but I also don't want to jump into a future that doesn't have you in it in this same way."

"Well, you know what… I've been thinking along similar lines. What if we take this further? What if we start to expand our compound to really support our joint operations. We can maintain our separate interests, and we'd do that outside of this. But the things we're interested in working on together? We could go all in. Maximize our resources. Build something great."

Wow. To think we didn't used to be able to get these guys in the same room together for more than ten seconds without a punch being thrown… it really does feel like a different time. Like her wild idea is an actual, tangible possibility.

"What have you learned from all this, anyway?" I glance at her.

"Oh god," Devon pleads, "please don't make us go around in a circle with the guys like some sad after-school special."

"No no, I was asking you in particular because I've seen you go through some massive hurdles and I'm mad proud of you." I shrug. "You've taught me that you can go through hurdles and you don't have to jump over them, by the way," I add.

"What do you mean?" Devon looks confused.

"Let's not pretend you're some type of dainty pole vaulter, gently leaping over challenges to get past them. You're all spit and venom, ignoring the rules, and bashing through the obstacles like a roller derby jammer in the final minutes of a close bout. But how you get to the other side rarely matters. It's that you get there."

"You're the best thing that ever happened to us, you know?" Devon says, her expression softening as she squeezes my arm. "I don't know if we'd even still be here unless it was for you. And now you've taken something that was okay... maybe even very good.. and you've made it into something amazing."

"I feel the same way about you," I say, reaching out to squeeze her hand. "My old life just seems drab and boring, like you and the guys have brought color and sound and light into it. We're nobody and nothing without you."

Devon smiles and her cheeks flush slightly. "You flatter me, but I feel exactly the same way about you guys. Everything seemed complicated and kind of... I don't know... empty, I guess, before I met you. And now it's just so... full."

Of course, Brick leads the guys into the room right at this moment, overhearing the conversation. He immediately cracks up and jabs Slade in the ribcage with his elbow. Slade laughs in turn, and the others soon follow. "We have no problem keeping you full, my dear," grins Brick.

"Oh stop it, you!" But I grin back. He's not lying.

"I don't like that this has made me trust strangers more than I did before." Slade complains.

Brick wiggles his eyebrows. "Oh Slade, has this cured you of your stranger danger?!"

"No, Brick." Slade shakes his head and scowls. "We are *meant* to have stranger danger. Stranger danger is a good thing! It keeps us alive!"

"What about accepting people as they are, and expanding our sense of community by surrounding ourself by people who may not be exactly like us?" Brick puts his pointer fingers to his thumbs and closes his eyes as if he's deep in meditation, humming to himself. When he eventually opens them again, they're twinkling with amusement.

"BRICK!" Slade explains, his eyes flicking to the dishcloth in his hand like he's contemplating swatting him with it. "Goddammit you are frustrating."

Brick smiles sweetly. "But you love me."

Slade sigh, visibly exasperated, but a little smile gives him away, tugging at the corner of his mouth like the hands of a toddler at the hem of their mother's shirt in the candy aisle at the grocery store.

"For real, though," says Slade. "A moment of truth...you'd think with everything going on it would just encourage me further into the shadows. To force
me into some hermit life, surrounded by the only person I can ultimately
trust—myself. Yet, here I am. And it's like this entire process has softened me
somehow. Normally I wouldn't like it, and god knows I've fought against it
enough. But with you guys—and Angel in particular—I guess you've helped
me to realize it's okay to trust. And even love."

My heart almost bursts with pride at Slade sharing his feelings with the group
in this way.

"Are you saying you love me, Slade?" Brick asks, grinning. Oh god, he just has
to keep pushing it. Slade's eyes narrow and for a moment I think he's going to
snap.

But instead, he opens his mouth to speak. "Yes, Brick." he says, squeezing
his mouth together in a thin line while his eyes meet Brick's. "I do love you."
As soon as the words come out, it's almost too much. Slade's body tenses, as if
waiting for a blow to come out of left field, just because he uttered those words.

Brick is unable to contain himself. "Slade, are you saying that if we were in
some world involving MM, where there were swords crossing all over the place,
you'd want to cross swords with me?"

I laugh and shake my head. This guy.

Instead of running to the kitchen to grab a sharp knife, Slade just laughs.
"Yes, Brick. I guess that is what I'm saying. Although it's purely hypothetical,
so don't get any ideas."

Brick beams. "Slade likes me. He really likes me."

I can't help but laugh again.

With Brick on my team, life will never be boring.

As if on queue, Brick reaches out and gently touches my jaw. "My sweet
Valkyrie. We have a surprise for you..."

CHAPTER FIFTY-THREE

ANGEL

Blindfolded and giddy with anticipation, I cling to Brick's arm as he guides me along the uneven ground.

"Come on, Angel. We're almost there," Slade says from behind me. His breath tickles the back of my neck, sending shivers down my spine.

"You're not taking me to some deserted warehouse to chop me into little pieces, are you?" I tease. My heart pounds with each step, a delicious blend of fear and excitement. These men could do anything to me, and I'd let them.

Brick chuckles. "My sweet Valkyrie, if we wanted to chop you up, we wouldn't waste time on a romantic date first."

I swallow hard. "Good to know." I know they love me more than anything, but my mind still likes to play pranks on me every now and then. I mean, they did kidnap me in the first place... muscle memory, I guess.

The air feels different here, heavy and salty. Seagulls cry out in the distance. We must be at the beach, although, to be fair, most places on this island are on it or close to it.

"Are we going to Aria's?" I guess. The guys are always spoiling me with trips to my favorite restaurant. And I don't just say that because the owner has become like a sister to me. Her food and drinks are seriously to die for, and not in a Tane Brown's henchmen kind of way.

"Nope." Slade squeezes my shoulders. "Somewhere even better, I reckon. But don't tell her that."

My mind races with possibilities, each one more tantalizing than the last. A private island? A secluded beach house? A yacht on the open sea, far from prying eyes?

I lick my lips, trembling in anticipation. "You can't leave me in suspense like this!"

Brick stops walking and presses his body against mine. I feel every hard line of muscle through our clothes. "Patience, little one." He kisses the tip of my nose. "All will be revealed soon enough."

Slade's hands slide down to my waist, pulling me back against his chest. I'm sandwiched between them, acutely aware of their strength and the growing bulge in each man's pants.

"Trust us," Slade whispers in my ear. "You're going to love this surprise."

I do trust them. Implicitly. These dangerous men are the four loves of my life, and they would never steer me wrong.

My heart flutters with excitement and nerves. Whatever they have planned, I know it's going to be an experience I'll never forget.

The pier creaks beneath our feet as we walk further out to sea. The sounds of the city fade behind us, replaced by the gentle lapping of waves. A salty breeze kisses my skin, carrying the fresh scent of the ocean.

My pulse quickens. We're definitely getting on a boat.

"Can I take the blindfold off now?" I ask eagerly.

"Not yet," Roman says from behind me. His large hand strokes the small of my back in a soothing gesture.

After a few more minutes of walking, we come to a stop. The pier sways under my feet as the guys untie my blindfold. I blink in the bright sunlight reflecting off the water, spots dancing in my vision.

When my eyes adjust, I gasp.

We're standing in front of a massive luxury catamaran, gleaming white sails billowing in the wind. Two levels of polished wooden decks are adorned with plush lounge chairs and an open bar.

It's the most stunning vessel I've ever seen.

"Do you like it?" Aidan asks with an uncharacteristically shy grin. From the way he runs his hand through his hair, I know straight away that he's been anxious about whether or not I'd like this surprise.

I throw my arms around his neck and kiss him soundly. "It's perfect!"

His shoulders readjust in what I can only assume is relief and perhaps a little excitement.

Brick sweeps me up in his arms, spinning me around until I'm dizzy with delight. "Only the best for our girl."

"The captain will take us wherever you want to go," Slade says, wrapping his arms around my waist from behind. "We have the catamaran for the entire day."

My heart swells with love for these men. They always know how to make me feel special.

"Then what are we waiting for?" I say breathlessly. "Let's set sail!"

The engines rumble to life as we board the catamaran. This is turning out to be the most romantic date ever. I have a feeling the adventure is only just beginning...

We cruise along the coast, soaking in the sun and enjoying glasses of champagne. The guys take turns feeding me bites of cheese, fruit, and chocolate as I lounge between them. "This is the life," I giggle, feeling like a fancy guest on *Below Deck* but without the cameras in my face or the staff on board acting the fool.

When the catamaran anchors in a secluded cove, they lead me downstairs to the main deck. My breath catches at the sight before me.

Lights are strung up along the rails, and blankets and cushions are strewn about. More champagne is on ice, along with an array of desserts.

It's the perfect setting for romance.

Brick pulls me into his arms, swaying gently to music only he can hear. "Dance with me, Valkyrie."

I melt against his chest, following his lead. Slade cuts in, then Roman, then Aidan. We dance and laugh, perfectly at ease in each other's arms.

As darkness falls, we cuddle up together to gaze at the stars. The sky is awash with constellations, the Milky Way stretching endlessly above us. The warm breeze carries the scent of the sea.

It's pure bliss being here with the men I love.

Roman nuzzles my neck, his stubble scratching my skin. "What would you like to do now, my love?"

A delicious shiver runs down my spine. I know exactly what I want.

"I want you to make love to me," I whisper. "All of you."

Brick growls low in his throat, eyes smoldering. "Your wish is our command."

They undress me slowly, their hands and mouths exploring every inch of my bare skin. The combination of their warm mouths and the cool air create goosebumps all over me.

I tug at their clothes in turn, craving the feeling of their hard bodies against mine.

When we're all naked under the starlight, I give myself over to pleasure. Tonight I belong to them, body and soul, and it's the sweetest surrender.

Slade captures my mouth in a searing kiss, his tongue dancing with mine. I moan into his mouth, desire pooling hot and heavy between my thighs.

Brick nuzzles the curve of my neck, scattering kisses along my collarbone. "So beautiful," he murmurs. "All ours."

Roman trails his fingers down my spine, making me shiver. "We're going to make you feel so good, baby."

I whimper in delight as Aidan strokes the inside of my thigh. "Please..."

"Patience, darling," Slade croons. "We have all night."

Brick's lips suddenly graze my thigh, his stubble rasping against my sensitive skin. I whimper, squirming against my restraints. Why did they have to tie me up? It's maddening not being able to touch them.

"Look at you, Angel," Roman murmurs. "You're absolutely perfect." He captures my mouth in a searing kiss, effectively distracting me from Brick's slow ascent.

Aidan and Slade continue their sensual assault, their hands roaming my body as Brick's mouth closes over my clit. I gasp into Roman's mouth, back arching off the cushions.

Brick's talented tongue works its magic, lapping and sucking until I'm writhing uncontrollably. He slides two fingers inside me, crooking them just so.

Stars explode behind my eyelids. I come with a muffled cry, inner walls clamping down on Brick's fingers.

He doesn't stop, drawing out my orgasm until I'm trembling. Only then does he lift his head, wiping his mouth with the back of his hand.

"So sweet," he rasps, dragging his fingers through my slick heat.

I whimper, beyond words. How is it possible to feel so much pleasure?

"You're so wet," he groans. "So ready for us."

They continue to lavish me with slow, sensual caresses, stroking and kissing every inch of my skin. I writhe beneath their skillful hands, aching to be filled.

Brick kneels between my legs again, this time guiding his cock to my entrance. He pushes in slowly, stretching me inch by inch.

I moan at the sudden intrusion, nails digging into his shoulders, although by this time I'm delirious with need.

He starts moving in a slow, torturous grind, dragging his cock along my inner walls.

"So tight," he hisses. "So perfect."

I cry out as he begins to move, hard and deep.

Roman claims my mouth in a searing kiss, muffling my moans.

When he pulls back, Slade slips two fingers into my mouth. "Suck," he commands softly.

I eagerly obey, swirling my tongue around his digits.

"That's it," he growls. "You're our good girl, especially when you're being bad."

Aidan kneads my breasts, rolling my nipples between his fingers.

Sharp bolts of pleasure shoot through me with every thrust of Brick's hips.

It's sheer bliss being surrounded by these men, all focused on giving me pleasure.

Brick's thrusts rock my body, pushing me closer and closer to the edge again. His hands grip my hips, fingers digging into my flesh as he pounds into me.

"Do you remember that scene from Titanic?" he pants. "Where Rose is leaning over the front of the ship, arms outstretched, while Jack stands behind her?"

A vivid image flashes through my mind and I moan, clenching around his cock. The fantasy of recreating that iconic moment with Brick sends a fresh wave of arousal coursing through my veins.

"I'm going to do that to you, Valkyrie," he growls. "Bend you over the railing and take you just like Jack did Rose... the way I like to imagine it really happened, not the clothed version in the movie. Would you like that?"

"Yes," I gasp. "Oh god, yes."

He chuckles, the sound dark and sinful. "I knew you would."

"But... what if I fall in?"

"Then we'll jump in right after you, of course," he says. "Not even the ocean could keep us away from you."

Without further words, he takes me by the hand and guides me to the front of the boat. He positions me so I'm front and center, facing out toward the dark ocean, its vastness stretching out before us under the twinkling stars.

He pushes himself in behind me and another powerful thrust lifts me onto my tiptoes. I'm already so close, hovering on the edge of bliss.

His power, and his sheer size behind me causes my pussy to clench like crazy, the coil continuing to tighten as he thrusts.

The noise of him slapping into me from behind rivals the slaps of the wave against the boat. The front of my body digs into the cool metal railing, but I don't mind the pain one bit.

A shadow falls over us as Slade approaches, desire burning in his cobalt eyes. Without a word, he lifts himself onto the railing as I move back to give him a little room, positioning his hips directly in front of my face.

I know what he wants. What they all want. To use me, to claim me, to mark me as theirs in every way possible.

The thought sends a fresh wave of heat flooding my core. I glance up at Slade through half-lidded eyes, my mouth falling open in invitation.

He wastes no time, guiding his cock between my lips. I take him in eagerly, humming around his length as I lavish the sensitive tip with my tongue.

Slade snarls, tangling his fingers in my hair. Behind me, Brick's thrusts grow more forceful, pushing me onto Slade's cock with every snap of his hips.

I'm dizzy with need and desire, caught between them as they plunge into me from both ends. This is heaven—this is home. Being filled and surrounded by the men I love, giving myself over to them completely.

We move as one, a well-oiled machine designed for pleasure. The coil in my belly winds tighter and tighter, fueled by their grunts and groans and the lewd sounds of flesh on flesh.

"Come for me, Valkyrie," Brick commands. "Let go and come for me."

His words tip me over, shattering my restraint. I explode around him with a scream, my inner walls clamping down on his cock.

"Good girl," he rasps, and then he roars, burying himself inside me as he finds his own release, his hips jerking against my ass.

Slade's cock throbs, a sure sign he's close. I redouble my efforts, hollowing my cheeks as I suck him deep.

A guttural cry spills from his lips. Salty warmth floods my mouth as he spills down my throat, his grip tightening almost painfully in my hair.

I gasp as Brick pulls out, leaving me empty and wanting.

But before I can protest, Slade guides me back over to the cushions where Aidan and Roman are patiently waiting, and settles between my thighs.

"My turn," he growls, grasping my hips. He sheathes himself inside me with one smooth stroke, stretching my walls.

I cry out at the sudden intrusion, my nails digging into his shoulders. He starts moving in a slow, torturous grind, dragging his cock along my inner walls.

"So tight," he hisses. "So perfect."

Roman and Aidan resume their sensual assault, their massive hands roaming my body as Brick plunders my mouth. I'm drowning in pleasure, every nerve ending alight with ecstasy.

I break away from Brick's kiss to moan, writhing beneath Slade as he pounds into me.

"That's it, Angel," Roman croons. "Let go. Come all over Slade's cock. Cover it in your delicious cum."

Slade picks up the pace, snapping his hips against mine.

I moan again, and I know I'm getting close. From the looks in their eyes, the guys see it too.

"That's it, baby," Roman croons. "Come for us."

The coil in my belly winds tighter and tighter until it snaps, sending shockwaves through my body. I come again with a scream, my inner walls clamping down on Slade's cock.

He growls, burying himself to the hilt as he spills inside me.

I cling to him, aftershocks rippling through my core.

Slade collapses on top of me, both of us breathless. The others wrap around us, a tangle of sweat-slicked limbs under the stars.

My heart overflows with love for these men. Together we've forged something rare and beautiful, a bond as deep as the ocean that surrounds us.

This is where I belong. In their arms, and in their hearts. Always.

No words are needed. They aren't necessary here—not in this place we've carved out for ourselves. A sanctuary from the world, filled with love and desire and passion.

This is home. This is heaven. This is everything.

We collapse onto the cushions, a tangle of sweat-slicked limbs as we struggle to catch our breath. Brick wraps his arms around me, pulling my back flush against his chest.

"I love you, my Valkyrie," Brick murmurs, pressing a kiss to my shoulder.

"I love you too," I whisper.

The waves lap at the hull of the catamaran, rocking us gently. I'm drifting in a sea of bliss, anchored only by the warmth of their bodies pressed against mine.

A soft kiss brushes my temple, followed by Aidan's gravelly tone. "Ready for round two, angel?"

I hum, nuzzling into his chest. As much as I'd love to stay here forever, we have only rented this boat for the day. And there are still so many wicked things I want to do with them before our time runs out.

"Greedy girl." Brick nips at my ear, hands roaming to cup my breasts. "You'll get your fill, don't you worry."

Heat pools low in my belly at his words. I tilt my head to capture Slade's mouth, tasting myself on his lips. By the time we break apart, desire has reignited in my veins—hot and insatiable.

Roman brushes a strand of hair from my face, eyes glowing with affection. ..and lust. "Where to next, Angel?"

I grin, pushing to my feet on shaky legs. The catamaran sways under me, but four pairs of strong hands keep me steady. "The netting."

Understanding dawns on their faces, followed swiftly by hunger. In unison, they lift and carry me to the front of the boat. Aidan climbs onto the net first, settling against the railing with his legs spread.

He retrieves a small tube from his pocket, and snaps it open, coating his cock with the viscous lube.

"Have a seat, Angel." His smirk is positively sinful, patting his thighs in invitation.

I moan as I realize the deliciousness he has planned. My pussy has been filled twice today, but my ass needs some attention.

I straddle his hips, gasping as his cock slowly slides into my ass and stretches me deliciously full. I lean back against his chest with a contented sigh, baring myself for the others.

Aidan nuzzles my throat, hands splayed over my ribs. "Look at you. So perfect, so willing. Our sweet, insatiable angel."

Heat suffuses my cheeks at the praise, heart overflowing with love for them. And when Roman steps forward, his beautiful cock in hand, I open my thighs wider for him gladly— ready to be filled and surrounded once more.

Ready to be home.

Aidan's leans back and his strong arms wrap around my waist, holding me steady as Roman sinks into my pussy with a groan. The sensation of being filled so completely, front and back, sends stars exploding behind my eyelids.

"That's it, Angel," Roman murmurs, brushing his lips over my collarbone. "Let us take care of you."

I whimper, beyond words, awash in pleasure and sensation. The catamaran rocks gently beneath us, waves lapping at the hull and carrying us along on their rhythmic pulse. We move as one, a single entity fused together in body and soul, chasing release and connection.

Roman's gaze locks with mine, pupils blown wide with desire, and I drown in those fathomless blue depths. "Come for us, Angel. Let go."

The coil in my belly snaps, pleasure ricocheting through every nerve. I cry out, vision going white, distantly aware of Aidan and Roman following after. We cling to one another, panting harshly, as the tremors fade into blissful lassitude.

Brick and Slade join us then, wrapping us up in strong arms and soft blankets. Their hands glide over my skin, grounding and soothing, as I drift in a sea of contentment.

"Thank you," I whisper, tilting my head to meet each of their gazes in turn. "For loving me, for giving me this—for being mine."

"Always, my love. Our sweet Angel," Roman murmurs, pressing a kiss to my forehead. "From the moment I first saw you, I knew you were meant to be ours. You have our hearts, now and forever."

The others echo his sentiment, surrounding me in a cocoon of love and warmth. I close my eyes with a smile, basking in the joy and wonder of having found my home—my family—in them.

CHAPTER FIFTY-FOUR

AIDAN

We're sitting around the large table in our compound. There's an air of anticipation in the room as we work to figure out what's next. All fourteen of us—Angel and us Brixtons, Devon and the Snakes, and Aria and the rest of the Unknowns.

I want to be happy with everything that's happened—after all, we just successfully executed our mission, but there's something holding me back from being truly excited about it. I sigh, hating to be the one to bring everyone down. "You know this isn't really over, right?" I run a hand through my hair.

Roman studies me, his intense eyes piercing through my doubts as if they're breaking them down piece by piece. "In what respect? Tane's gone now."

"He's right," Dimitri speaks up. "The chapter with Tane may be over, but the threat hasn't gone away. We're just at the start of establishing ourselves in this new capacity, and while I'm very pleased that Tane is dead, now is not the time to get complacent."

"What do you mean?" Roman asks. "I thought we'd have a moment to breathe, to relax and enjoy life for a minute."

"You know he's not going to be the last person to try and take power of these islands, right?" Dimitri explains. "There's always going to be the next group coming for us, with ambition to take over this precious turf. The islands may be relatively small compared to some hubs on the mainland, but they're lucrative with the sheer quantity of tourists coming in and out. Plus, they're a strategic access point for substantial drug funneling and human trafficking. To anyone wanting that for themselves, we'll be like their Tane. But less into human annihilation and mass graves. Compared to him, and despite his eventual demise, we look comparatively soft."

"Yeah, but in practice it's easier to stand strong at the top of a platform while people try to make you crumble by your knees, than it is to topple that person off," Skyler adds. "It's physics, psychology... all of that stuff in one. Since we took Tane down we've become the biggest fish, with home court advantage. Someone won't be able to come in and just oust us. It would be possible, but it'd be much, much more difficult."

"Well, we'll be ready and waiting. Anticipating," says Roman. He turns his attention to Dimitri. "So what's new with you guys, now that all that is over? Any plan to leave the other island and come here any time soon? Are we all going to live together in one giant house?" I grin at the image.

"Nah, no way!" laughs Dimitri. "I actually do really like coming here for a visit, but any more than a week or so and I start to get itchy feet. It just feels... no offense, by the way.... commercialized. Built for tourists and everything. We like our little slice of nature."

"Well, I can't disagree with you there," I nod. "But, that said, it is how we make a lot of our money."

"Yeah. I know. It's not totally different where we are. Anyway, I'd still be on one of these islands than anywhere else. I know that much." He smiles. "Besides, Aria's going to be here regularly to check on the restaurant. When she's not flitting around checking out new locations, that is. We've bought her an apartment right near the restaurant, and we'll be coming with her a lot of the time."

"Oh good," says Slade, out of nowhere. "I'm really starting to like you guys."

"Wait, did hell just freeze over?" I say, staring at Slade in surprise.

The entire room laughs. This is really starting to feel like a team.

CHAPTER FIFTY-FIVE

DEVON

The next few months pass by in a blur as we figure out everyone's respective new roles in this new organization. Of course, there are some speed bumps here and there–some miscommunications and minor misunderstandings that are to be expected in any new venture like this. But, through strong communication, we're able to navigate the potentially treacherous waters and establish our new structure.

I take a deep breath as I start to write a note to my friend Donkey. An old school letter, written with pen on paper, the old school way. There's so much to update him on, and our usual conversation has been reduced to exchanging memes on an almost-daily basis. Now that Tane is gone, I intend to strengthen some of my friendships outside of this circle, starting with my dear friend:

Donkey, my dear friend – I hope this finds you well... there's a lot to update you on and it would be easier to tell you about it in person. Maybe one day you'll actually agree to show your face on a video call. But, this serves as something tangible that you can keep and think of me, so here you go...

Rake is exploring standup comedy and performing at local mic nights. He's actually pretty hilarious and he's developing a bit of a local following.

Dom has opened a nursery full of rare plants and started a YouTube channel helping others to channel their efforts into growing the most finicky varieties. One of his special skills has turned out to be growing very spicy chilis, and he's working on developing his own hot sauce line (which he has other people test on his behalf, and he takes their word for it). He particularly enjoys helping people grow their own food in their gardens, and hopes that for some people this means they will never know true hunger again. He still enjoys violent video games, and breaks skulls on the side as needed. I can't wait for you to meet him.

Brick and Slade have partnered on a culinary project exploring vegan cooking. Slade secretly holds meat-based popups, and thinks Brick doesn't know about them. Brick secretly uses the popups to lure deserving victims and murders them when Slade isn't looking. Neither of them asks any questions, but Slade does wonder why the number of guests often dwindles over the course of the event. I'm deciding whether I want to get involved by telling one or both of them, but for now I'll just let things play out...

Skyler's surfing business continues to take off. He has a range of beachy merch that represents his love for the ocean, and of course, prominently features snakes. A percentage of all sales goes to a charity that helps young people on the islands. He now wears his father's legacy as a badge of honor, and part of who he is, but firmly realizes he is his own person, and that's all anybody ever expected him to be.

Angel's and my athleisure range is thriving. Focused on strong, badass women, the range is trendy, size-inclusive, and of course, edgy. We plan on expanding our empire in ways that help women to feel comfortable in their skin and do whatever it is that brings them joy.

Zeke is content running the Snake's operations from a business perspective, spending his days just how he likes them—wading through spreadsheets and other documents, with plenty of quality time set aside to spend with me.

Aria's has taken off way beyond expectations, and Aria is expanding her concept to each of the islands. Her signature booze-free drinks are one of the most popular menu items, and she's working on developing a ready-to-drink version which will be available in stores everywhere. She's been invited to appear on Shark Tank, which the guys find hilarious given the name. I'll send you some samples when they're available.

Florian's band is doing well. One of their songs just became part of a viral trend on social media, and he tries to avoid watching people turn his song into skits and choreographed dances. You should check it out on YouTube. I'll send you the link as soon as I mail this.

Anyway, that was a lot. I hope one day you can visit and meet everyone, and see some of this for yourself.

Remember that no matter how far away you are, I see you and I love you, and am always here for you,

Devon xx

Smiling to myself, I tuck the letter into the envelope and place it in my purse to mail later today. So many exciting things going on all around. For the first time in a long time, I feel hope and excitement for what will happen next.

Rake

I visit the cemetery on the anniversary of my brother's death, clutching a bouquet of his favorite flowers. The grief still gnaws at me, but it's less sharp than before. Therapy has helped me understand that children under poor supervision are prone to accidents. My pain is valid, yet now is the time to move forward.

I've started doing stand-up comedy, channeling my trauma into humor on open mic nights. The crowds are small but appreciative. Their laughter eases my soul. My brother would be proud to see me transforming hardship into healing.

Though shadows of our pasts still loom, rays of light now pierce through. We've found constructive outlets for our pain and new purpose in uplifting others. The future shimmers with promise. Our bonds remain unbroken, ready to explore life's next chapters together. For the first time in long while, a sense of hope and inner peace blossoms within me. I am a good person, and I am enough. I'm also hella fucking funny.

Skyler

The salty ocean breeze ruffles my hair as I gaze out at the shimmering turquoise waves. It's a perfect morning to catch some barrels. After waxing down my board, I paddle out, waiting for the next set.

A smooth swell rises, and I spring to my feet, dropping in. The wave walls up, and I carve across its face, feeling the pull of the barrel as it forms around me. For a few seconds, I'm enveloped in aquatic bliss.

Surfing keeps me centered these days, just like it always has. My merch business is blowing up, peddling board shorts, bikinis, and other beach swag prominently featuring snakes and representing a shared love and respect for the ocean. Sales benefit island youth charities, paying forward my good fortune.

I've made peace with my past. My father's choices no longer define me—well, they never really did. That was all in my head. His reckless legacy is now my badge of honor and a cautionary tale. I'm my own man, living each day to its fullest, and I've never felt more free.

The wave spits me out and I kick out, watching it crash in a cascade of white water. Back on the sand, I'm greeted by whoops and cheers. My friends await, their surfboards underarm, ready to seize the day. A wide smile spreads across my face. This island paradise will always be my home, and these brothers, my family. As we all charge towards the surf, my only thoughts are of the next wave and new beginnings.

Aidan

I glance up from the spreadsheets scattered across my desk as Angel bursts into my office, her face glowing with excitement.

"The new athleisure samples just arrived!" she exclaims. "These turned out even better than I imagined."

She holds up a sports bra and leggings set in sleek black fabric with metallic snake print accents. I can't help but grin, knowing our clothing line is about to slay the market.

"It's perfect," I say. "Sexy yet functional. Edgy with a hint of glam. Our customers are going to go wild over these."

Angel nods enthusiastically. "This is only the beginning too. Once sales take off, we'll expand into shoes, bags, swimwear. Anything to make badass women feel like the goddesses they are."

Her passion is contagious. When she and Devon first dreamt up this business, their vision was clothing designed to boost confidence. Seeing their creation come to life is beyond rewarding.

"I'm proud of you, Valkyrie." I pull Angel close and plant a kiss on her forehead. "Now go get changed. We need some fierce promo shots of you rocking your threads."

As she heads to the changing room, I turn back to my desk, sifting through paperwork. Running the Brixton's operations is my forte, though paperwork isn't glamorous. But seeing Angel thrive makes it all worthwhile. Her joy is mine. For her, I'd happily spend a lifetime swimming through spreadsheets.

Zeke

I nod in satisfaction as I review the latest figures. Business is booming across all our enterprises. The clubs and casinos are pulsing with activity day and night.

Backroom deals ensure our pipelines stay full and our pockets lined. On the surface, we're legitimate businessmen. Underneath, the machine hums as we pull the strings.

A knock at my office door stirs me from my thoughts.

"Come in," I call out.

Aidan enters, his presence commanding as always. "Morning, Zeke. Just checking in on the status of things."

"All good on my end," I assure him. "Profits are up, our partners are happy, and any whispers of dissent have been silenced."

Aidan's mouth twitches in a hint of a smile. "Excellent. Can't have anyone getting ideas about challenging our rule."

He's not one for small talk, preferring to get right to business. It's what makes him invaluable as my second-in-command. Aidan sees threats before they materialize, snuffing them out swiftly.

"Anything you need me to handle?" he asks.

I shake my head. "We're solid. But keep your ear to the ground. The second there's a rumble, I want to know."

"You got it." He turns to leave but pauses. "Oh, Roman mentioned something about a side project with Angel. Some do-gooder dating app. Wanted to give you a heads up."

I chuckle under my breath. Once a player, always a player, even if now he does it vicariously through others. "Appreciate it. But I trust Angel to keep him in line."

Aidan nods then takes his leave. As the door shuts, I lean back, contemplating our empire. All is well in our kingdom. For now, the streets belong to us.

I nod, satisfied with Aidan's report. Our operations are secure, at least for the moment. There's always another threat on the horizon, but we'll face it when it comes.

My thoughts drift to Aria and her success with the restaurant chain. I know she's got big plans to expand to the other islands soon. I make a mental note to check in with her later, see if she needs any help greasing the wheels. Her ambition impresses me. Just like Devon and Angel's.

A buzz from my phone shakes me from my reverie. It's a text from Florian, a photo of the latest music charts showing his band's single rising up the ranks. Underneath he's typed: "Who would've thought taking down a crime boss could be good promo lol."

I chuckle. Florian has a knack for finding the humor in just about anything.

Replying quickly, I write: "Don't get too famous on me now."

His response is swift. "Never :)"

Setting my phone down, I take a deep breath and gaze out the window at the city below. The view from up here is commanding, but lonely too. Power comes with a price. But surrounded by family—of blood and bond—I know I'll never have to bear that weight alone.

This kingdom is ours. And together we'll defend it, whatever comes next.

Dimitri

I take a long sip of whiskey, savoring the slow burn as it slides down my throat. From my vantage point at the window, I have a panoramic view of the city sprawled out beneath me. An empire that is now partly ours.

My phone buzzes again, drawing my attention back to the present. It's a text from Josef this time.

"Got an offer to write an advice column for the local paper," he's written. "Pretty sure you guys set this up just to mess with me."

I chuckle under my breath. Josef's not wrong—the idea of our resident hitman doling out life advice to the general public is too funny to pass up. But his writing talent is real, even if his day job is less than savory.

"Could be good for your author profile," I tap back. "Your call, though."

Josef's reply comes a few minutes later. "Yeah, yeah, laugh it up. I'll think about it."

I grin, picturing his exasperated eye roll. Josef likes to play the tough guy, but underneath he's a softie at heart.

My amusement fades as my thoughts turn down a darker path. To the blood on my hands, and the lives I've taken to get here. Power always comes at a price.

But looking out at the city lights glittering below, I know it's a price I'd pay again.

This is our kingdom now.

Whatever comes next, we'll face it together.

For now, we reign.

Check out my other books here.

C(r)ouch Bind Set (Sports romance – Rugby Why Choose)

- Rucked (Book 1)

- Quick Tap (Prequel Novella—coming late 2024)

- (Book 2)

- (Book 3)

Blood and Sand (Dark Reverse Harem Mafia Romance)

- Sea of Snakes(Book 1)

- Sea of Sinners(Book 2)

- Sea of Rage (Book 3)

- Sea of Pain(Book 4)

- Sinners, Rage & Pain: The Brixton Trilogy(Books 2, 3 and 4)

- Sea of Demons(Book 5)

- Sea of Redemption(Book 6)

Standalones

- Pretty Lovely Lies (FBI/mafia romance, single parent, international)

- Ruthless Choices(romantic horror)

Palm Falls Series (mafia romance – interconnected standalones)

- F*CKBOYS(dark revenge romance, second chance, enemies to lovers)

- Bronson & Wren's story (title TBC) – preorder. Releases July 2024

Billionaire's Takeover Collection

- Irreversible Decision

- Compelling Proposal

- Love Merger

- The Billionaire's Takeover Collection (all 3 of the above!)

Novellas

- Love in a Seedy Motel Room

Sign up for my newsletter herefor the latest on new releases, promos, giveaways and events!

Join me on social media:

Facebook: @heidistarkauthor

Instagram: @heidistarkauthor

TikTok: @heidistark_author

Twitter: @heidistarkauthr

Websitehttps://heidistarkauthor.com

Thank you to everyone who has joined me for this journey with Devon and the Snakes, Angel and the Brixtons, and Aria and the Unknowns, right from the beginning.

It's wild to think this is now a complete 6-book series (6!!). What started as one book—my first foray into dark romance—soon took on a life of its own. Ever since Sea of Snakes, the characters have had more to say. And the tension and friendship arc between Devon, Angel, and now Aria, is something I've really enjoyed watching over time.

Thank you to Rossy, for your support throughout this process, including working with me on the PR boxes. I had fun working with you!!

I'm so grateful this series has reminded me of some important things. Like that within darkness, you can find humor. As well as friendship, kinship, healing, and redemption. And from the darkness you can grow again, wiser and stronger than before.

Stay true to yourself, because that's the best you. And keep surfing.

Heidi Stark is an indie romance author who loves writing romances featuring strong females, morally grey men and, occasionally, athletes.

Heidi grew up in New Zealand and now resides in the US. She's inspired by the locations she visits on her travels, and the people she meets along the way.

When she's not writing, you can usually find her voraciously reading dark romance, listening to podcasts, dreaming about her next book, indulging her reality TV obsession, roller skating, swimming, or snuggling with her cat, Fang.

Learn more about Heidi Stark at her website. Sign up for exclusive content and her newsletter here.

You can also find out more about Heidi and her upcoming books on social media:

Facebook Page

Facebook Group

Instagram

TikTok